The Case of the Three Species

(The Mare, the Elephant, and the Pink Flamingo)

A 'Before Watson' Novel

(Book Four)

Further Reminiscences of P. S. T.

(Based upon notes newspaper clippings, and correspondence received from Sherlock Holmes)

By A. S. Croyle

Paperback ISBN 978-1-78705-400-4
ePub ISBN 978-1-78705-401-1
PDF ISBN 978-1-78705-402-8

Published in the UK by MX Publishing
335 Princess Park Manor, Royal Drive,
London, N11 3GX
www.mxpublishing.co.uk

Cover by Brian Belanger

To **Heather Edwards** - A friend and first reader whose insights and suggestions were invaluable. Thank you for your patience and persistence!!

And to **Rae Griffin** – BFF and constructively critical when I need it the most.

PROLOGUE

3 September, 1945

The war has officially ended!

I did not think I would live to see this day, a day that did not come easily. I think even Sherlock Holmes would have broken in character to express joy and relief.

Four months ago, the Western Allies invaded Germany and Soviet troops captured Berlin. Adolph Hitler, we were told, committed suicide and the Germans surrendered. On 8 May, thousands listened intently as King George's speech about this was relayed by loudspeaker to those who had gathered in Trafalgar Square and Parliament Square. Earlier, Mr. Churchill broadcast a message to the nation from the Cabinet room at Number 10, telling us that the war with Germany was over and that the ceasefire had been signed on 7 May at the American advance headquarters in Rheims. In his message, he paid tribute to the men and women who had laid down their lives for victory, as well as to all those who had 'fought valiantly on land, sea and in the air.' Huge crowds, many dressed in red, white and blue, gathered outside Buckingham Palace and cheered when the King, Queen and two princesses came out onto the balcony.

My daughter Hope was there with her husband Keith. They were told by their employers that the war was likely to end and, if so, to take 8 May off. So Keith and Hope walked across the bridge to Trafalgar Square. I live with them but at the age of almost ninety, I am no longer mobile enough to participate in such gatherings. When they came home, I clasped her hands and said, "Tell me everything!"

Her eyes lit up. She has my dark eyes and hair—though now that she is in her mid-fifties, her hair is turning gray. Her brilliant smile and zest for life—those attributes she inherited from her late father.

"Mum, there were bonfires on some of the bomb sites and lights in some of the shops. Nelson was lit up by a searchlight."

'The Nelson' to whom she referred was Nelson's Column, a monument in Trafalgar Square in central London built to commemorate Admiral Horatio Nelson, who died at the Battle of Trafalgar in 1805.

"Long after dark, people were still flooding the streets," Hope told me. "Many gathered around the different monuments, floodlit tonight specially for the occasion. There were fireworks, too, and burning effigies of Hitler. We pushed our way into the square, but a car was in our way. As we went around it, a girl in uniform tripped and literally fell into Keith's arms. With a big smile she planted a kiss full on his mouth!" she laughed. "Everybody spent the evening dancing and celebrating and Mr. Churchill was greeted by cheering crowds as he made his way to Whitehall and appeared on the balcony of the Ministry of Health."

I had heard his speech on the BBC. Mr. Churchill said, 'We may allow ourselves a brief period of rejoicing; but let us not forget for a moment the toil and efforts that lie ahead. Japan with all her treachery and greed remains unsubdued.'

We were still at war with Japan. She refused to surrender.

Just a few months later, on 6 August and 9 August respectively, the United States dropped atomic bombs on the Japanese cities of Hiroshima and Nagasaki.

On 15 August, streets around the world were flooded once again with giddy, boisterous crowds. Paper littered the Strand; civilians and service personnel carried and waved the stars and stripes and the Union Jack, as they surged through Piccadilly Circus. On hearing of the surrender, ladies poured out on to the sidewalk and did the Lambeth walk, a jaunty dance that supposedly mimicked the way a cockney struts and which was made popular in a musical called *Me and My Girl*. Hope saw a New Zealand sailor and three GIs express their glee by chairing a London policeman in Piccadilly Circus. Russian, American and British soldiers cheered together. The King and Queen drove from Buckingham Palace to the House of Lords for the opening of Parliament and thousands lined the route and assembled in Parliament Square, giving their Majesties a tumultuous welcome rarely seen in London.

With the Soviet invasion of Manchuria, the invasion of the Japanese archipelago imminent, and the possibility of additional atomic bombings, Japan finally surrendered yesterday, 2 September. The signing of the unconditional surrender document occurred in Tokyo Bay aboard the battleship *USS Missouri*, officially ending World War II.

Jubilation has replaced much of the devastation and despair. London is ready to rebuild from the rubble.

As I drifted off to sleep last night, I was filled with memories of the happy and confusing times of my youth, of cheering crowds that gathered each November for the Lord Mayor's Show in London. I remembered the last time Sherlock Holmes and I attended the parade together.

3

It was November 1880, just a few months before my brother, Dr. Michael Stamford, introduced Sherlock Holmes to Dr. John Watson. By that time, Sherlock wanted very much to move into a home owned by Mrs. Hudson on Baker Street. 221B Baker Street, to be exact. He said it was likely too much for his purse. He had considered looking for someone to share the flat. But he was still pondering who on earth, aside from me, would ever want to live with him. He had not met Dr. John Watson yet.

Not quite yet.

1

My last adventure with Sherlock Holmes began on 9 November 1880.

Shivering and standing near Mansion House, the Georgian town palace that is the official residence of the Lord Mayor of the City of London, I was surrounded by an assortment of little children, some well-dressed like my nephew Alexander and little Billy, my aunt and uncle's ward—and some less affluent toddlers and youth, dressed in tattered clothing, worn boots and threadbare coats. The latter group was comprised of Sherlock Holmes' homeless helpers . . . Rattle, Ollie, Ivy and others, all of them led by their self-proclaimed leader, one Archibald William Wiggins, known to most simply as Wiggins.

Ivy, an adorable little girl whom I longed to dress in petticoats and velvet dresses, fancy hats and fur muffs, tugged at my sleeve. She asked, "'ow did all this 'appen, Miss? 'ow did it all start?"

"The parade, you mean, Ivy?"

She nodded. So I explained to the little girl, as best I could, the origin of the Lord Mayor's Show.

"Well, Ivy, it all began in the sixteen hundreds."

"Is that a long time ago, Miss?"

Smiling, I said, "Yes, a very, very long time ago."

I told her that the King had made life very difficult for the people of London with taxes, and that the people felt like baronial hostages for a very, very long time. (My explanation to Ivy became a bit more simplified when she asked what a baronial dispute was.) "So," I said, "King John tried to win the love of his people by allowing them to choose their own Mayor. But he insisted that immediately after the election, the Mayor had to leave the safety of the City of London, travel upriver to distant Westminster, a very inconvenient journey, and swear loyalty to the Crown."

I explained that over the centuries, this event became one of London's favourite rituals. The parade moved from river barges to horseback to the magnificent State Coach, and around it grew the rowdy and joyful medieval festival and parade that is known as the Lord Mayor's Show. It has marched . . . and floated and trotted, and occasionally fought through hundreds of years, despite two bouts of the plague, the Great Fire of London, and countless wars.

"There are fewer sword fights these days but the floats are grander than ever," I said.

"Sword fights?" Rattle asked. "Like with real swords, Miss?"

"Indeed," I laughed. "It's a great day out, isn't it Wiggins?"

Wiggins shrugged but his wide smile betrayed his appreciation for the festivities.

Sherlock Holmes suddenly appeared at my side. It took me by surprise because he so rarely indulged in such "frivolous events."

He sighed and said, "You do not plan the parade before you win the championship."

"What on earth are you talking about?"

"Things are still unsettled in the East. When our troops were emulsified at the Battle of Maiwand in Afghanistan a few months ago, it severely dampened morale and I fear more battles will erupt there."

"Sherlock, Uncle Ormond said that the Battle of Kandahar at the beginning of September was the end of the conflict. Your brother Mycroft told him that total evacuation is scheduled to begin after the first of the year. Besides, if we wait to partake in gaiety until all wars have ended, we shall wait forever."

"Yes, and I believe we shall. There will be other wars. Humanity is in an ineluctable decline."

I shivered. All the gold of summer was gone. Now the wind was blowing across the city and everything was bleak and gray. Sherlock made it sound like the world might forever be darkened by the graying dust of war.

"Does it not seem that when one ends, another begins?" he continued. "It is not epic betrayals that destroy nations, Poppy, nor men with ideals and great plans who seek to stop the suffering throughout the world only to see their great plans fail. It is not mass depression. It is destructive tribal spirit. It is the little things that clutter our daily lives, Poppy. The tedious monotony. The greed, the lust, the envy."

"Nevertheless, Sherlock, a war's end should be celebrated and there is also much to celebrate in daily life."

"Daily life is tedious," he grumbled.

Clearly, Sherlock Holmes was bored.

"You are in need of a case, Mr. Sherlock Holmes. You are always most disagreeable when you are between adventures."

Little did I know that very afternoon, my brother Michael would furnish Sherlock with some new cases to solve, precisely what he needed to lift his spirits.

When the parade ended, Sherlock and I went home to have lunch with Michael and received some startling news. This time, the parade did not end with an investigation into mutilated swans and corpses as it had the year before. Instead, we were about to embark on a case involving pink flamingoes…

2

    As expected, my brother was waiting for us at my residence in Regent's Park, where I lived with my Uncle Ormond and my Aunt Susan, my mother's sister. But I was surprised to find him seated on the loveseat that faced the fireplace next to Kate Dew, our new cook. This was odd for Kate rarely came into this part of the house.

    Sherlock and I had rescued Kate from her life as a prostitute after she had helped us solve our last murder case. Now she and her young daughter Mary lived here. I was not only thrilled to have had a hand in giving her an opportunity to right her ship but also to have the pleasure of eating the fabulous meals she prepared. I adored her and thought of her as a friend.

    And my Aunt Susan doted on little Mary.

    Aunt Susan and Uncle Ormond had never had children. They thought of me as a daughter because I had lived there since I was a young girl. My parents had asked them to watch over me in London while I attended a girls' school and then nursing school at St. Thomas. I continued to reside with them during medical school when one finally was opened which admitted women, and afterward, when I set up my small practice near the British Museum.

    Now the house was filled with the joy and laughter of small children again. Not only did they have Mary underfoot, but Billy, the younger brother of Wiggins, the leader of Sherlock's homeless band of beggars, stayed with us off and on and my nephew Alexander was a frequent guest as well.

My nephew Alexander dropped my hand and ran to his father. Michael hugged him fiercely but then told him and little Billy to run along to the morning room to see Aunt Susan and Mary.

Puzzled, I asked, "Why did you shoo your son away? We just got home."

"Because we need to talk. Is Sherlock with you?"

"He'll be along momentarily. He ran into his brother Mycroft at the corner and they are chatting."

"I am glad that Sherlock is detained," he said softly. "I need to speak with him, but first I have some things to talk to you about privately."

I realized now that Michael's face was ashen and Kate was digging her nails into her palms. Something was clearly amiss. "Michael, what's wrong?" I asked as I removed my cape, hat and gloves and sat down across from him.

"One of several very troublesome things on my mind, Poppy. I told you John Watson joined the British forces in India, with the 5th Northumberland Fusiliers. Then he became attached to the 66th Berkshire Regiment as one of their medical officers."

"Yes, I remember."

He held up a letter. "This letter is from a man named Will Murray. He was John's orderly in Afghanistan."

"And?"

"Murray writes that John was wounded at the Battle of Maiwand last July. He was struck in the left shoulder by a Jezail bullet which grazed the subclavian artery, and then on top of that he contracted enteric fever."

"Typhoid."

I had never treated the fever but had read about it during medical school. Left untreated, the patient's fever would become very high and he could dehydrate and die.

"Michael, is he . . . has your friend?—"

"No, no, Poppy, John Watson is alive. In fact, for some reason, Murray went back to India and his letter was much delayed. John was sent back to England on the troopship *HMS Orontes*, invalided to the port of Portsmouth, and I received a letter from him just days after Murray's arrived."

He held up another letter. "John writes that he will eventually make his way back to London when he recovers fully. He will have a small pension, I assume, but I shall write back to him so that he knows that I shall help him when he gets here."

I had been so busy trying to make a go of the practice of medicine, and was often so embroiled in my own emotional war, trying to put aside my feelings for Sherlock, that I had paid little attention to a war that was so far away. But I knew that the British had entered Afghanistan in 1878 to install a British-friendly regime across the border from India. When we defeated the Afghans, a treaty was signed and all seemed well until September 1879 when a mob of Afghans attacked the envoy's house and he and his small military escort were massacred.

After that, our army marched on Kabul, occupied it and hanged the ringleaders of the massacre. Kabul and Kandahar were garrisoned.

"Murray," Michael said, "writes that their regiment arrived in Kandahar at the beginning of 1880. But in May, an army of eight thousand fierce Afghans and Ghazis, led by Ayub Khan, marched eastward. Khan vowed to expel the British.

Michael heaved a long sigh. "It sounds like this Battle of Maiwand where John was injured was brutal. According to Murray, Brigadier-General George Burrows had never commanded in battle before. He writes, *We were fighting on a dusty plain at the height of the Afghan summer. We were not used to the heat which reached almost 50 degrees Celsius. And we were almost out of food.*

"*Most of us had not eaten all day and our supply of water ran out early on. Our rifle barrels became so hot we had to wrap cartridge paper around our fingers to stop blistering.*"

"It appears that most of the 66th was destroyed," Michael said. "Murray says the escaping British and Indian troops streamed up the road towards Kandahar, pursued by the Afghan cavalry, but they were unaware that what was left of the infantry was fighting to the death behind them."

Michael read more of Murray's letter.

"*We were quite literally hacked to pieces and the wounded were in a terrible condition. We were cut to ribbons. It was an impossible fight against thousands of bloodthirsty tribesman. Wave upon wave of fanatical, screaming white-robed Ghazis rushed at us. Many were mown down but others made it to the British lines. They grabbed British and Indian soldiers and hacked them to pieces with their long knives. We were outnumbered ten to one and outgunned. The Afghan artillery pounded our lines relentlessly and Afghan cavalry thundered towards us in charge after charge.*

"*Burrows finally realised the battle was lost and finally gave the order to fall back. But a ravine lay between us and safety. Some managed to negotiate the ravine — only to face the* most desperate fighting of the day. *Others stumbled down its steep sides and fell on their swords.*

"*Dr. Watson was deserted by the stretcher-bearers and left lying on the ground in the dust and the heat. But I put him on a horse and then loaded him into the first available gun carriage with other wounded. We were forced to halt in one village as the exhausted horses could go no further. Dr. Watson lay helpless on the wagon for a couple of hours while the villagers fired at us continuously. There weren't enough transports for all the wounded, so many were left to their fate. They knew what it would be. The Afghans are infamous for mutilating the wounded and the retreat was even more terrible than the battle. Men could hardly speak. When the wounded opened their mouths, their tongues were dried and parched. We later learned that a young officer went in search of water and was taken prisoner. His captors cut his throat.*

"*In the end, only a handful of us were left. In fact, we few are all that is left of the 66th Berkshire, us and our faithful dog Bobby. His furious barks were soon lost in the deafening din of battle.*"

I heard my bull terrier, Little Elihu, barking outside behind the house and was reminded that he had often interceded when Sherlock or I were threatened. I could imagine Bobby's fierce attempts to stave off the Afghans and protect his masters.

Then Michael handed me the letter from John Watson. I felt my hand shake as I took it. After the death of his wife Effie— my best friend—my poor brother had so grieved that he thought about enlisting. It could have been him lying in a hospital in the back of beyond.

I forced my hands to stop trembling as I read some of John Watson's letter. He wrote:

I am told by Murray that the retreat through the whole night was fearful. We had no water for 32 miles. Some men died of thirst. I have no memory of it but even as late as August 6, according to Murray, the ordeal was still not over. Ayub Khan's army besieged Kandahar. It was not until General Roberts marched from Kabul with an army of 10,000 to relieve the garrison that we could withdraw to India in some safety.

Murray tells me that we finally prevailed in September. I am glad of it. I was treated at the base hospital in Peshawar but then contracted enteric fever. I was sent to Portsmouth to further recover. I hope to be back in London before the end of the year.

I handed the letter back to Michael. "I shall pray for his rapid recovery, Michael. Hopefully, he will be home soon."

I stood up, intending to nudge Kate to help me see about lunch, although I thought it unlikely that I could manage to eat anything after reading about the horrors of the war.

Michael looked at Kate and then down at his shoes.

"Michael, what is it? What else is troubling you?"

He cleared his throat but could not seem to find his voice. Kate drew in a deep breath and tucked a strand of wavy blonde hair into her bun. Her deep blue eyes misted as she focused on me. Then she looked at Michael, waiting.

"Michael, for heaven's sake, what is going on? Tell me."

"Well, for one thing, there is a little crisis at home."

"Home? As in Burleigh Manor?"

That was our ancestral home in the Broads, where our parents still lived.

"What kind of crisis?"

"Loke has been arrested."

"Loke! Arrested on what charge?"

"Well, you know that he left our parents' employ to tend the stables at Victor Trevor's estate."

"Yes, I know. He and Marie have lived there since they married."

"Well, it seems that one of the horses maimed someone and Loke has been implicated somehow."

"Loke would never do such a thing—accidentally or intentionally. There must be a mistake."

"I don't have enough facts. I was rather hoping Sherlock might look into it."

"I will certainly ask him."

I looked at Michael closely. He was clearly very agitated. "What else do you wish to tell me?"

He cleared his throat, glanced at Kate again and tapped his fingers on his knees. "Yes, well, Kate and I—" He paused.

"Yes?"

"Kate and I have a mutual friend who is in trouble. She's . . . well, she runs a brothel. It's called The Pink Flamingo."

"A brothel," I repeated.

"She's in trouble and we were rather hoping Sherlock would look into it."

"What kind of trouble?"

"Well, we can wait for Sherlock to explain what we know. But here's the thing. I think you should know something of a preliminary nature. Kate and I know her . . . well, I know the madam at The Pink Flamingo because—"

"Yes? Because?"

"Because in the past . . . in the past . . . ." Kate stuttered. She swallowed hard and her tears of sorrow seemed to weave like a chain of pearls down her cheeks.

"Kate, tell me."

"Because, in the past, Michael occasionally availed himself of services at The Pink Flamingo," Kate explained. "I met Michael there."

The strings of my heart snapped. Its beat seemed to stop and I reeled forward crazily, heavily, like a hinge creaking under a heavy burden. "What?"

"It was he who referred me to you when I was ill during the Great Fog."

I stared at Michael, mouth dropping. "You? You referred Kate?"

He nodded and took her hand. "And in fact we have become . . . well, very fond of each other."

Biting back harsh words, wanting to scream at him for engaging in such behavior, I sat quite silent for a minute. His wife, my dearest friend Effie, had been gone for several years now and I understood his loneliness. I understood also how one could be swept away in passion. But this was a shock. My brother? Involved with a former prostitute?

Finally, regaining some of my composure, I said, "I see. Michael, how did you come
to . . . to find this establishment?"

"You can guess, I am certain."

"Jonathan," I said flatly.

Jonathan Younger, his friend, his best man at his wedding, frequented such places. Sherlock had in fact revealed this to me after I'd had lunch with Jonathan, in an attempt to persuade me not to pursue the relationship further. I had spoken to Michael about it because I thought he should know of his friend's secret sordid behavior. But Michael had not mentioned his own foray into the seedy side of life in London.

Kate pulled her hand away from Michael's. "Poppy, I know all of this comes as a shock. There is much more to explain. But we are seeking your help because our friend is in imminent danger."

"Imminent danger?"

I turned my head toward the door. It was Sherlock parroting Kate's words as he entered the library. "Sounds like I am in the right place."

3

Michael rose and shook Sherlock's hand. Sherlock turned to Kate and said, "Hello, Kate. So who is in imminent danger? I am all attention," Sherlock said as he removed his hat and cape. His hair was slicked back, and he wore a tightly tailored blue suit with brass buttons, French cuffs, a spread collar and a perfect half-inch of pocket square showing.

Michael sat down and Sherlock sat next to me on the divan.

"I . . . ." He paused and looked at Kate. "We have a friend who is in need of your assistance."

"Go on," Sherlock urged.

"Her name is Margaret Mayhew but everyone calls her Maggie May," Kate said. "I worked with her briefly . . . at a—" She stumbled and stuttered over the words. "We worked together at a brothel. She owns the house now, and several others. One in St. Giles, one in Shadwell, not far from The Three Crowns and The White Swan. And also one in Tothill Fields."

"Tothill Fields, you say," Sherlock said. "Near where the old prison was? The one that closed a few years ago?"

Kate nodded.

"Kate, I am confused," I said. "You call this Maggie May your friend. But you told me that when you discovered that you were pregnant and told the woman who owned the brothel—the woman to whom Mary's father Cecil Gray had sent you—she turned you out."

Kate squirmed. "She did turn me out, Poppy. But that was Maggie May's predecessor, a wretched old woman. When Maggie bought the house where Michael and I met, I stayed

18

there for a while before I decided to try to make a go of it on my own. A huge mistake," she added with downcast eyes. "It's round the corner from Whitehall. She calls it The Pink Flamingo."

Michael fidgeted and fixed his eyes on the window, clearly uncomfortable with discussion of Kate's past. I followed his gaze. Sheets of rain and harsh thunder booming, the rods of lightning splintered the sky.

"Wait! Round the corner from Whitehall you say?" Sherlock asked. "The Pink Flamingo is a house of ill repute near Whitehall?"

"Yes," Kate said.

He laughed. "Whitehall. Brother Mycroft's sacred government complex. So, Kate, do tell us the nature of this proprietress's troubles."

"Well, as you mention government, Mr. Holmes, it may have to do with that. Apparently, there are many men in high places who are well known to Maggie and someone has ransacked the place trying to find her list. She fears for her life if she does not hand it over."

"List?" Sherlock asked. "She has a list of the men who frequent The Pink Flamingo then?"

"But why would she keep such a list?" I asked.

"As a way to have the upper hand with her clientele," Sherlock proffered.

"Yes," Michael agreed. "The list serves to protect her. These men . . . most men would not want to be exposed."

"Including you," I said flatly. "You did not want to be exposed either."

Kate's eyes darted from me to Michael and back.

Suddenly memories of Effie flooded me. I glimpsed Kate's left hand, half expecting to see Effie's exquisite engagement ring there on Kate's ring finger. There was, to my relief I must admit, no sparkling bauble on her hand.

But when my eyes travelled to her throat, I noticed a necklace I had not seen before. Hanging from a long chain was a floral pendant, with the flower buds studded in sapphires and the leaves rendered in gold. The flower head shivered with Kate's every movement in a new and popular technique called *en tremblant.*

Noting my gaze, Kate clutched the pendant and slipped it beneath her blouse. She rose and stepped into the center of the room. Her golden hair, bright as the first gleam of dawn after a deep and silent night, fell softly to one shoulder. Fastidiously she pushed her hair back into its twist. "I'll go see about lunch," she said as she left the room.

When the door closed, Michael turned to me. "To be honest, dear sister, yes, my reputation at Bart's does mean something to me. And Mother and Father—"

I stood up. "Michael, a word. Alone."

I marched out of the room and waited in the hallway. When he exited the library, I walked to Uncle's office. He followed me and shut the door behind him.

4

I walked to the window and listened to the rain beat against it for a moment. Then I turned to face him.

"Michael, when I told you about Jonathan Younger, about his . . . entertainment, what did you tell me?"

He opened his mouth to speak, but I pushed forward.

"You told me you knew nothing about it, that it shocked you. You said in all the years you had known him, you would never have suspected him of such behavior. You said that you were glad Sherlock found out about Jonathan's nocturnal activities and that you were angry that he had attempted to worm his way into my life. You said he was beneath me. And *now* I find out that Jonathan directed you to brothels to engage in . . . to . . . well . . . Michael, I don't know what to say. And a relationship with Kate Dew. You with—"

"Stop!" he shouted. "Just calm down for a moment."

I heaved an exasperated sigh.

"Sit down."

"I will not."

"Sit. Down."

I slumped into the chair behind Uncle's desk and let out another sigh.

"Poppy," he said striding over to me. He knelt next to me and took my hand. "You remember what a tailspin I was in after Effie died. The heavy drinking, the insomnia."

I touched his face. I loved my brother so much. He was a good man, a kind and gentle man. A good doctor and a wonderful father. We had all felt the incomprehensible pain of losing Effie when she died in childbirth, a pain that persisted deep in my heart to this day. Even when I tried to shutter it off, a part of me was always inconsolable, always weeping and wailing for the loss. I had memorised all my best days with Effie. We were never going to see each other, ever again, and it was almost unmanageable. I could not imagine how difficult it was for him.

I turned away from him and stared out the window. The cold rain pelted hard against it and I recalled a time when Michael and I had been out riding together and a sudden storm like this one rose up. We had huddled beneath an old willow tree. Though we were disappointed that our pleasant ride had been interrupted, we talked for an hour, waiting for the rain to slow. We spoke of secrets we'd kept even from each other; we shared our dreams of becoming doctors and living happily with some yet unknown perfect mate. We had turned something miserable into something good. I remembered that afternoon now, and the words of Henry David Thoreau. "Cold and damp—are they not as rich an experience as warmth and dryness? So is *not* shade as good as sunshine, night as day? "

Thinking now of Kate, I realized suddenly how much she reminded me of my departed friend. Effie was the opposite of me in so many ways. Like Kate, Euphemia O'Flahertie Stamford had flaxen curls, skin like alabaster, dove's eyes and a brilliant smile. She had a tiny waist, delicate bones; she was slender as a sapling. My hair was dark and I was tall and clumsy. Smiling came to me with difficulty; Effie was always optimistic. She would say, "No matter how dark life may get, there's a light just waiting for you if you are only willing to stretch to grasp it." She felt that appreciating the lovely moments is the best way to arrest the most downward spiral of a life and stop all pernicious influences.

Though Kate had had a hard life, she, too, found beauty in small things . . . the throbbing sound of the wingbeats of a swan in flight, cooking a wonderful meal, receiving a shred of respect coming from someone from whom she least expected it, raising her little girl though she was not married and had to do it alone. The daughter of a Deputy Swankeeper, after he died, Kate had masqueraded as a boy to try to take her father's place tending to the Queen's swans. Then she'd become involved with a married man, Sir Cecil Gray, a member of the Privy Council, and bore his child. She'd supported herself and Mary by lying on her back. She'd helped us apprehend Gray's killer. She persisted and always looked forward by exercising sheer will and compassion.

Kate's life was as different from Effie's as night from day; they came from very different backgrounds. But did their differences really matter that much?

Did Michael overlook the differences and see the value in both women? Did he feel that despite the differences between his first love and this young woman . . . the sunshine versus the shade . . . the experience of loving Kate could bring him great happiness?

"Poppy, look at me."

I turned my head from the window and stared at him. His jaw set, his eyes intense, he said dryly, "You disapprove of my soliciting prostitutes and you disapprove of my relationship with Kate."

The precision of his words startled me. I was not unfamiliar with London's underworld. I had seen for myself the daily life of beggars, thieves and prostitutes. As a nursing student, I had often accompanied Uncle Ormond to district clinics where he volunteered, areas of our city that most genteel young women never see, that which was beneath and beyond and into its beating heart. I'd seen the infuriating grime and grit and tears and rage. I had seen street prostitutes ridding themselves of the rank smell left by customers who had had them in an alley. I saw their corpses and I was aware of the risk of catching a disease from one of the bodies. I'd treated young women like Kate Dew who had been forced by circumstances to swindle or beg or trade their bodies for money to buy food to eat.

But the thought of my brother . . . .

"Michael, it simply caught me off guard. I was, as you know, most disturbed to discover that your best friend, a man who expressed interest in courting me, found his entertainment in brothels. And when I told you, you feigned surprise."

"Yes, I lied to you, Poppy. And for that I am sorry and beg your forgiveness. But I am not sorry I met Kate. And I am forever in your debt, and Sherlock's, for the way you helped her in the Gray murder case and for persuading Aunt Susan to employ her here."

"When did this relationship with Kate begin? At the brothel?"

"No, Poppy. I did meet Kate there and we talked a great deal but we were not—" He paused and took a breath. "At any rate, I got to know her well only after she moved in here and started to look after Alexander when Aunt Susan was busy. But even before that, at Maggie May's place, we talked for hours. She was instrumental in getting me back on the right track. She listens. She cares."

I remembered Kate telling me of her prior involvement with Sir Cecil Gray, the unhappily married man whose murder she had witnessed. He was lonely and forlorn and she said they would talk for hours and hours. She was a good listener and compassionate. I had few friends since Effie died and Kate had become a confidante to me as well.

"Does Aunt Susan know anything of this? Does Mum?"

He shook his head. "No. And from what Kate tells me, you have never told them of her past either, and I am grateful for that as well. The past is past."

I squeezed Michael's hands in mine. "But Michael, even forgetting her past, forgetting what she did to survive, Mum and Papa will never accept her. She has had a child out of wedlock. And she is a cook. She's Aunt Susan's cook."

He jerked his hands away and stood. "Really, Poppy, you . . . *you* of all people should know that you don't really choose with whom you fall in love based upon their occupation or anything else. It just happens. You know that from personal experience."

"What? I don't understand what you—"

"Priscilla Olympia Pamela Price Yavonna Stamford!" he shouted as he threw his hands up in the air.

Oh, I knew he was aggravated now. He never called me by the litany of names from whence came my nickname unless he was beyond frustrated and peeved. No one, except Victor Trevor, my childhood sweetheart, ever called me Priscilla.

"Yes, you do understand. While Sherlock Holmes is the son of a respectable country squire and attended the best schools, he is not exactly the personification of what our parents would prefer in a son-in-law."

25

"What are you talking about, Michael? Sherlock Holmes and I—"

"Have a special and I suspect intimate relationship. It is at the very least obvious how *you* feel about him, Poppy. It has been for years. And again, while he might be considered suitable in some respects, there is little question that he would be a poor choice for a husband, but that did not stop you from loving him."

"Michael, I don't—"

"Oh, Poppy, you still run to him if he crooks his little finger."

"That is not true."

"Even if it is not, you still ignore the facts."

"What facts?"

He started to pace. "The fact that he plunges into danger with no thought to his safety or anyone else's. The fact that he cavorts with garret thieves from Hackney Road to Kingsland, from Seven Dials to Russell Square, and with homeless children whom he uses with little concern for their safety. If it serves his purpose, he loiters about with accomplices in every possible illegal trade from jewelry robbery to selling immoral books and obscene prints to grave-robbing. He is cunning as an old fox, that much is true. But don't for one moment think that our parents approve of him. Nor does Uncle Ormond for that matter. And one day he will likely receive a blow during one of his investigations from which he will never rally. For years now, we have all held our breath, hoping you would escape unscathed when it happens, given you always seem to be by his side when he places himself most in danger! But did I try to dissuade you? Did I?"

Before I could reply he said, "You must know that we all hoped you would marry Victor Trevor. Mum has mentioned him many times since he left for India.

"And he's coming back to England soon, by the way," he added.

I jumped up and went to the window, trying to gather my thoughts. Oh, he had turned the tables on me. He should have been a solicitor as he had just delivered a most criminal indictment of my bias and shortcomings. Then his last sentence hit me. I touched the locket at my neck, which I always wore.

Sherlock had given me the locket last Christmas—a huge surprise and entirely out of character. Inside it I had placed a photo of Sherlock, Effie, Victor Trevor, and me. It had been taken at a dinner party in the spring of 1874, shortly after I met Sherlock. I opened the locket and looked at the image now, remembering Victor. He was handsome, tall and lean with sinewy arms and his father's broad shoulders and intense blue eyes. I had known Victor Trevor all my life. My trust in him was marrow deep and vice versa . . . until he discovered that Sherlock and I cared for each other. I had betrayed his trust, as had Sherlock, who Victor had befriended at Oxford when no one else gave a fig about him. Sherlock and I did not mean to hurt him; we did not mean to care so deeply for one another. Once our feelings were revealed, everything changed. Sherlock could not forgive himself for betraying his one, true friend. Even worse, despite our mutual affection, Sherlock could never again place his trust in a woman, not even a woman he loved—and I believe he did love me—for she—*I* had had betrayed the man whom I had all but promised to marry—Victor. It was a quagmire from which none of us could recover. It was why Victor had left for India and his family's tea plantation as soon as he graduated from Oxford. I had not seen him in over five years.

I turned around. "Victor? Victor is returning from India?"

"He wishes to expand his holdings in India. He is coming back to sell the estate in Norfolk. Mum told me when she mentioned this incident with Loke and the stable and the rest of it."

"Oh," I said with a nod. "When? When is he returning?"

"Before Christmas. He won't be here long. There are some troubles in the area near his tea plantation."

"I see," I whispered. "Troubles? What kind of troubles?"

"Apparently, many of his workers are members of a tribe from West Bengal, I believe. Do you remember twenty or so years ago, there were reports of rebellions and witch hunts?"

"I remember Father spoke of rebellions and that many of the tribal leaders accused anyone who aligned with the British of witchcraft. What has that to do with Victor?"

"Only that many of his labourers from Nepal and Chota Nagpur blame illness or a bad harvest or pretty much any other difficulty on witchcraft or the British or both. They think it can mean only one thing—a curse of some kind. Earlier this year, some of Victor's tea gardens did not do well. The workers have converted some of the forests nearby into villages and seem to get on well with Victor but recently the witch doctor convinced some of his people that the poor harvest was a curse because . . . well, because Victor is British. There have been some incidents."

"Is Victor in danger?"

"He doesn't seem to think so, but he decided it was a good time to take a break, to let things settle down a bit before harvesting season."

"And when is that?"

"March to October."

"I see," I mumbled again.

It unnerved me that Victor might be in danger. I had never thought of him being in harm's way at his plantation in the Teri-Duar. The area was famous for its tea gardens and there was a heavy British presence there. For years, young women had sailed to find husbands among the ranks of our military or government or the many men, like Victor's father, who had opened the tea plantation there not long before he died. The British had essentially launched the tea industry by offering land south of the Himalayas to cultivate tea for export.

I had thought of Victor often, especially in the last several months when I had endeavoured to completely rid myself of my feelings for Sherlock. I had wondered what life would be like with Victor, what life I had passed by. Lately I was weighted with memories of our times together and the awful way we had parted. He was free of those burdens; he was no longer here. He had kicked the relics of his life, this world, away like a used, tattered ball. He had broken the knots of memory, chosen a new liberating path where he could claim new stars, new dawns in a new world.

Now Michael took my hands in his. "Never mind Victor, Poppy. What happened between you is your business. What happens between you and Sherlock is your business. Your life is your business. But my life is *my* business.

"Kate is a wonderful mother, and she loves my son and he loves her. We have made no solid plans but I do love her, Poppy. Not the way I loved Effie. I will always love Effie and I carry her in my heart every single day. For a while, it was like my mind and heart were a cage that held her memory. But I have escaped that ever-falling darkness finally. I want you to be happy for me. Can you forget about Kate and me for the time being? What we ask of you right now is simply to be silent on that subject and help us help our friend."

Before I could answer, Sherlock threw open the door and asked, his voice dripping in exasperation, "What is keeping you? Dr. Stamford, we have a case to solve."

I drew in a breath and looked at Michael. As his eyes pleaded with me, I recalled once again Effie's hopeful words. "No matter how dark life may get, there's a light just waiting for you if you are only willing to stretch to grasp it." Michael was stretching for the light. How could I fault him for that?

"Two actually, Sherlock. One at Victor Trevor's estate in the Broads. And one here in London at The Pink Flamingo."

5

Sherlock said nothing about Loke's arrest, which Michael had also spoken to him about, but by Wednesday evening, Sherlock, Michael, Kate and I were ready to embark on the first step in the Pink Flamingo adventure.

"Should I find a way to take lodging at 221B Baker," Sherlock said as he put on his cape and scarf. "I will give audience to prospective clients there. It is most inconvenient to be tramping around all of England to make a living."

I smiled. "You enjoy it, Sherlock. Admit it."

"On the contrary, I would much prefer for people to show deference by coming to me. I would even endeavor to make part of the flat comfortable for them."

"And just how would you do that?"

"Comfortable chairs, of course. For you and I, that is."

"And an uncomfortable chair for the person we interrogate?"

"Of course."

Michael helped Kate with her coat. She buttoned little Mary's coat and Alexander's and then put mittens on both of them. Kate and Alexander rubbed noses and it took but a moment to glean that they adored each other. Michael hoisted little Mary into his arms and kissed her cheek. In that fraction of a second, I determined that I would support my brother's decision to pursue a relationship with Kate. I tied my cape and was putting on gloves as we were about to leave, but then I felt a tug at my elbow. I turned and saw Uncle.

"A moment, Poppy?" Uncle asked.

I recognized the look on Uncle's face. I'd seen it many times. He was going to ask me to tell him the truth because he could always tell when I hadn't.

Our pretense was that Sherlock, Michael and I had been invited by Mycroft to join him at a post-parade party. After the Lord Mayor's Day parade, banquets were held all over London, the largest and most extravagant attended by high government officials, so we said that Kate was going to look after Michael's son and little Mary at his house while we went to the party. Michael had in fact retained his regular babysitter and we were taking the children there before going on to Maggie May's brothel. It was a thinly veiled deception. Just as Sherlock had warned when I devised the lie, Uncle obviously saw through it immediately. He and Mycroft were old friends and Uncle knew that Mycroft never participated in such frivolity.

"You three go ahead," I said. "I'll be right there."

Michael wrinkled his forehead and gave me an anxious look but pushed Sherlock out and closed the door behind him. I turned to face Uncle.

"Where are you really going, Poppy?" Uncle Ormond asked.

"I told you, Uncle, we are—"

"Going to a party, yes. With Mycroft Holmes. Really, Poppy?"

"Uncle, I—"

"Susan and I have no plans. We could have watched Alexander here. There is absolutely no reason for Kate to take Mary to Michael's to watch the children. What are you really up to?"

I hesitated and his eyes bore through me.

"Kate and Michael . . . I mean, Michael has a friend in need of some assistance from Sherlock."

"Michael has a friend. Not Kate?"

"Well, perhaps Kate knows her as well. I just—"

"You just don't lie very well, Poppy."

Uncle had a crisp way of speaking his mind.

Uncle Ormond was tall and slender, graying and stately. I suddenly felt as if he towered over me though I was but a few inches shorter.

"It's a case, Uncle. One which Kate and Michael brought to us. It's nothing dangerous."

"So you say each time you accompany Sherlock Holmes on one of his capers. The last time you said it was nothing dangerous, you went off with Sherlock to Chippy and confronted a deranged maniac who cut off people's heads! And I had to ask Mycroft to go after you."

"Really, it's nothing to worry about," I protested. "Michael and Kate just need our help on a little case—"

"There is no such thing as a little case in Sherlock's world. He would tell you himself that he leaves those to Inspector Lestrade," he chuckled. Sighing, he added, "Oh, Poppy, it must be difficult to live so close to the ocean and be unable to catch any fish."

I gazed at him a moment, trying to read his penetrating eyes. Before I could think of a reply, he said, "Poppy, have you become aware of your brother's affection for our cook?"

"Pardon me?"

"Do you know that Michael is involved with Kate?" he asked, his voice shifting sharply louder in key.

"Michael's business is Michael's business."

"I agree. But thank you for the confirmation. Run along, now. And do be careful."

I took a few steps toward the door but then turned and stopped abruptly. "Uncle, do you disapprove? Of Michael's involvement with Kate Dew?"

"I thought you knew me a bit better than that, Poppy. I am not given to such judgments. If Michael is happy and if she is good to him and his child, why should anyone interfere?"

A tingling sensation slowly crept up my back and neck. I had a feeling Uncle knew much more than he let on. He usually did.

"Good night, Uncle. I shan't be late."

"It's already late, young lady. Do be careful," he said again, concern written all over his face.

I caught up to the others and we quickly made our way to Michael's townhouse, settled the children, and then went on to The Pink Flamingo.

A black fence encircled the house and the center gate opened to a white paved walkway which led to the front door. The exterior was brick but in the darkness, I could not confirm the pink hue that Kate had mentioned. Above the door to the left was a sign with an artfully drawn pink flamingo.

We were greeted at the door by a young woman whose dark braids twirled atop her head. She wore a green evening dress that highlighted her hourglass figure. The bodice was fitted with an open neckline and sleeves ending in extravagant puffs.

The gored skirt swept the floor. It was a dress that my dear Effie, always fashion-conscious, would have adored.

Michael did not appear to know her nor did Kate. When he introduced us, she said, "My name is Sarah. Ms. Mayhew is expecting you."

She ushered us in and led us to a room at the back of the house. The home was luxurious and well-appointed. It might have easily passed for an upscale boarding house. Off the entrance hall were several rooms: a reception room, a study, a double aspect drawing room, a kitchen and breakfast room and a large dining room. I assumed all the bedrooms were upstairs. Several lovely ladies appeared to be deep in conversation with gentlemen, and a group of men sitting in the dining area were playing cards. There was not a hint of any unseemly activity.

Sarah knocked on the heavily ornate over-sized door and I heard a woman say, "Come in." Sarah opened the door, stepped aside to allow us to pass, and closed the door as she left the room.

The room was large; it appeared to span the full width of the house and huge windows gave a view of a large arboretum. On each side of the room were tall bookcases and a one- cylinder roll secretary with glass bookcase doors, top drawer and lower right door. The finish was a deep cherry. Seated behind an enormous writing desk in a similar cherry finish placed in the middle of the room was the Madam of the house.

How to describe Maggie May?

Like Sarah and the others, she was dressed in elegant evening attire. Her dress had a white satin underskirt, kilted in front and trimmed with Mechlin lace, and a garland of pink roses. The overdress was of pink silk with a low neck and short sleeves, and was trimmed to correspond with the underskirt. It was embellished with a low corsage and a bertha of lace and flowers. The flowers in her chestnut hair matched those on her dress; her lustrous tresses coiled up in a twist and delicate tendrils framed a perfectly oval face. Around her neck was a collar of pearls. Her cheeks were pink as cherry blossoms, as were her lips. According to Kate, she was almost forty, but her face was devoid of wrinkles and her skin was flawless. She was exquisitely beautiful and looked no more than thirty.

She had grey eyes like thick, icy cold rain. I doubted that the deepest, most painful emotion could possess them enough to brim over with true sorrow. She looked at us as if squinting into the wind. Silently, she motioned for us to take seats on the two divans that flanked her desk.

Michael sat down on one and I sat down next to Kate on the other. She seemed agitated, deeply affected by being in this place again. I touched her hand.

On the way there, Kate had spoken about her friend at great length. She said that Maggie May had a keen sensibility to sudden changes of fortune and capitalized on them. She had listened eagerly to those men who could give her sound financial advice and never forgot a single detail; she made a note of references to matters of an intimate nature when necessary. According to Kate, she could easily weep soft tears with all the frailty of a woman's heart when it seemed useful to appear to be struck by the contagion of a man's grief. Kate said that if and when needed, she could give vent to a shriek or allow tears to gush forth from her eyes as if on cue.

She spent evenings smoking pipes, playing cards, chatting about politics, horses, cows or whatever it was that made a man rise in the morning to make a living. She manifested no deep affection for family or acquaintance, "except for the girls," Kate said. For them, according to Kate, she would go face to face with the Devil himself.

"Maggie May," Kate said, gesturing to Michael. In a hesitating voice, full of anxiety, she asked, "Do you remember?—"

"Remember him? Of course. It's lovely to see you, Dr. Stamford. "

Her voice was as exquisite as her appearance, like an ocean wave, translucent, rolling, and sparkling like diamonds in the sunlight.

"And this is Michael's sister, Dr. Poppy Stamford."

I said 'hello' and she eyed me closely. "A doctor. A female doctor. I could utilize your services, Dr. Stamford. My ladies would feel so much more comfortable with a female doctor, and their well-being is important to me."

I didn't know how to respond.

"Just think about it," she added quickly. "And you," she said, walking over to Sherlock, "must be Sherlock Holmes. Your reputation precedes you."

"Reputation, Miss Mayhew?" he asked as a satisfied smile appeared on his face.

"Maggie, please," she insisted in the sweetest possible intonation. "You must know that you are well known now as an imminently qualified detective and chemist. At least that is the word in the circles I keep. I am very pleased to meet you," she added, extending her hand.

Sherlock gently kissed the back of her hand and I squashed the tinge of jealousy I felt.

"Now to the matter at hand. I have straightened up quite a bit, but Michael and Kate can attest to how this office looked two days ago. It was ransacked."

Before another word was uttered, Sherlock's eyes darted about the room. He went from the desk to the bookcases to the secretary and back to the desk. He ran a gloved hand across the front of the desk and down the sides and then took out his lens to peer further.

"What are you doing, Sherlock?" Michael asked.

Without answering, Sherlock walked over to the windows and inspected the sills and frames. He kept shaking his head. "We would need a comparison, of course."

I replied. "He was certainly hoping we could get fingerprints."

"Fingerprints?" Maggie asked.

"Sherlock has been in contact with Sir Henry Faulds, a Scottish surgeon who established a mission in Japan. Faulds is experimenting with the use of fingerprints to identify criminals. Faulds says that the pattern of ridges on each person's fingers is unique to each individual."

Maggie's eyebrows raised up in surprise.

"When his hospital was broken into," I continued, "the local police arrested a member of his staff, whom Faulds believed to be innocent. You see, Dr. Faulds started a collection of prints when he studied ancient fingerprint markings on cave walls."

I went on to explain how Dr. Faulds had studied grooves and imprints and how he had proved his staff member innocent by employing his study of fingerprints. "On the strength of his evidence, the police released the man they had suspected of the crime and eventually caught the true thief."

Sherlock looked at me, his own eyebrows now raised in surprise. "You remember all that? All that I told you about Faulds?"

Maggie laughed. "Obviously she does! I do admire a bright, assertive woman."

"Yes, well," Sherlock muttered. "Without a comparison, I suppose it's pointless. And the Yard still does not look for fingerprints on a routine basis. Speaking of that, I don't suppose the Yard found anything."

"I did not contact them," Maggie stated, "for obvious reasons. And we had quickly cleaned up everything, so I don't know that you would find any fingerprints anyway."

"Well, the Yard lacks vision," Sherlock grumbled. "I don't believe they have paid any attention to Faulds' work or its implications in solving cases."

Finally, Sherlock sat down. Maggie stood right in front of him. Staring straight at him and rather obviously ignoring the rest of us, she asked, "Would you like some tea? Or perhaps something stronger? A glass of port, perhaps? I am going to have a glass and I hate to drink alone."

He nodded. "Yes, that would be fine, Miss . . . Maggie."

I had never seen him quite so tongue-tied.

She went over to a small table and poured port into two glasses from a crystal decanter. She handed one to him and lingered before him. Then, as though she realized she'd been purposely oblivious to the rest of us, she said, "Dr. Stamford, Michael, Kate, can I offer you anything?"

Simultaneously, we declined. Swirling the red liquid in her glass, she sat down behind her desk.

"How could that have occurred?" Sherlock asked. "This ransacking you mention. I presume you are rarely alone here. There must have been some activity about. Someone must have noticed or heard something."

"In fact, that was the evening that many of the ladies were at a gathering at the St. Giles house and I and some other ladies were escorted to a performance of Berlioz's *Faust* at St. James Hall."

"So whomever ransacked your office likely was privy to these events and knew the house would be empty."

"I would presume so," she said.

"Hmm," he said, folding his hands beneath his chin as if in prayer. "A concert at St. James, you say? Poppy . . . Dr. Stamford and I attended a concert there last May. Hallé conducted, I believe."

Maggie's face brightened. "Indeed, as he did when *Faust* was performed."

Their eyes held a moment, the silence clutching the air, and I watched as she savored, succored, prevailed as if with a prey caught.

Michael cleared his throat and said, "About the list you told us about."

Maggie broke eye contact with Sherlock and turned to Michael. "Yes, the list. A list of my clients. I believe that is what they were looking for, either because the burglar was himself listed on it or he wishes to blackmail those who are. It could have been any number of men, or quite possibly and more likely, someone who wishes to blackmail one of them. But there are one or two who would have more fear of being compromised than the others. They have made dealings that . . . well, let's just say that Inspector Lestrade would certainly march them to gaol were they discovered."

"May I see the list, Miss Mayhew?" Sherlock asked.

"Maggie," she corrected. "Certainly, you may."

She returned to her desk and opened the middle drawer with a key. We all gathered around Sherlock as she handed it to him.

"Code," he whispered. "It is entirely in code."

"Yes, of course. So I would have no fear of anyone being able to trace any of my clients."

"Then even if it had been discovered, what risk—"

"Because anyone who finds it would know that the list of names and secrets is really all up here," she said, pointing to her temple. "In my head. Trying to get anything out of that which you hold would be like penetrating viney wood or quarried rock. Except perhaps for you, Mr. Holmes. And there are a few who know that I have an almost infinite memory and no need of lists. . . . so my fear is not so much that the list will be found and deciphered, but rather that an intelligent person will realize that the only real thing they need to acquire is—"

"You," Sherlock said.

"And I do not believe I would fare well under inhospitable conditions. Or torture."

6

Sherlock continued to chat with Maggie May while Kate wandered about to see some of her old friends. It occurred to me that despite all my experiences as a doctor—diseases, train wrecks, ships colliding on the Thames, not to mention my various cases with Sherlock that exposed me to thugs, mentally unstable deviants and murderers, I still often saw the world through rose-coloured glasses. I'd never been inside a brothel and it seemed to me that this establishment of Maggie's was by no means a small accomplishment. Obviously, she was not convention-bound and yet the atmosphere reminded me of Mycroft's favourite place, the Diogenes Club. It was quiet, refined. And Maggie was stupendously refined yet beautifully human. I was, to say the least, surprised.

I glanced now and then at Sherlock. I still found him incredibly intriguing. He could be exasperating and eccentric, yet if you paid the right kind of attention to him, absorbing his riffs and digressions as well as his melodies, you would find yourself no longer wishing to fly solo. You wanted to be part of the duet. At least I still did and from the looks of things, Maggie May might like to join the chorus as well. For me, much of the attraction was that Sherlock was simply himself. I had realized long ago that is not necessarily one's deepest fears or personality traits or cultural differences that bring about the devil, but rather their repression. I still worried about the demons Sherlock hid.

"I have some suspects. All speculation, of course," Maggie said.

"But you have some evidence, I presume?"

Sherlock was not disappointed in his expectations.

Maggie handed him three large, bulky file folders, not unlike those one might see in a large bank vault. "These are the three men I trust in the least," she said.

"You are convinced then that it was not a prankster or someone trying to steal something of value?" Sherlock asked.

She shook her head. "There is little of value kept on the premises, but nothing was taken, even items that might be sold on the streets for a shilling or two."

I took notice of the vague thrill in his eyes—an expression that always erupted whenever he smelled the scent of a serious crime.

As he opened the top folder, she said, "Bertrand Littlecode."

On the left inside flap was a sketch of a man who stood, leaning on a silver-topped ebony cane, much like one that Mycroft Holmes always carried. Behind small wire-rimmed glasses and below ragged brown brows were intense, grey eyes. He was quite tall with wide shoulders. His blondish-brown hair was immaculately combed to one side with little curls at the temple, but he was ruggedly handsome.

"He has been involved in several fraudulent activities that have brought him to the brink of . . . well, let's just say that that the fortune he inherited appeared to be evaporating, but he is now involved in several new schemes. He leads an opulent life. He rather thinks of himself as a plutocrat. He feeds his greedy appetites—for women, luxury and travel. But indeed he is a swindler. He works on the London Stock Exchange but was previously in his family's banking business."

Sherlock scanned the file and suddenly muttered, "Eton."

"Pardon me?" Maggie asked.

"It says here that he went to Eton. That he played sports there."

"He's quite proud of that. He is in general quite braggadocious. He played the Wall Game there, a form of football."

"I've never heard of it," I said.

"It's similar to rugby," Michael said.

"Littlecode was a member of both the Oppidans and Mixed Walls," Maggie said. "Though he was not a King's Scholar, he brags about this constantly. He is bright enough," Maggie said. "After all, he was able to get into Cambridge."

"Cambridge," Sherlock scoffed.

"He was at Trinity College there, a non-rowing member of the Trinity Boat Club. A social hub, mainly. And he was expelled from the Magpie and Stump."

"The what?" I asked.

"A formal debating society that inducts about fifty Trinity men each term," Michael said.

"At any rate," Maggie said, "Littlecode entered his family banking business but then wandered into the arena of stocks and bonds. He has engaged in some very questionable deals. He has some new scheme, something about a cathedral."

"A cathedral?"

She nodded.

Sherlock turned to the next folder which contained a sketch of a stocky man in his forties who wore a full beard. He had strange, pale eyes. "Gerard Hamilton?"

"He says that his family owns a grand estate near the Birmingham canal. I know little else about him but that he is an

44

obsessive gambler and owes money to some nefarious people."

"And this third gentleman?" Sherlock asked, turning to the last folder. The sketch was of a small bird-like man, balding as if his feathers had wilted. With large, dark eyes, a close-cropped moustache, and an enormous scimitar-like nose, he looked a bit menacing.

"Arthur Barclay. Also a gambler. He looks much more ominous than he is. He was managing a sisal plantation in the Bahamas but it has not gone well, I'm afraid. He has entered into such projects as re-insurance and public subscriptions to various theatrical ventures. I understand that he is attempting to procure benefactors for the building of an abbey as well."

"Interesting," Sherlock muttered.

"There are others who would have an interest in what is kept here, of course. Jewels, for example, though most of the genuine jewelry is not kept on the premises. I truly believe that the list of my clients was likely the target."

"So you are convinced that whomever ransacked your office was looking for the list to blackmail one or all of them?"

"Yes, or that he is on my list of clients himself and is afraid of *me* blackmailing him."

"And would that be a correct assumption?"

Maggie arched an eyebrow, then chuckled. "I am not above doing it but have never had need to do so. Nor am I so inclined at present."

I urged him to conclude his inquiries as we needed to get going. Michael had to get home to Alexander and Kate needed to fetch little Mary and get back home as well or it would raise suspicions with Aunt Susan.

We rose and Michael and I started walking toward the door. I stopped when I heard Sherlock say, "Maggie, I just have a few more questions."

"Please," she said.

Michael left to find Kate and I lingered.

"The code? Yours?" Sherlock asked.

"Yes, my own invention. But it was inspired by an American Civil War spy. Elizabeth Van Lew."

"I am not familiar with her. She was—?"

"A spy during the Civil War, Mr. Holmes. Miss Van Lew was a member of the Richmond elite, but she defied convention and the Confederacy and fed secrets to the Union during the American Civil War. She was educated in the North and fervently opposed slavery and secession, but she always pretended to be a loyal Confederate. She quietly focused on helping the Union and sent valuable intelligence to Union officers, provided food and medicine to prisoners of war and helped plan their escapes. She ran her own network of spies."

"Really? Intriguing," Sherlock said. "I have always asserted that a woman's mind is quite indecipherable but not necessarily inferior in any way to a man's."

Maggie laughed. "Well, thank you for that astute observation, Mr. Holmes. Miss Van Lew was most creative. She passed information to prisoners using a custard dish with a secret compartment and communicated with them through messages hidden in books. She bribed guards to give prisoners extra food and clothing and to transfer them to hospitals where she could interview them.

"When Grant finally captured Richmond, Virginia in April 1865," Maggie said, "Miss Van Lew received personal thanks from him and several other Union officers. Unfortunately, much of her personal fortune and all of her social standing were gone."

"Because now she was labeled a spy?" I asked.

"Exactly, Dr. Stamford. Her fellow Richmonders couldn't forgive her."

Sherlock leaned forward, then retrieved a pipe from his pocket and lit it. He puffed on it slowly. He had been listening very intently, his keen eyes focused on her face. He did not wish to miss a single word that she said. "And after the war, what happened to her? Was the brave lady rewarded for her espionage efforts?" he asked.

"Her difficulties slightly improved when Grant became president in 1869; he appointed her postmaster of Richmond. After all those years of imitating Anna Smith Strong—or Anna Bates, depending on which side you were on—I suspect that was quite boring."

"Too quiet. Too sedate," Sherlock proffered.

Maggie May's eyes narrowed and she smiled. "Yes, it would have been quite disappointing, wouldn't it? To suddenly be so . . . ordinary."

"Indeed," Sherlock said with a nod.

"You mentioned Anna Smith Strong. And Anna Bates?" I asked. "I have never heard of them."

"Anna Bates was a British spy during the American Revolutionary War. On the other side of the coin was Anna Strong. She sleuthed for the Americans." She sighed. "Anyway, Miss Van Lew needed to work after the war so she toiled at the postal job. But, four years ago, when Rutherford B. Hayes was elected President, Van Lew lost that job and had almost no one to turn to for help. She contacted one of the Union officers she'd helped during the war, the grandson of the famous Paul Revere. The family, along with other wealthy people in Boston whom Van Lew had helped during the war, regularly give her money."

"*How* do you know all this?" Sherlock asked.

She paused a moment, then said, "My young nephew works for a newspaper in Boston. He is but sixteen and mainly runs errands but he hopes to be a journalist one day. He has been researching spy networks of the American Revolution and the Civil War."

"I see. And you admire Miss Van Lew."

"Yes, Sherlock," she said, but she looked directly at me. "I do admire all women who make their way in a man's world."

"Miss Mayhew, the sketches in these folders?" Sherlock asked. "Your work?"

She nodded.

He slapped the folders down on the desk. "Miss Mayhew, you are clearly very bright, innovative, educated, articulate, and creative. Your artwork shows great talent. What are you doing here?"

Her lips turned up in a wry smile and she stared at him with her obscure eyes. "I'm talking to you about a case, Mr. Holmes."

"No, I meant, what are you doing here, with your *life*? Running a brothel?"

Her smile faded. "My reasons are my own, Mr. Holmes. They are none of your business."

I tugged on Sherlock's sleeve and pulled him toward the door.

As we left, Maggie said, "Do your investigation with speed, Mr. Holmes. I do not like feeling vulnerable and I have a business to run."

7

Michael and Kate went back to his place to collect the children. He said that he would put Kate and Mary in a hansom to take them home, so Sherlock and I walked home in the fog. There was always the fog . . . but at least it was nothing like it had been earlier in the year. That impenetrable 'soup,' as Sherlock often referred to it, smelt of sulphur and coated every surface. It was as black as the death it caused. Now it varied from grey-yellow to orange, but always it seemed to swirl about our feet.

Again, I thought of Victor Trevor in India. He had described his environment in letters to Michael many times and it sounded so different from London, so sunny and beautiful. He wrote of the throb of crickets, the moonlight that flooded the night sky, the trees trembling in the breeze, and the baskets of colorful, unusual flowers—jasmine and jãtĩ and cãpä—often wilting in the blazing sun at the markets. And the magical mixture of blue above and green below and all the mysteries of his exotic new country.

"What are you thinking about, Poppy?" Sherlock asked, as he pulled up his pocket watch to check the time. "Sleep, no doubt."

Suddenly pulled back to cold, damp reality, I shivered and gave him a shrug. "No, not sleep. But of nothing important. You?"

"Art."

"You are thinking about art, really? You?"

"You used to sketch. I remember that design you were sketching the day we met. A brooch you envisioned for graduates of your nursing school, wasn't it?"

I nodded.

"It had symbols from the coat of arms of St. Thomas's. The Tudor rose, a fleur de lis, and the shield with the sword of St. Paul. And you used to make sketches of St. Paul's, as well. You do not draw anymore."

"I've been a bit busy, Sherlock. With medical school and then my practice and with our cases. What makes you bring this up? Is it Maggie May's sketches?"

Instead of directly responding, he replied, "I would think artwork is not unlike music. I play the violin; I listen to music. It is soothing."

"Well, I am not all that fine of an artist."

"That does not matter, Poppy. I am not a virtuoso on the violin either but—"

"But what? Tell me, Sherlock, does playing the violin aid your thoughts, or is the playing simply the result of a whim or fancy?" I blushed and laughed. "Oh, never mind. You are not given to whim or fancy."

"Well, like meditation or distancing oneself from a problem for a while, I suppose it enables the thinking process. When I listen to Sarasate play, for example, I must admit I am genuinely pulled away from the ordinary boredom of life."

"Pablo Sarasate . . . you have mentioned him before."

"Yes, he's astounding. He is the son of an artillery bandmaster. He picked up the violin when he was just four or so and played a passage of music perfectly that his father had been struggling to play for a long time. He began studying the violin at the age of five. He appeared in his first public concert at the age of eight."

"So you have you seen him in concert, Sherlock?"

"I have. He first came to England when he was seventeen. He played at the Crystal Palace in 1861. I was but seven years old but Mycroft and I went with our mother."

His eyes grew distant for a moment. He rarely spoke of his parents. I knew little about his mother except that she had forced him to read *Romeo and Juliet* once and that she died in a freak hansom cab accident.

"I was also privileged to see him and hear him play at St. James in May of 1874," he continued, "not long before we met. He played Lalo's *Violin Concerto in F.* It was exquisite. He is an excellent composer as well, but he absolutely *sings* on his instrument. He has purity of style, brightness of tone, excellent flexibility and facility. Never have I heard anyone play Mendelssohn's *Violin Concerto* with so great a speed, such fire and dash," he exclaimed, his hands now animated as if he were plucking strings himself. "But he can play a Chopin nocturne equally well and with tenderness and grace and charm.

"I shall never play the violin like Pablo Martin Meliton de Sarasate y Navascues, and the more cases that come my way, the less time I have for such an indulgence at any rate. But that does not keep me from playing. You should not let your art fall away if you enjoy it."

We walked along silently for a few minutes. Then he asked, "What do you make of all this? This intrusion into Miss Mayhew's home. Her suspects."

"I'm not sure yet, Sherlock. You?"

"I think we must interview all of these men without them realizing it. This Littlecode . . . I find that chap interesting. Kate mentioned Tothill Fields and Maggie May mentioned a cathedral scheme and that got me to thinking. There were three separate gaols at Tothill Fields, one for male prisoners and debtors, one for male convicts, and one for women. Inmates were put to work treading the treadmills to power cranes. They were widely used in the Middle Ages to lift the stones in the Gothic cathedrals, you know."

"No Sherlock, I did not know that. But what has that to do with the break-in at The Pink Flamingo?"

"Perhaps nothing. Perhaps everything. Prisoners have been transferred to Millbank Prison and the old gaols will soon be demolished," he said. "Mycroft was just telling me that there are rumours that the prison foundations will be used for a new cathedral. Westminster, I believe he called it. He said that Cardinal Manning is negotiating the purchase of the land to erect the cathedral in memory of his predecessor Cardinal Wiseman. But the archdiocese needs money."

I doubted that this proposed abbey's spires would ever soar into London's sky." It is unlikely that project will ever come to fruition, Sherlock. Uncle Ormond knew the original architect, Henry Clutton, and his plans were scuttled long ago."

"Yes, Clutton started work on the cathedral a decade ago. The archdiocese could not afford to implement his plans."

The space between his close-set eyes seemed to narrow even more. He was thinking. He was mining data in his brain attic. His mind was like a palimpsest, a manuscript—a piece of writing material on which the original writing has been effaced to make room for later writing but of which traces remain. He was good at acquiring and building a knowledge base of that which he believed would be helpful in his work. He'd relax by playing the violin or smoking a pipe—and sometimes by using cocaine or other deleterious substances—and let his brain sort through the data of a specific case until it all came together. His was a powerful mind, a quiet mind that was present, reflective, mindful of its thoughts and its state. He did not allow trivia into it unless it served a purpose. He always said that problems with evidence can result from hasty, incomplete, or biased interpretation.

Sometimes Sherlock was like a lonely, brooding sentinel, gazing out across an endless tide of crimes to be solved . . . and I was caught in the hypnotic spell of his heroic dimensions.

But why he thought the history of financing this fantasy cathedral was important, I had no idea.

"Sherlock, for someone who claims to keep his brain uncluttered, you certainly can collect useless information."

"But, it may not be useless. There is an appeal for benefactors to come forward and—"

"And?"

"And the information is not useless if it has to do with the need for benefactors and a man who might be trying to convince them to invest in a cathedral." He drew a breath and said, "Incidentally, I believe Maggie May needs protection."

"Will you talk to Lestrade?"

He laughed. "Now why would I do that? No, I shall ask Wiggins to keep an eye on Miss Mayhew. He'll see to it that no one accosts her or breaks in again until we sort all of this out."

"Wiggins is a bit young to be . . . well, I mean he is impressionable and—"

Sherlock laughed out loud and clapped his hands together. "Wiggins? Impressionable? The boy has been arrested for grave digging and skirted the law on numerous occasions. Poppy, dear Poppy, he is anything but impressionable."

He saw me to the door and said, "About the problem with Loke, the stable boy. He still works at the Trevor estate?"

I nodded.

"Well, that must be sorted out as well, I suppose. Perhaps once we solve this Mayhew matter, we can travel to Norfolk. It has been some time since you saw your parents, has it not?"

"Quite a long time, yes. Because of the illnesses caused by the fog, I was not there last Christmas, as you know. So I must definitely make an effort to be there this year. But Loke is in trouble, so it really can't wait. I could see about it while you work on the Mayhew case."

"No, Loke is a good lad. And for now, he is safe."

"I don't understand, Sherlock."

"Oh, yes, I should have told you about the telegram your mother sent to Michael. Loke is out on bail. Your mother posted it. And he and Marie are living back at Burleigh Manor now, away from the Trevor Estate and the man who accused him. The Scottish chap who worked for Victor's father . . . you may remember him, Henry MacLean. He left a few months ago. He was replaced by a man named Mansell. He is the one who says that his injuries are Loke's fault, that it is because of his training that the horse attacked him."

Flabbergasted, I stuttered the next words. "M . . . m . . . my . . . mother posted bail? But she threw Loke and Marie out when she discovered they were involved. That's how they ended up working at Victor Trevor's estate."

"I know. She had a change of heart. She always liked Marie, and Loke, as well. She does not believe that he would intentionally hurt anyone."

"My gracious," I whispered. Like Aunt Susan, my mother was very rigid about what her employees could and could not do. When she discovered that Marie and Loke were seeing each other, she had turned them both out but because Loke was so wonderful with horses and Mrs. Hudson was leaving, Victor hired them both.

"I think Loke is safely out of his reach but nevertheless, I shall make certain that nothing happens to him until I have a chance to investigate. I will deal with this man Mansell. As soon as I figure out what has been going on at The Pink Flamingo," Sherlock added.

I did not even ask how he planned to delay a court case against Loke. If Sherlock Holmes said he would do something, he did it.

"Shall we meet for lunch tomorrow to discuss this further?"

"I am meeting Oscar tomorrow, Sherlock. At Pagani's."

"Oh, well . . . Then—" He paused and quite impulsively, I assume, pecked my cheek. I resisted my natural impulse to lean toward him and kiss his lips.

He said, "Good night," and turned to walk down the dark street.

As I closed the door behind me, I leaned against it and closed my eyes. Then I walked to the library and over to the window. I stared up at the sky. It was cold and clear. It seemed that in the deep silence, a million stars smiled and whispered among themselves, mocking my heart, my frailty.

Sherlock was a confirmed bachelor; his life was controlled and planned. He would not allow his carefully tailored life to be disrupted by love. He seemed, at times, almost nihilistic, convinced that life was without objective meaning or purpose, with the exception of solving cases, at least. I had become a fixture in his life. I think I flattered him and gave him companionship. He would allow nothing more, but occasionally, he showed his vulnerable side to me. Those moments were increasingly and exceedingly rare, but on those occasions, despite my Herculean efforts not to allow it, he still tugged at my heart, just a little bit.

8

In the deep silence of the night, which was only occasionally broken by the sound of Little Elihu whimpering and moving his paws as he dreamed at the end of my bed, I could not find my way to slumber.

Aunt Susan had placed a vase of flowers on my dresser, the blossoms clipped, no doubt, from pots in the small greenhouse she'd had erected behind her music room, which was reached by French doors. The flowers sweetened the air with their perfume and I instantly recalled the morning after I'd spent the night with Sherlock in a small cottage at Holme-Next-the-Sea. It had been almost six years but I remembered every detail. Waking up alone in a strange bed the following morning to the sound of screeching seagulls in the distance. Hearing the marvelous sound of waves crashing to shore. Seeing the most beautiful display of floral jewels on the fainting couch near the window. Wild flowers of every kind were strewn the length of it—blooms in gold and violet and blue and red that Sherlock had gathered at dawn. The memory jolted my heart, just as it had when I'd realized he had left that shower of flowers cascading across the deep red velvet couch in the cottage.

I crawled down to the end of the bed and rested my palm on Elihu's chest, feeling it rise and fall. Then I turned over on my back and stared at the ceiling. I had managed to bury my feelings for Sherlock, outwardly at least, and we had fallen into a somewhat pleasant rhythm of friendship. Rarely was that romantic interlude mentioned. But I wondered—even though I could forget my feelings during my wakeful hours, why did I still carry some disappointment with me into my dreams?

I sighed. Uncle said it was difficult getting over your first love. On that we agreed. I was in the spring of my life, yet sometimes felt like a cloudy autumn, like the remnant of a leaf uselessly floating in the sky.

Elihu woke briefly, shifted, and scooted up to lay his head on my pillow. I joined him there, plumped up another pillow, put it behind me and let my thoughts drift. I knew the best cure for me was to concentrate on my career and the people in my life who did not hesitate to show their feelings for me. Oscar Wilde, Effie's cousin, was one of them.

I reached into my night stand and retrieved notes and letters from Oscar since I would be meeting him for lunch the next day and anticipated he might ask me my opinion of his works-in-progress.

Oscar was living in London, now with little intention of returning to Ireland. The woman he had planned to marry had instead wed Bram Stoker, the man who would one day write *Dracula.* Oscar had only been back to Ireland twice since she announced her engagement to Stoker. Now twenty-six, the same age as Sherlock, Oscar shared rooms with an artist named Frank Miles at 3 Tite Street in Chelsea, where he was busy writing every day. He also popped up everywhere in literary circles and seemed omnipresent in boxes and dress circles of theaters. He had just published *PAN, A Villanelle*, in *The Pall Mall Gazette* in September and several sonnets and several poems in *The World.* Just as Sherlock's reputation as a detective was growing exponentially, Oscar's success as a writer seemed preordained.

Oscar had sent me fragments of something that would soon be published, *To Helen,* about Helen of Troy, and I loved some of the lines. *The waning sky grows faint and blue, It wants an hour still of day*. He'd also sent a few lines of another poem he was writing, one called *The Artist's Dream*. In it, he said, *I too have had my dreams; ay, known too well The crowded visions of fiery youth. Which haunt me still.* I had often felt like that, wanting something I could not have, haunted by dreams that I knew would never materialize, like breaking down the male bastion to become a surgeon at Bart's and purging Sherlock Holmes entirely from my heart.

Sometimes, to my deep shame, I felt embarrassed by Oscar Wilde. He was so flamboyant and unusual-looking. He was tall and bulky and had dark, flowing hair, glowing eyes, a pale face with large lips, heavy cheeks, a high forehead and a firm jaw. He dressed meticulously but with eccentricity and always carried a walking stick from his large collection of them. Papa called him outlandish. Michael said he was 'fanciful.' Sherlock had little use for him.

I put the bits and pieces of Oscar's literary works aside and opened Effie's last journal. I read it in fits and starts because it was so difficult, knowing that she'd written it while she was carrying Alexander. He was now three and a half years old, a year older than Kate's daughter Mary. The image of his mother, sweet and full of life.

Now I turned in Effie's journal to a prediction she'd written just weeks before she died that I'd suddenly recalled. She had actually titled it, 'The Case of the Three Species.' I had previously read it as I so often did, quickly and through a veil of tears, but I distinctly remembered her mentioning pink flamingoes.

You will have another adventure with Sherlock, she wrote, *and I take, dearest Poppy, this moment to once again remind you that he is not good for you.*

I closed the journal for a few minutes, remembering. On the night of the dinner when the photograph in my locket was taken, she has issued her firtst warnings.

"He'll suck you in, Poppy . . . your feelings for him are going to draw you in."

"You're wrong," I had scolded. *"You're being irrational."*

Her eyes narrowed and her entire face took on a cat-like expression, as if she were about to growl and pounce. *"Who is being irrational?"* she had purred.

Later that night, she and I had a longer discussion about Sherlock. We had returned to Effie's house after dinner and Effie slipped into my room just as Little Elihu and I were settling under the covers. *"He's callous beyond belief,"* she said. *"He's not good for you."*

"Who?"

"Sherlock Holmes."

"What would make you say such a thing?"

Of course, I knew why she had said it. It was plain that Effie had jumped to the conclusion that I had fallen for Sherlock Holmes.

"He is using you. And as so often occurs when a woman falls in love, you do not see it. I used to think that your heart was made of cast iron—and I do not mean that in a derogatory way.

I know you care very much about people and about your friends. But I did not think that a man could cloud your judgment."

"I truly do not understand what you're talking about, Effie," I'd protested.

"Sherlock Holmes wants to crack this baby farmer case to show up his brother. Nothing more . . . "

At that time, we were in the middle of the very first case we had worked on in a partnership, a case involving baby farmers, despicable individuals who paid unwed mothers for their infants and then sold them to adoptive couples, or sometimes killed them to make room for more.

"He doesn't give a fig about your safety," Effie had continued. "He just wants to solve this riddle. You're in love. You're too blind to see how wrong he is for you. It's not without precedent, you know. It happens."

"I will not reproach you, Effie, for surely you are joking. You would never say such a wicked and absurd thing in earnest."

"Poppy, I can see how you would be attracted to his mind. I can see how you would find him exciting, mysterious."

"Effie, I am almost engaged to Victor Trevor. You said it yourself."

"You certainly did not sound 'almost engaged' when you argued with him tonight."

"Everyone has spats now and then, Effie. That's all it was. If he asked me to marry him, I—"

She interrupted me. "You would say no. You would be miserable with Sherlock, but now—" Then she paused, tilted her head and sighed. "Now, unfortunately, you would probably be miserable with Victor. I

62

am sad for you. You may have been settling for Victor Trevor, but I believed that he loved you enough for both of you. Now, with Sherlock in the picture . . . Victor can never be Sherlock, Poppy."

"Effie, you don't know what you're talking about."

But she had pressed on.

"Poppy, dearest, you have fallen in love with Sherlock Holmes and Victor is not blind or stupid. Sweetest, it's written all over your face."

I remember how I'd flushed. My cheeks felt as though I'd been in the hot sun all day.

"Normally, I would be so happy for you," Effie said. *"I've wondered if you would ever feel love. You are so logical and practical, but to live in this world without love is to live in a great, sucking void. I so wish I could help you through what is coming,"* she said, tucking a strand of my hair behind my ear as if she were tucking the pain I was going to feel out of sight.

Now I wiped away a tear, remembering my dear friend's face, her silky blonde hair, her soulful eyes, her impish humor and unfailing optimism. She was soft as pure air, like a violet peering from a hiding place, afraid only of her own fragility and her strange and secret psychic life, a morning star with an open heart. She took great joy in everything, especially fashion and nature with all their colors. Be it a fancy, floral hat that she had created, or white lilies, or butterflies in burnished brown and gold in a pasture, or little birds charming her with songs in the woods, Effie adored them all. Often she would twirl on the banks of the rivers in the Broads and burst into song herself. She had a bright vision of the world, so different from my own tortured, tormented pessimism about my future back then when I so longed to be a doctor and could not get into a medical school without leaving England.

Sighing now, I focused on the words she'd written.

It was an odd dream, this. I cannot fathom what is fated but I know it is unavoidable. You will encounter, of all things, pink flamingos. They are bright and beautiful but there are secrets beneath their flamboyant, startling wings. Do not be fooled by their long slender legs and graceful necks or their friendliness. There is more going on beneath the tucked wings I see.

And then I saw a mare—she was out of control, kicking and lashing out. I kept seeing Victor Trevor in the dream which makes no sense. I don't know what to make of it.

And finally, just before I woke, I saw a parade of elephants. At first I thought I was dreaming of the London Mayor's Parade—you know the ones—the gorgeous, magnificent, triumphant elephants dressed in their Oriental trappings and howdahs, ridden by young boys. But they were not dressed like that. They had diamonds on their toes and were fitted with bloomers like the ones I used to sew for us to wear when we went biking at Oxford. Most unusual.

And as is so often the case, I have no idea what it means. But be careful, Poppy. Especially of the elephants.

So she had predicted a case relating to pink flamingoes and one involving a horse. But elephants in bloomers?

Exhausted and puzzled, I closed the journal and extinguished the light, hoping to catch a few hours of sleep.

But visions of raging horses and pink flamingoes with wings arched and thundering elephants in white bloomers kept sleep at bay.

9

When I met Oscar Wilde on Thursday for lunch, he was, as usual, fashionably late for our lunch at Pagani's. And, in keeping with the norm, *his* norm, he was dressed in a dark purple vest, waistcoat, pants and cape, with a dark fur stole draped over his shoulders.

"Poppy!" he exclaimed and held out his arms to embrace me. He gave me a tight hug and then escorted me to our table in the Artist's Room. I had never been to this this restaurant, but I could see why Oscar wanted to dine there.

The main dining room was very pretty with blue paper on the walls and soft blue curtains at a little bow-window at the back. But the décor of the Artist's Room was quite different. When we came to the little room with its ruby velvet curtains and mantel drapings, I saw that the walls were pasted with squares of brown paper at about the height of a man's head and were covered with drawings and writings protected by glass. There were framed drawings and paintings and hundreds of notes and signatures of famous patrons, including actress Sarah Bernhardt and the famous Italian composer, Giacomo Puccini. The owner had even installed shaded electric lights, quite the new invention at that time.

This was astonishing. Earlier that year, the very first home in the world to use the incandescent lamps invented by Joseph Swan was Cragside, the country house in Northumberland owned by William Armstrong, an industrial magnate, scientist and inventor.

And one of the little lamps shone on Oscar Wilde's signature.

I don't recall what I ordered that day, but Oscar's meal was unforgettable. He made it clear that he was starving by ordering bortsch soup, tournedos aux truffes, haricots verts sautés, and soufflé au curaçao. "I pondered the calf's brains and lark-and-steak pie but that seems a bit heavy for mid-day."

I laughed. "Oh, yes, a bit heavy indeed. How are you, Oscar?" I asked, squeezing his hand. "You are such a prolific writer now. Getting so famous."

"I am having some success, yes, despite so many people doubting it would ever be so."

"I have never for a moment doubted your greatness, Oscar. You've come a long way since winning the Newdigate Prize. That was just the beginning."

He smiled.

"And so, you have not gone to America yet. You are well settled in London now?"

"Yes, for the time being. And behaving."

"Meaning?"

"Bram Stoker just offered me tickets to a performance at the Lyceum Theater and I accepted. You know that Stoker manages the theater now."

"So you are speaking to him now? I thought after he married your Florence—"

He waved his hand through the air. "We are artists. And who can blame Florence? He has a steady income and the theater is doing well. This year opened with *The Corsican Brothers* and on 3 January, Henry Irving will perform in Tennyson's *The Cup*. It is highly anticipated. Critics predict it will be one of the most beautiful stage productions in which Irving ever starred."

I had seen Henry Irving in *Hamlet* in 1874, the year I met Sherlock, with Uncle Ormond and Aunt Susan. He was tall and thin and wiry with a beautiful face and expressive features, but I had heard he was very proud, self-centered and egotistic.

"Do you enjoy Irving's performances, Oscar?"

"I do. And Stoker certainly does. Frankly, I think he has great affection for Irving. He is drawn to his devotion to his work and dedication to the dignity of his art, and his sensitivity. Irving has a certain genius, even though his speech can be a bit slow and his peculiar pronunciation and monotonous voice are distracting. But I saw him alternating as Othello and Iago and he also showed a very different and new Shylock in *The Merchant of Venice*. He was the grandest and most sympathetic figure in the play. Irving is remote; Stoker is gregarious and emotional. They complement each other. And as for Irving, why, I could feel affection for him, too!"

"Are you saying that Bram Stoker . . . that he feels some peculiar affection for Irving?"

"I think Stoker has some untapped desires that Florence cannot quench. I think Irving makes him whole."

I lowered my head, not just because Oscar had insinuated that Stoker might have romantic feelings toward Irving, but because he had struck a nerve with his words. I often felt that Sherlock Holmes quenched some untapped desires within me and that he alone could make me whole. I was relieved when our lunches arrived.

We were halfway through lunch before Oscar asked me if I had ever finished reading the journal written by his cousin Effie.

I placed my fork down and pushed my plate away. Immediately he noticed and, always sensitive, said, "I'm sorry, Poppy. No need to talk about it."

I shook my head. "It is just that I miss her so. But I was reading the journal again just last night."

He scowled. "Don't tell me, more predictions."

I nodded. "Something about mares. Horses."

"Horses?"

"Yes, horses and elephants, and pink flamingoes."

He looked at me, puzzled. "That is odd. Even for my late cousin."

"Yes, it is."

A few moments later, our lunch was abruptly interrupted. Twice.

10

"Wiggins!" I said, as young Bill Wiggins approached, marching in with his usual air of superiority, despite being dressed in overalls and a dirty shirt. I was amazed he'd been permitted to enter but Wiggins was nothing if not persistent.

"Oscar, you remember Archibald Wiggins?"

"Ah yes, still a little scarecrow."

"'ello, Guv'nor."

"What are you doing here? How did you find me? And aren't you supposed to be keeping watch over Miss Mayhew?"

"Mr. 'olmes is with Miss Maggie. 'e said you would be here. She sent me. Yer know that Mr. 'olmes pays us a shilling and expenses and a guinea if we gives 'im a clue about an investigation."

"Yes, I know," I said, hiding a smile behind my napkin.

"Well, Miss Maggie offered double that to bring yer a message."

"I am all attention, Wiggins. What is her message?"

"She would like t' see ya. She 'as a . . . a propo . . . a proposit . . . a—"

"A proposition?" Oscar asked. "How intriguing." He turned to me. "Who is this Maggie?"

I felt myself blush. "A friend."

"She owns a place down on Whitehall. Th' Pink Flamingo," Wiggins said.

"The brothel!" Oscar said, his usual lyrical voice escalating to an almost shrill. "Do tell us what kind of proposition that might be!"

"She'll tell yer 'erself," he said to me. "Come at three for tea, Miss."

I glanced down at the watch pinned to my bodice. "Three, you say. Is it urgent?"

He shrugged.

"And she will pay you when you return?"

"If ya say yes."

I smiled again. "Then tell Miss Mayhew I shall be there at three."

He turned and ran out of the restaurant and Oscar clapped his hands together. "A proposition from a brothel owner. Dear Dr. Stamford, what have you—"

"It's nothing, Oscar," I hissed. "Just stop."

"Oh, this could be even more interesting than the Prince's affair with Lily Langtry."

"Ssshh."

We had barely finished the rest of our lunch when once again we were disrupted. This time it was Sherlock.

"What are you doing here?" I asked.

"Hello, Oscar," he said as he sat down between us. "I'm glad you are here. I have a proposition for both of you."

"Wiggins was just here with a message for me to come to see Maggie because *she* has a proposition."

"Yes, I know. I have an idea which I need to discuss with you. I've already talked to Maggie May about it. It's a scathingly brilliant idea and one which involves you as well, Oscar."

"Me?"

"Yes, to help with a case. You are becoming widely known in literary circles, are you not?

"Of course."

"People come to hear you speak. To hear you recite your poetry?"

"Yes."

"Well, then you can be of great help in this venture."

"Is it dramatic? Theatrical? Amusing?"

"All of those things."

Oscar raised his wine glass and said, "Count me in then. Whatever it might be."

11

When we left the restaurant, Oscar hailed a hansom. Stretching my fingers into my wool gloves, I said, "Oscar, you really must get more exercise and eat less!"

"To stay young forever, I would do anything, Poppy! Except get up early, be respectable or *exercise*!"

I laughed, waved after him, and Sherlock and I started walking toward Maggie May's.

"He and Mycroft . . . both of them, broad and fat," Sherlock grumbled. "Mycroft walks round the corner into Whitehall every morning and back every evening. He takes no other exercise, is seen nowhere else, except the Diogenes Club. They both shall be sorry for it."

"No doubt, Sherlock, but they are grown men and set in their ways. Just like you."

He ignored my last comment. "Now, tell me what you think of my idea. You seemed rather subdued in there when I proposed my plan."

"That is because I think it is insane!"

"It's perfectly logical."

I stopped in my tracks and faced him. "Sherlock Holmes, you want Mrs. Hudson to allow you to use her boarding house as a fake Grand Opening of a new brothel to which the suspects are invited. As extra incentive, you want Oscar to do a reading to draw them in. You want *me* to masquerade as a prostitute and *you* intend to appear as an actor who is promoting a new play. It is very insane."

"It is not. I am simply trying to get to the bottom of this and to protect Miss Mayhew and her ladies."

"Sherlock, it is not like you to defend the common women of the street."

Sherlock had, in fact, made some rather derogatory comments in the past about the ladies of the night who migrated from St. James or Marylebone to Covent Gardens or from the Strand to St. Giles.

"Well, getting more fully acquainted with Miss Mayhew has enlightened me a bit. Common is not an apt description. She is quite a superior woman. And often we are formed by our environment, are we not?"

"So if I partake in this ruse, I would be disguised as a *superior* prostitute, is that what you are saying?"

"I am simply saying that it our duty now to uncover the criminal scheme behind the burglary at Miss Mayhew's establishment. The point is there is a criminal game afoot and the ladies are quite vulnerable. You would not want anyone to be harmed as a result of our negligence, would you?"

"Well, no, but—"

"As I spoke with Maggie today, several stories similar to Kate's history emerged. Take, for example, Sarah, the girl who met us last night at the door. She was an unfortunate. Her father was a stonecutter in Derbyshire. She wanted to visit London to see the fine shops and so on and so she visited an aunt. She stole out one evening when her aunt was under the weather and wandered about and got lost. She ended up on some dark street, knocked on one of the doors and told the woman who let her in that she was lost, that she needed to get back to Bank Place. The woman pulled out a bottle of gin. The drink was drugged. You can imagine what followed. Sarah never got free and was sent from a bawdy house in St. James to one in Portland Place and then to one on Cuzon Street and finally to one in near the Guard's Club. She tried to steal something to exchange for food. Maggie witnessed this and took her in."

"Maggie May could have sent her home," I noted.

"Apparently by then, Sarah did not want to go home, Poppy. She likes being free of restraint. She is content at Maggie May's maison de passé. There is lust in the aristocracy . . . illustrious lords, noble dukes, princes of royal blood—these are the men who frequent The Pink Flamingo. The house is frequented by men who have plenty of money at their command and spend it quite freely and this allows Maggie to educate the ladies, to dress them well and feed them well. Should they choose to leave, they take with them their clothing, accessories and education.

"And Miss Mayhew's accomplishments are not superficial, I assure you," he added. "She is originally from Liverpool. Her father went to jail and her mother died when she was young. She went to work as a maid but tired of the drudgery and rules, so she struck off on her own. Somehow she educated herself and her sister. Her sister married very young and moved to America. She is the mother of the nephew Maggie mentioned, the young apprentice journalist in Boston. The father is dead; he joined the Union Army during the Civil War and was killed in battle."

"But, Sherlock, even such a difficult upbringing should not push a woman into—into such a profession."

"Maggie did not want to mind a shop or tend to domestic matters or engage in sewing, though she has a love of fashion and display. Those trivial matters do not gratify her. Apparently, she took up with a young man and they came to London but tired of one another after a few months. They were apparently eager to take their leave of one another. She lived for the moment and gave little thought to the morrow. She was an artist's model for some period of time after that but realized she had more talent than most of the artists for whom she posed. But she was unable to make a living with her artwork—*why* escapes me—and ended up in one of the houses of ill repute. She is shrewd and clever. Never reckless. Truth be told, I think she is one of the most charming women I ever met, and might be most useful in such work as we have been doing. And her life has been full . . . she told me that she buys a new bonnet once a week and several dresses a month. She likes casinos, she takes dancing lessons; she has a box at the opera. She was charmed with Cremorne and is quite interested in Equestrian exercise."

"Cremorne, the famous racehorse?"

"The same. The one who won the Ascot Gold Cup in 1873. Maggie was there."

"And she engages in Equestrian exercise?"

"One of her benefactors is a country squire and she frequents his estate where he keeps a horse for her. She is quite knowledgeable about horses and I made inquiry about Loke's predicament. Michael received another telegram about Loke's predicament from his wife. Didn't he tell you? I have more facts to explore on that matter."

"But, Sherlock, they are still—" I stopped. I thought of Kate again. She was a former prostitute, now a cook and sometimes a nanny. And someone my brother had come to love. Uncle was right; we had no right to judge. "Oh, never mind."

Then I thought about the plan further. "Sherlock, I cannot be seen in such a place. You know that Uncle Ormond is well known in Parliament and the Privy Council. I—"

He put a finger to my lips to quiet me. "Poppy, you will be fine. You'll be with me."

I instantly recalled what I'd re-read and re-remembered last night. Effie had said, *"He'll suck you in, Poppy . . . your feelings for him are going to draw you in."* And my brother Michael . . . his words ricocheted inside my brain. *You still run to him if he crooks his little finger.*

"Poppy, you will be dressed differently. You will be . . . well, painted! You will likely be unrecognizable. Think of the great fun it will be to fool all of them whilst we interrogate right under their noses."

They were right, Effie and Michael. They were both right. So I started to protest.

"Sherlock, I don't think that I should—"

"Please, Poppy. Do this for me."

I paced for a few moments, thinking. I'd read a poem recently—not one of Oscar's but one by a young man from India I'd met the previous year. It went something like, "The daylight hides in the dark of his hair, His arms hold life and death in their power. The world falls silent to hear him."

Damn you, Sherlock Holmes, I thought.

But suddenly I realized it wasn't just Sherlock that drew me into these precarious situations. It wasn't *just* Sherlock anymore. It was really something far more intoxicating.

It was the *adventure.*

12

Sherlock and I arrived at The Pink Flamingo promptly at three and tea was served at once, but Sherlock was asked to take his cuppa and wait in the library. Reluctantly, he left me alone with Maggie in her office. She wore a lovely day dress now, a navy plaid with a high collar, not unlike those that Queen Victoria favored when she visited Balmoral, her castle in Scotland.

"Dr. Stamford," she said, "before I discuss the plan that Sherlock has hatched to ferret out the criminal, I want to explore something else with you."

"Yes?"

"I am certain that a woman of your position and background is reluctant to associate in any way with my kind of woman—"

"No," I interrupted. "It's—"

She cut me off. "Obviously, you are a woman of privilege. You were likely brought up in a strict moral environment. I understand if you have a low opinion of the services my ladies provide."

"Maggie, I—"

"But you have never known hunger. You have never known what it is like to not have a scrap to eat. You come from a family of some means."

"Maggie, I am not judging."

"Whether you do or not matters little to me."

"But I—"

She put out her hand to cut me short. "What I know is that you have been kind to Kate. You exhibit great fondness for her."

"I am very fond of Kate."

She took a sip of tea. "I want you to know something about my establishment. It would be a great mistake to suppose that my ladies are without friends or morals or honour. Their male acquaintances are select and they travel in a brougham or a carriage and at a fashionable hour pay visits to their friends and leave calling cards. Though they have several lovers, they are quite discreet. They are in the habit of receiving them at different times and escape detection, of course.

"One of my former ladies now calls herself Lady Waller and his Lordship purchased a home for her in one of the terraces overlooking Regent's Park, where I believe you reside. He allows her four thousand pounds a year and she passes time when not in his society with a box at the opera or the pit tier and lives very well. She receives precious jewelry from him and beautiful dresses.

"Another lived similarly until she was caught at a performance with a younger man, after which her elderly amour gave her congé and five hundred pounds and tossed her out of the house he had rented for her. Very foolish and unwise of her."

It occurred to me that Sherlock's congé—his unceremonious dismissal of me after our one night of romance a few years before—did not include the sum of five hundred pounds. I wondered if I should feel slighted.

Before I could get a word in edgewise, she continued. "I am very careful as to who I admit to these rooms. We have a supper room and the men who come here must have the intention of spending ten pounds at least. They would shrink from being seen on Haymarket but not from my establishment. Many of the ladies are like Kate. They fell on misfortune and they found their way to these houses. But many of my ladies were dress-makers, milliners, shoe-binders, pastry cooks and were simply fatigued of the monotony—something to which I can relate—and longed to frequent fairs and theaters and dancing rooms.

"One of the girls met a man at Sam's last year and they were married at St. George's at Hanover Square a few months later. My ladies dress well, they can converse on a variety of subjects. They insinuate themselves into the hearts of men by appealing to their passions and their occupations.

"I am sure it is difficult for you to comprehend why a woman would stray or stumble into this life. Be that as it may, as an assertive, ambitious young woman, you pushed through the barriers you face. So can you understand why a person might struggle to purchase some freedom, especially in the face of a secret, creeping awareness of failure or anguish or a tragic childhood. Take Sherlock, for example."

"Sherlock? Excuse me?"

"I suspect that he is who he is because of a difficult childhood . . . or some emotional turmoil or a perceived failure on his part. These things affect men as well. Some people sob from the soul. Some turn inward."

She drew a deep breath. "Sherlock tells me that you are an excellent doctor. Kate affirms that. And I understand you are calm under pressure. The Thames boat disaster, for instance. All of us went there to help in any way we could. Rolling bandages, comforting the children." She paused and met my eyes. "You stood out, Dr. Stamford. You were so attentive and tender, even with the corpses."

I gasped, remembering the hundreds of corpses lined up after the boat collision on the Thames. People came from everywhere to look for survivors and deal with the dead, even inmates from workhouses. But I had no idea that Maggie's lot had been there.

"Now, nothing I tell you is going to extinguish the fact that what we do for a living is unseemly in the eyes of someone like you, Dr. Stamford. Nevertheless, if you can look past that, as you have with Kate, I have a proposal."

I really didn't know how to respond so I just nodded and waited.

"My ladies should have good medical treatment. More importantly, the people who live in the area of my other two establishments do not have access to good doctors and hospitals as do most of the residents in this area. I should like to pay you to look after my ladies' medical needs and should you agree to do so, I shall open a clinic in the building in Shadwell. The clientele there is comprised mostly of sailors and men of the sort I would rather avoid. Also, there is too much competition. One man alone owns thirty brothels nearby. But my ladies need attention and the people in that area likewise are in dire need of a free medical clinic."

My ears perked up. A free medical clinic. A place to treat everything from skinned knees to traumatic injuries, to give good prenatal care and deliver babies. Something I had always dreamed of.

"If you will attend to all my ladies at no charge, I will pay you quite handsomely to render medical services to anyone who walks in the door of the new clinic."

I swallowed hard. "You're serious."

"Completely."

"Well, I . . . I don't know what to say. A clinic. Truly, a medical clinic to run myself?"

She nodded. "There is one condition. You must agree to help Mr. Holmes and me with his plan at . . . what was her name? Oh yes, the home of Mrs. Hudson."

Now I shook my head. "Oh, Maggie, I don't know about that. I—"

She stood up and walked over to me. Her hands on my shoulders and staring straight into my eyes, she said, "It will be absolutely glorious." Leaning in even further, she added, "It will be like spying, and Dr. Stamford, I assure you, the spy game is thrilling."

13

There was a knock on the door and Sarah, the tall brunette, poked her head in. "Maggie, we need you. A little dispute."

Maggie frowned and said, "I'm coming, Sarah." She excused herself and left me in the office alone. For some reason—perhaps Effie's words . . . *Do not be fooled by their long slender legs and graceful necks or their friendliness. There is more going on beneath the tucked wings I see* . . . I decided to snoop around. I am not proud of it, but I barely knew Maggie May; I'd met her just twice. She was offering to set me up in a free clinic, to have free rein, something I'd dreamed of. But she ran a brothel. Some of her clients were men who obviously couldn't be trusted. I wasn't even sure that her bawdy houses were her only means of income. Who knew what else she might have her hands in or what she might be hiding?

I rose and walked around the office, my eyes flitting from one corner to another. I zeroed in on a photograph on the roll top, which was open. I walked over to take a closer look.

The photo depicted a fair-haired young woman and a handsome young man with a sculpted face and dark, wavy hair. He was dressed in a Union Army uniform. I glanced down and saw that one of the drawers was open. I pulled it open further and leafed through it. I should have felt ashamed, sneaking around like this, rummaging through Maggie's personal effects. But I had suddenly donned Sherlock's detective hat and that tug on me was far stronger than respect for her privacy.

I found another photo. It was of the same young man, the Union soldier, only in this photograph, he wore tattered clothes and he was at least two stone thinner than in the photo on

Maggie's desk. He stared back at me with vacant eyes, as if his very soul had been extracted. I remembered a case Sherlock and I had solved last year. One of the murderer's victims had been a former soldier in the Union Army who had spent considerable time in a Confederate prison camp called Andersonville. This photo looked like Civil War photos my Uncle had in his own office at home . . . photographs of prisoners, Union soldiers, incarcerated at Andersonville in Georgia. They were emaciated, broken. Some fifty thousand soldiers languished under the brutal torture of the man in charge. Nearly fifteen thousand perished.

Beneath the photograph was a letter. Before I unfolded it, I returned my eyes to the first photo. Then I twirled around, as if something called to me. Across the room was a painting of Maggie. Still holding the letter, I walked across the room and stood in front of the painting.

Earlier, Sherlock had told me that for a time, Maggie was a model for artists. This was clearly a depiction of her in her younger days. The same chestnut hair, only it fell in long, soft curls to her waist, barely covering her breasts. The same icy grey eyes. The same high cheekbones.

I went back and looked at the first photo again. The young man could have been her twin.

I opened the letter and read it. It was dated 1864.

My dearest Margaret,

This is what they have done to Malcolm, my husband. Your brother. This is what your government has helped the Confederacy do to him. He is too weak to write to me anymore, even if he could find any paper and pen. He is in a space four by six feet. He is lucky to get a ration of unboiled cornmeal with the cob still on. He has but once or twice been offered rice or beans and foul-smelling meat. He and his cell mates scrounge for fire wood to keep warm. His only water is from Stockyard Creek which flows through the prison yard.

Our child is due any day and he shall never see it. He shall never hold it.

He is dying and your country's government supports the very people who have imprisoned him.

Despite your network of contacts, you do nothing. And I can do nothing.

Ellen

Network? I thought. *What network?*

I walked over to the desk and looked at the photographs again. In one, Malcolm was strong and healthy and had his whole life ahead of him; in the other, he looked like he could barely stand.

I quickly put the letter and photograph back in the drawer. But I found an old newspaper article and could not resist reading it.

It was from May of 1862, an American paper called *Harper's Weekly*. The first line jumped out at me. **Mr. Gladstone and the English**. I read it as quickly as I could. Halfway through the article, the author said:

"England did everything she could do to assist the rebels short of actually declaring war upon us . . . Her newspapers, great and small, with a few bright exceptions, elaborately decried us and vaunted the rebel cause. They derided our army, sneered at our navy, strove vigorously to break down our credit; while, in the same breath, they lauded the rebels, talked of the chivalry of their soldiers, the sagacity of their leaders, and the utter impossibility of subjugating such a people. From being furious abolitionists, they became mild apologists for slavery."

I replaced the newspaper article.

Once again, I chided myself for having so little sense of military history. Had Britain actually assisted the Confederacy in the American Civil War? And what did Maggie May and her brother have to do with England's affairs of state? What was it that the author of the letter, Ellen, thought Maggie May could do?

Then with a start, I turned to gaze at Maggie's portrait again. The artist's rendition captured perfectly every detail. Her face, her flawless skin. She wore a cape of pink feathery fabric, draped around her body but sloping down one shoulder. The cape was partially open, revealing her beautiful swan-like neck and her long legs from the top of her thighs. It puddled on an oriental carpet. I stared at it a moment, again remembering Effie's journal. *Do not be fooled by their long slender legs and graceful necks or their friendliness. There is more going on beneath the tucked wings I see.*

Barely able to breathe in that moment, I blew out a long gasp.

The door opened and I twirled with fright, somehow afraid Maggie would burst in and catch me out. That she would somehow know I'd been rifling through her things. It was Sherlock.

"Sherlock!" I cried.

Eyebrows pinched, he asked, "What is it? You look like you've seen a ghost."

Trying to disguise my state I gave a little nervous laugh. "But you don't believe in ghosts."

"No, I do not," he said as he strode toward me. "Poppy, really, what is it? You look quite shaken."

"Sherlock, where is Maggie?"

"She's still mediating some sort of dispute. One of the ladies accused another of taking something."

"Sherlock, look at this photograph," I said pointing to the photo on Maggie's roll top.

He gave it a long look, then look at me, puzzled. "Yes, what is it?"

"Maggie said that her sister went to America and married a Union soldier. Look closely at the young woman. She is short with blonde hair. But now look at the soldier. Do you see the resemblance?"

His eyes revealed recognition. "I do. He could be . . . he could be Maggie's twin."

"Indeed. And I found a letter which makes made clear that this young man was related to Maggie. She doesn't have a sister. She has . . . had a brother."

"You've been snooping through her things?"

Blushing, I nodded.

"Well done, Dr. Stamford. Bravo! A very logical thing to do while you had the office to yourself."

"I shouldn't congratulate myself on having done such a thing, Sherlock. But you see, she has lied to us. She lied about her background. If she lied about that, she may be lying about other things."

I related to him the contents of the news article and asked, "Why would she keep an article about British sentiments toward the Rebel cause?"

"It deserves further inquiry, certainly. And I assume you don't want us to become involved without being fully apprised, correct?"

"Exactly."

He thought for a moment as he paced. A look of dismay clouded his face. "The photograph—I should have observed this the moment I entered the room."

I almost said, 'But you were too distracted by the by Maggie May's lovely profile,' but thought better of it.

"Queer thing to lie about, is it not? Brother rather than sister? Let us keep this between us for now. It may be pertinent to the case or it may be totally irrelevant. "

"But—"

"For now, Poppy, let's keep this to ourselves."

"But—"

"The best way of acting a part is to be it. We must immerse ourselves in our play at Mrs. Hudson's building and for now, we must immerse ourselves in our endeavors to investigate the intrusion into Maggie May's home, not extraneous assumptions. For the time being at least."

There were footfalls outside, a turn of the knob and Sherlock said, "Ah, I hear our mysterious friend coming back."

The door opened and Maggie appeared.

She seemed a bit flustered but quickly collected herself. "I do apologize for the interruption." She turned to me. "Now, we do have an agreement, do we not, Dr. Stamford?"

She was referring to the clinic, I was sure. I nodded.

"Perfect. Then shall we discuss the grand opening of . . . hmm, what shall we call this new brothel?"

14

"Sherlock," I said, as we walked toward my medical office, "why must we do this at Mrs. Hudson's? Why not simply rent out rooms at a nice hotel?"

"Maggie's clients must be convinced of the ruse of the new brothel. We need to be able to meander about, talk with each of the invitees."

"But Sherlock, there are many places that would accommodate such a . . . party." I rattled off a list of hotels in Central London: The Albmarle, the Brunswick, the Burlington, Fenton's on St. James, Haxell's on the West Strand. "Or what about the Tavistock in Covent Gardens?" I asked. "Or the Westminster on Victoria Street. Uncle was at a gathering there not long ago and he says it is quite luxurious. Members of Parliament and people frequenting the law courts and foreign visitors stay there. And it has gentlemen's and ladies' coffee rooms and several committee rooms and dining rooms—"

"And do you think the gentlemen who frequent such places as Maggie May owns would wish to be seen by members of Parliament or solicitors they might run into? Poppy, be logical. Yes, these hotels do have nice rooms, single rooms. They would not easily replicate an establishment, such as Maggie May would consider purchasing and refurbishing. Why are you so opposed to Baker Street?"

"I hate to involve Mrs. Hudson again, Sherlock. She has made a nice, respectable home for herself."

"That is very evident but don't be childish. She'll be fine with it, I assure you. Now simply adjust your thinking because next Friday night, you shall be transformed."

"And will I have a pseudonym, I assume?" I asked with some asperity.

"That would be appropriate. What would you like to call yourself?"

I pondered this for a moment and then remembered the bogus name that Kate used when we first met in my medical office. "Penelope. Penelope Potash."

"An odd choice, but as you wish. I am famished. I should like a chop and a pint of ale. I've heard Blanchard's in Soho is quite good."

"I had lunch with Oscar, remember? And I must get to my office."

"Very well. I shall come over this evening to further discuss our plans if that is convenient. We also need to arrange a visit to the Broads, Poppy so that we can gather exculpatory evidence for your poor stable boy."

I bid him goodbye and went to my medical office for the rest of the day. There were just three patients—now that the Great Fog had virtually disappeared, so had most of my patients. The opportunity to open a free clinic . . . Maggie's proposal sounded more appealing by the minute.

15

The following Monday morning, I went to the brothel that Maggie was turning into a medical clinic. There was no evidence of the home's previous use. There were no dark drapes, no sumptuous divans or other elegant furnishings. There was a small room equipped as an operating theater and the shelves were lined with bandages, ointments, salves and other emergency medical supplies. It seemed almost overnight, Miss Mayhew had transformed a house of ill repute into a working medical clinic.

As I stood in awe, I heard a light knock on the door frame. I turned to see Maggie, again dressed in a lovely day dress of blue and white stripes, a cape draped over one arm. She removed her long gloves and put her hands on her hips. "Well, what do you think?"

"I came as you requested because I thought I would be helping to put it all together. But it seems you have everything in order. How did you . . . where did you get all of these supplies and—"

I stopped short when I saw Uncle Ormond enter the room behind Maggie. "Uncle! What are you doing here?"

To my shame, I must admit a fleeting thought that Uncle may have, like my brother Michael, availed himself of the services that Maggie's ladies offered.

"Miss Mayhew, may I have a moment alone with my niece?"

"Of course, Dr. Sacker," she said, smiling. "I'll go check on how the examination rooms are progressing."

She left us and closed the door.

"Uncle, what on earth on are you—"

"Have a seat, Poppy," he said as he pulled up a chair for me and sat down on a stool.

I sat down in the chair and waited.

"Are you upset?" he asked. "That this has been done without your input?"

"No. Stunned."

He removed his coat. He was wearing a starched, white shirt beneath a dark blue suit and a navy blue tie. As always, Uncle cut a dash. The gray at his temples seemed to enhance his good looks rather than detract from them. He always struck the eye as ineffably dapper, with a hint of the sacerdotal. Sometimes as a little girl, I would watch him pull on his dark, silk socks and buff the toe cap of a shoe, and then wield a hairbrush, sweeping his lightly silvered locks with care, as if robing himself for some solemn, provincial occasion.

Now, as carefully and quietly as he could, he explained the sudden transformation of the clinic and many other things.

"Sherlock told me of Miss Mayhew's endeavors."

"He did?"

"Yes, and though she has the money, she knows next to nothing about what would be needed here. Of course, you would know the 'what' but not how to obtain things quickly so Sherlock asked me to step in. He is quite anxious for you to begin your work here."

"He is?"

"I think he has an ulterior motive."

"I don't understand, Uncle."

"I believe that Sherlock is afraid that you might not stay in London unless you have a very good reason to do so."

"Why would I leave London? My office is here. Now the clinic. And Michael and Alexander and you and Aunt Susan are here." *And Sherlock and our cases*, I added mentally.

"There are several things that are about to change, Poppy. For one thing, your mother has written to Aunt Susan that your father is not feeling very well. She is wondering if you would consider going home to look after him."

"Papa? She has told me nothing of this."

"She did not want to worry you. She wrote to Susan to try to get some idea of how you would feel about the matter."

"What is wrong with Papa?" I asked, my heart beating faster.

"I want him to go to the Royal Infirmary. His physician believes he has an ulcer but I would like to have him examined by others."

"Others," I repeated. "As in specialists. In what field, Uncle?"

He grimaced but did not immediately respond.

"In what field?"

His expression was solemn and I gripped the arms of the chair.

"Your father has been experiencing nausea and vomiting. He has severe cramping. I am concerned and that's why I will go in your stead so you can get this clinic moving."

"But you have your own work. How can you leave Bart's to look after Papa?"

"About that, yes," he said, looking at his feet. "I've consulted with a surgeon at the Royal Infirmary. I may suggest taking your father to the hospital where I'll be teaching so that I can—"

"A hospital, yes, of course."

Then all of his words hit me. "Wait. A hospital where you will be teaching? What are you talking about?"

He took a deep breath, then said, "I will be leaving Bart's shortly. I have been offered a position at the University of Edinburgh Medical School. I'll have the chance to work with Dr. Joseph Bell. You've heard me speak of him."

"Yes, you said Sherlock reminds you of him."

"He's about my age, perhaps a bit younger, but already is getting quite famous in the field of forensic medicine. He has a remarkable ability to quickly deduce a great deal about a patient. I've watched him on my visits to Scotland. He observes how a person moves; he looks for things, small things that identify where a person is from, what he does for a living, much like our Sherlock."

"Much like you, Uncle."

I held back tears. I'd lived with Uncle Ormond and Aunt Susan for so many years that I could not imagine them living anywhere else, away from London, away from me.

"It's an excellent opportunity to grow in this new field, Poppy." He took my hands in his. "It is not without difficulty that I've . . . that Susan and I have come to this decision. We have become very fond of Wiggins' little brother Billy, but Wiggins does not want to let him go with us. So Susan wants to make some arrangement for him . . . perhaps with Michael. He gets along well with Michael's son and Kate's daughter. We've also considered asking Michael to move into our house because his is rather small and if he and Kate—well, the two of them and two children, or possibly three with little Billy—it would be cramped. But that is entirely dependent on what you wish."

"What I wish? It is your house, not mine. And what I wish is for you not to go away!" I blurted out, like a petulant child.

"Poppy, we will not live forever, Susan and I. One reason I considered taking this position is so that you start to stand on your own two feet. With this clinic now, I think you will. The house is yours. You've always known that. You know that when we are gone from this earth, everything we have is yours. You are like our own daughter."

Now I was weeping, despite my efforts not to. "Oh, Uncle."

"So it is up to you. If you would rather your brother not move in, or if you wish to make yourself a home elsewhere for now . . . what do you think?"

"Think? I can't even think—" I started to say something and then all words completely left my mind. For a fraction of a second, the thought occurred to me that I could move in with Sherlock. I could be the roommate he was searching for. But of course, nothing would have been more indecorous and ridiculous.

"But before I go anywhere," Uncle continued, "I'll be going to your parents' home, to examine your father myself and to consult with his physicians."

"I need to go with you. Mum needs me if Papa is ill and—"

"Poppy, it is not necessary for you to leave this new clinic right now. Let me see what I can find out before you turn your life upside down. I have already cut back my hours at Bart's."

"But I was going to go to Burleigh Manor soon anyway. There is trouble with Loke."

"Yes, yes, I heard about that as well. But Loke is out on bail right now. Why don't you get settled in at the clinic and just go home around Christmas as you planned?"

"How long will you be there?"

"I don't know. A few days, a week. I have to get a handle on the situation."

I nodded, feeling the tears drip down my cheeks and land on my bodice. "No, I should go home."

"No, you should stay here and do what you do best. Help people. And I will take care of your father. I'll keep in touch. I will send you telegrams. I promise."

Nodding again and brushing tears away, I said, "You mentioned something about Sherlock having reason to believe I might not stay in London? Do you mean because you are leaving?"

"And because your father is ill. He knows that you will worry and that you will be concerned for your mother. And one other thing."

"What? What other thing?"

"He knows that Victor Trevor is coming back from India soon."

"What has that got to do with anything?"

"He believes, it seems, that if Victor is returning to the Broads, it is really to draw you away."

"What? That's insane."

"Perhaps. But Sherlock does think that Victor will try to persuade you to go back to India with him. I believe it is

Sherlock's hope that becoming the director of this clinic will keep you firmly in London."

I sat, feeling numb, feeling dizzy. Uncle left to go back to the hospital and when Maggie returned, I barely acknowledged her. She introduced me to a young woman—I could not even describe her, I was so distraught. "This is Dr. Olivia Robertson, Poppy. She just graduated from the same school as you did and your uncle plucked her out to work here and learn from you."

I looked up. "Because she cannot get work anywhere else, I suppose?"

"That's right," Olivia agreed. "That's exactly right. But if your skills are anything like Dr. Sacker has described, I'd be honored to assist you here and learn from you."

"Do you want to see the examination rooms? One is completed," Maggie said.

"No," I replied. "No, not right now."

I grabbed my cape and gloves, and said, "I have to go now," as I hurried out of the room.

As I left the building, fog swirled around my feet, and I felt like I did not know myself or anyone else at that moment. I felt like I was caught up in some heavy, murky mists of hell again.

16

I spent the rest of the day wandering around London. I think I walked every street and byway that I had ever walked with Uncle or Aunt Susan or Sherlock.

Sherlock had extraordinary familiarity with London . . . its squares and streets and neighborhoods. He knew it from the terraced homes of Regent to the mansions of Mayfair, from the bustling West End to Covent Garden and Haymarket. He knew all the hotels on the Strand to the East End; he knew it from Brixton to St. John's Wood. We had traveled Cockspur Street to Trafalgar Square, Charring Cross to the Lowther Arcade, from the publishing houses on Fleet Street to the austere seat of government at Whitehall.

I took a Four-Wheeler down to Limehouse Docks where, long ago, Sherlock and I had gone looking for Oscar Wilde in an opium den. I went over to Queenhithe Dock and Bell Wharf, one of the handling facilities of ships on the Thames where he'd gone looking for one of his street urchins who had gone missing.

Leave London? Leave London where I'd gone to school, lived with Uncle and Aunt Susan, practiced medicine . . . and followed Sherlock around like a puppy dog? Unlikely. Impossible.

By late afternoon, I found myself at St. Bart's and sought out Sherlock. He was, as usual, in the lab, staring through a microscope at something.

"Sherlock Holmes," I said in a commanding voice as I entered.

He didn't look up. His face was set grimly, his bushy eyebrows were pinched together in intense interest. "One moment, Poppy," he said. "One of Lestrade's many unsolved cases hangs on the balance of what I find on this slide."

"Sherlock, I must speak with you."

He continued staring into the lens. I walked over to where he sat and kicked at his stool, nearly knocking him to the floor.

"Dear me, Dr. Stamford," he cried, his eyes as mischievous as the first time we'd met. "I do believe you have some point of contention."

"Indeed I do. I spoke to Uncle a few hours ago and he told me that you have connived with Maggie Mayhew to open this clinic as quickly as possible because you fear I might leave London."

"You flatter yourself," he said flatly. "And I detect a querulous fluting in your voice. Really, Poppy, you are free to do whatever you wish."

"You are impossible!"

He lit his pipe and with a hint of mockery asked, "Are you here to ruin my evening?" Then he mumbled, "Or my entire life." Then he sat puffing, waiting, as my face surely revealed that his answer had completely confounded me.

"You do not wish me to stay in London then?" I asked with some reserve.

He pulled a few puffs and said, "I did not say that. I simply said you are free to do whatever you wish. I certainly think that this medical clinic could be quite stimulating and successful."

"Did Uncle tell you that my father is ill?"

"He mentioned it, yes."

"And you now know that Victor Trevor will be coming to England shortly."

"And returning to India soon thereafter, I presume. You should remember that it would be quite extraordinary for him to suddenly give up his estate and plantation there. He has been gone five years, hasn't he? So clearly, that would not be a reason for you to leave London and your medical practice. Or is it an unwelcome truth—that secretly you hope he will not return to India?"

"Don't be ridiculous. Uncle said—"

"Whatever your uncle told you I said was obviously misinterpreted. But so long as we are on the subject, I think it would be unwise of you to give up your careers here."

"Careers? Plural?"

"Quite so. As a physician and as my partner. You are doing what you love. What would ever make you wish to leave? It would be a most reckless course to take."

He stood up and came over to me. "I understand you will want to go to see how your father is and we do have to take care of Loke's little matter. Hopefully both things will be resolved to your satisfaction quickly and we can get back to normal."

"Normal," I repeated. "Sherlock, you are the most arrogant, self-centered—"

His eyes actually flushed with pleasure at my indignation and he continued puffing as he waited for me to finish my sentence. When I didn't, he said, "The little gathering at Mrs. Hudson's is Friday evening. Are you prepared for it?"

"Am I prepared to masquerade as a prostitute? Hardly."

"That is not what you are doing," he said, his voice slightly intensified with exasperation.

"You are investigating. You are helping me solve a case. That is what we do. You will see. Things will turn in our direction and I believe we shall pull this off."

He patted my shoulder and added, "I depend upon you, Poppy. You know that."

I felt some reflection of his confidence and promised that I would do my very best at the charade.

"I knew you would not shrink from your duty. This is your avocation, Stamford. And we are getting very busy. This cannot be stopped; new cases pop up like mushrooms after rain."

I shook my head. "It has come to be an avocation, yes. But Sherlock, don't you see, can't you see—" I was pleading now—"Can't you see that being possessed by the quest for perfection in your work to the exclusion of everything else . . . these obsessions can cramp the soul?"

"That has never occurred to me. I am not the least bit sure of the existence of a soul."

"Oh, you are so aggravating. Do not think for one minute that you can sway me from my duties to my family or my patients. And do not think for one second that I stay in London because of you, Sherlock Holmes."

Clearly amused, he said, "Of course not." Then I saw a tenderness in his eyes I had not seen in a very long time. He added, "But I am glad of it—of any reason that you do stay in London, Dr. Stamford."

I gathered my things quickly and was about to leave when he called out to me.

"Poppy, has it never occurred to you that when you seek to strike a Faustian bargain, one in which you get your heart's delight, you eventually realize that the price was far more than you expected?"

"What?"

"I do want you to stay in London. However, is that what you want? Is that what you need?"

Silently, I left him staring once again through the lens of his microscope.

As I walked home, it dawned on me that this latest exchange was reminiscent of our very first encounter at Oxford . . . after his encounter with Little Elihu, my bull terrier, extracted a bit of flesh from his ankle and I tended to him. Our banter that day was acidic, a test of wills, each of us with our giant egos on full display. Sherlock's draw was immediately magnetic. I suppose, as I look back, that I was of an age at which first love strikes with all its force.

The man I was with that day, Victor, was handsome, attentive, gentle, sensitive and intuitive, all qualities that should have appealed to the vulnerable core hidden beneath my willful, confident exterior. But we'd grown up together. I knew him so well. Sherlock, on the other hand, was still a mystery to me. His enigmatic personality, his brilliant mind and his elusiveness created an enormous gravitational pull, one that was irresistible and exciting. The fact that any passions we exchanged later were a secret just added fuel to the intensity, the tension of it all.

I was unlocking the front door to Uncle's house when one of Sherlock's little homeless helpers tugged at my cape. "A note, Miss. From Miss Mayhew."

As I took it from him, I said, "Ollie, I believe you've grown five inches. Soon you will be as big as Wiggins."

His smile widened and he puffed out his chest. "I will," he agreed.

"Has she paid you for your errand?"

He nodded. "G'day, Miss!" he hollered over his shoulder as he ran down the street.

I unlocked the door, and put my cape and bonnet on the coat tree. I lingered there for a moment to touch the stand tenderly. It was made of oak and Uncle's initials O. R. S.—the R. stood for Remington, his mother's maiden name—were carved into it. The hooks were cattle horns from his grandfather's farm in Herefordshire, and the rail had been fashioned from parts of an old haywain. Uncle rarely spoke of his father; he had no use for him. But he had fond memories of time spent on his grandparents' farm.

I found a note from Aunt Susan on the marble table near the door. The notecard leaned against the tiny silver bird perched on the rim of the ornate calling card holder on the table. It was where Aunt Susan always left notes for me and Uncle Ormond.

Ormond had an emergency surgery and I have gone over to Mrs. Landing's to discuss raising money for the entrance scholarships for chemistry, botany and physiology at Bart's. Kate has gone somewhere with little Mary. I won't be late...

I went into the library and poured myself a glass of port. Sighing, I picked up Uncle's most recent copy of the *Student's Journal and Hospital Gazette*, a fortnightly news publication. I flipped through it and a headline caught my eye. *The School of Medicine for Women.*

It was the medical school I had attended, the first in England to open its doors to women. The article stated that two scholarships had been awarded, thirty pounds per annum. Applicants were directed to contact Mrs. Thorne at 30 Henrietta Street, Brunswick Square. I did not recognize the name, Dr. Norton had been our Dean. And certainly no scholarships had been offered when I entered the school. Things were changing. It felt like everything in my life was about to change as well.

I wandered around the empty house, sipping my wine and thinking how morbidly hollow it would be without Aunt Susan and Uncle here. I had lived there longer than I had lived with my parents at Burleigh Manor. I loved this home. This *was* my home.

It was a stand-alone terraced-house, built in brick and stucco, with a slate roof and surrounded by a wrought iron privacy fence. Constructed in 1850, there were six bedrooms— Aunt Susan had planned on a large family that had never arrived. As I wandered from room to room, I chuckled, remembering that my fellow nursing students at St. Thomas had referred to it as "Dr. Sacker's Grand Mansion."

Below street level was the 'area,' the entrance which was used by servants and various delivery people. The enormous kitchen and scullery, food storage compartments, and wine-cellar were located there. Family members and guests entered through the front door into the entrance hall with its pattern of black and white marble squares and Uncle's beloved coat tree that his grandfather had made. The dining room was to the right. It boasted the highest ceilings I'd ever seen . . . I didn't know how on earth the maid cleaned the woodwork or the top of the chandelier.

The library was at the back of the ground floor, and across from the parlour. I quietly walked into the library and over to the marble fireplace and touched it. How many evenings had it kept me warm?

I walked down the hall, passed Uncle's study, and opened the door to Aunt Susan's morning room, her favourite room. Often in the morning, Aunt Susan would play even before she had a cup of tea. It was so different from the crowded clutter of my mother's morning room in our home in Norfolk—Mum's room was typical of what the magazines called 'romantic disorder'—it was filled with large ferns, birdcages, seashell collections, paintings and Japanese prints. But Aunt Susan's room, like Uncle's study, was sparsely furnished with a loveseat and one chair and her piano. The walls were papered with a delicate pattern of yellow rosebuds. She told me once it reminded her of the early days when she and Uncle were courting and he brought her yellow roses each week.

I could sit and listen to Aunt Susan play for hours. She had tried so hard to teach me to play, a futile effort, but I loved listening to her renditions of *Chopin's Sonata No. 2*, or Debussy's *Suite Bergamasque*, both pieces that Uncle adored.

I left the morning room to go upstairs. Standing at the bottom of the stairs, one hand on Uncle's statuary of Hippocrates, I steadied myself. Being a doctor meant the world to him, and to me. How could he give up his work at the hospital to teach? I wished I had asked him that. I decided I would. Maybe he could still be talked out of this.

As I climbed the stairs, my hand slid across the smooth, glistening mahogany bannister until I reached the torchère at the top of the steps. The moonlight shown through the tall windows at the landing. I crossed the red and gold carpet, opened the French windows, and stepped out on the tiny wrought-iron balcony. I sucked in the fresh night air.

I remembered the note from Maggie; I went back inside, walked to my bedroom and lit a lamp to read it. *Have you something to wear to the 'grand opening'? You and I are about the same height and weight. I am sure I could come up with something. Please let me know. And I hope you were not upset with me this afternoon. You left so abruptly. Meet me at Mrs. Hudson's on Baker Street in the late afternoon on Friday and we can get you ready!*

"Hmm," I whispered. "Ready." The word never sounded so ominous.

I went to my wardrobe. My dresses were rather drab. Plain brown. Plain blue. The occasional plaid. Nothing that would make me look glamorous or seductive. I had some lovely pieces of jewelry but I hardly ever wore them because it would just get in the way of my work.

I opened the top drawer of my dresser and lifted out a small wooden keepsake box that Aunt Susan had given me last Christmas. She'd said it was to "keep my secrets or fine jewelry."

Inside I stowed a few precious pieces that my parents and Uncle and Aunt Susan had given me over the years. I took out an elegant lavalier from my parents. It was crafted in platinum with three large diamonds and sprinkled with smaller ones in the drop and the delicate, stationed chain. It was shaped like a violin, which, of course, always brought Sherlock to mind. It matched graceful drop earrings with a diamond pattern that Uncle and Aunt Susan had given me the same day, for my birthday and for my graduation from nursing school. I'd worn the pieces only once, the day of Effie and Michael's wedding.

I placed them in the velvet pouches they'd come in and then I walked over to my wardrobe again. My fingers trickled over to the dress I'd worn as Maid of Honor in Effie and Michael's wedding. Effie had designed it and made it of pale lavender satin. It had a corset-like cuirasse bodice. It looked and felt like I was encased in armour when I wore it that day. Effie had been so forward thinking. I did not normally follow fashion, but after Effie's death, I would occasionally look at ladies magazines to see if her predictions about *haute couture* were correct. And they were. In fact, the dress she had made for me was, incredibly, almost identical to the ones in the very latest magazines.

So the very fashion-forward dress that Effie had designed over four years ago was now in style and would probably work for this little ruse. I pulled it out, held it up in front of me and looked in the mirror.

What do you think, Effie? I said to myself. *Have you made me a dress that will entice gentlemen to tell me their secrets?*

17

I arrived at 221 Baker Street around three on Friday. Mrs. Hudson met me at the door.

We had not seen each other since Victor's father's funeral but she had not changed a bit. She was a short, plump, woman. She wore her silver hair in a bun and she looked as bedraggled as ever. She gave me a hug and a wide smile. "Dr. Stamford, it is wonderful to see you. Come in, come in! Welcome to Hudson House."

I laughed. "Is that what they are calling it tonight?

She nodded and ushered me into her first floor flat. "Would you like some tea?" she asked as she whisked the carefully wrapped dress away from me.

"Well, I'm supposed to be meeting Miss Mayhew and-"

"Never mind that. They are upstairs making it all ready. I am rather glad that I have not finished remodeling the upstairs suites. I have a few boarders down below here—some rather undesirables, I must admit, but they pay the rent, indeed. I hope to change the character of my renters a bit in the future."

I had to smile at that. Despite her unkempt appearance, her flat was very tidy, as I'd expected, given she had been Victor's father's fastidious housekeeper for many years. It was modestly but nicely furnished; I even recognized a few pieces from Victor's house in the Broads. So I wondered how she might react to having Sherlock Holmes as a boarder. He was anything but tidy. He would probably be the worst tenant in all of London, with his strange scientific experiments, playing the violin at all hours, and the likely congealing of every sort of client, rich or poor, violent or timid. But Mrs. Hudson had the highest regard for him, I knew, for he had helped her greatly in the Trevor blackmail matter, orchestrated by her ex-husband. Sherlock had convinced Victor and everyone else that her compliance with the scheme was out of fear. Still, I wondered how she might feel if she wandered upstairs to collect rent from her often surly tenant and found him in dishabille or wrapped in nothing but an old, tattered purple robe. All the same, I was somewhat heartened by the fact that if Sherlock moved into '221B,' Mrs. Hudson might be about to watch over him and to seek help for him if he needed it.

"Tell me what you have been up to, my dear," she said sweetly. "Sherlock says you are quite the accomplished physician and now you will be director of a new medical clinic."

I nodded and started to reply but she jumped in. "Have you heard from Victor Trevor? He wrote and told me that he will be coming to England soon."

Again, when I opened my mouth to speak, she interrupted. "I have a letter from him here somewhere," she said, jumping from her chair. She opened a desk drawer and rustled through it. She retrieved a letter and held it up. "Here it is."

She opened it as she sat down again and started to read.

Early in the day, sometimes I sit in the grass and gaze at the sky and wonder what the sky is like back in the Broads. Not like this, I am sure. Never so blue, even on the loveliest of days. I watch the insects—different sorts of creepers and those who take flight on the summer breeze. Some give off light in the night like golden pennons flying overhead. Certainly no Norfolk hawkers are about. But the insects' chirping and fluttering swell in melodies just the same.

"Doesn't he write beautifully, Dr. Stamford? Did you ever think him to be such a poet?"

A bit stunned, I shook my head.

I watch the tribesmen as they set about building two guesthouses—not that I have great hopes of visitors. Time glides by and no dust flies from the wheels of a carriage coming to my door. This is when I am given over to memories, joys and sorrows mixed, but the sorrows seem to make up only the most fleeting moments of my life.

One of the new homes has risen from the ashes of an old shed. Like the new India that is emerging, this abode will likewise materialize from something old and worn. The walls are whitewashed. I will paint everything white, I think. The walls in the other house will be sheathed in red Indian-limestone plaster. Siddarth, my main builder, says it is a very old technique and easy to maintain. He says it is a traditional Rajasthani material.

This first house, soon to be finished, is small. Just one bedroom. The floors are also red limestone; the roof is thatched; the ceiling beams are of eucalyptus wood. Siddarth has made some muddha chairs of bamboo. He is also making a charpoy, a traditional Indian woven bed, and some chairs of mango wood and rope. His wife is making pillows and pillow covers in bright colors.

While the main house looks straight out of England, I have grown fond of the Indian ways—the copper pots, the meals of lentils, peas, cauliflower and okra. I love to sit out on the terrace and listen to the village people play their music.

The tribal women tend to the gardens—not just the vast tea gardens but trees . . . lemon, tamarind, jacaranda, mango and acacia. There are guava orchards and custard apple and roses and jasmine for scent and color.

The beauty here is priceless. I know now that you do not need a ten bedroom home or a large dining hall to be happy. I have connected with this place in a way I never dreamed of.

Mrs. Hudson looked up and smiled. "He adds, *I hope this finds you well, Mrs. Hudson. There are those I miss who are still in England and you are one of them.*"

"What a lovely, lovely letter, Mrs. Hudson. He sounds well. Happy."

"I think he is, Dr. Stamford, but I think he needs a wife. All men need a life companion, don't you think?"

All men except Sherlock Holmes, I thought.

"Mrs. Hudson, I believe I should go find Miss Mayhew and—"

"Here I am," Maggie said as she stepped through the doorway. She was followed by three young women. "Time to get you ready."

She introduced the others. Sarah was the tall brunette we'd met before. Louisa was short with blonde ringlets that framed her pretty face. Ann's height was somewhere in between and she had light brown hair.

"Did you bring a dress?" Maggie asked.

Mrs. Hudson fetched it and took it from its wrapping.

"I hope it's . . . um, suitable," I said, gulping.

"Oh," Maggie whispered. "Oh, my."

"I can wear one of yours or—"

Maggie took the dress from Mrs. Hudson, swept up the skirt and draped the garment over her arms. "Dr. Stamford, I had no idea you were so . . . well, that you had such modern taste in fashion. This particular style is all the rage in Europe."

"Well, I have seen in magazines—"

Maggie turned to the others and said, "This replaced the Polonaise styles several years ago. You see, like this one, they are absent a waist seam and the bodice and skirt are cut as one. But the very latest fashion houses show dresses with a bodice line similar to this very tight-fitting bodice. In Paris, they make the whole of the dress in Princess-line style with shoulder to hem panels. The silhouette is very form fitting."

Holding up the dress, she said, "You see how the bodice reaches the thighs, then dips even deeper both front and back extending well down the hips? This creates a very form-fitting dress, giving the look of a body—"

"Encased in suit of chain mail," I quipped and they laughed.

"It's lovely," Sarah said.

"Indeed," Maggie agreed. "Dr. Stamford, I must admit I am quite surprised. I rather thought you were given to wearing—"

"Plain things?" I said with a smile. "I am. Ordinarily. I have worn this dress only once, to a wedding about four years ago. I was maid of honor in my best friend's wedding. Effie designed it."

"Effie. Michael's wife?"

I nodded.

Then Maggie's eyebrows arched. "Four years ago, you say? But this is the very latest in fashion. How—?"

Determining it best not to go into details about Effie's psychic abilities, I simply said, "It's complicated."

Oh, Effie, you would be so very proud, I thought.

"Well. Well, we'd best get started. Mrs. Hudson, would you be kind enough to draw a bath for Dr. Stamford?"

"A bath? But I don't need—"

Pushing me toward the privy, Maggie said, "You are going to be reinvented from head to toe, young lady. Transformed. Starting with a bath in perfumed oils."

"But—"

She put her finger to my lips. "Not a word. This will be just what the doctor ordered."

18

"Lavender . . . to match your dress," Maggie said as she poured oils into the steaming bath water in Mrs. Hudson's fantastic claw foot bathtub.

"It smells wonderful, Maggie."

"Now, you just soak and soften for a bit. Here's a magazine to keep you occupied. It belongs to Sarah. She keeps talking about moving to India to start over and find a husband."

Smiling, se handed it to me and they left me alone to relax but I kept wondering about what would come next. Who knew what else they would do to make me look like an authentic, albeit elegant, lady of the night?

India, I thought, as I started to leaf through the magazine. It was called *The Complete Indian Housekeeper and Cook*. The more I looked at the pictures, the more intrigued I became.

Victor's father had told me a great deal about his plantation in India. He often visied thre before his death. He said the plantations were called tea gardens and born of the East India Company's ambitions. It was a trading company founded in the early seventeenth century. Its charter went all the way back to Queen Elizabeth I and it lasted until 1874, the year I met Sherlock. The company accounted for more than half of the world's trade in tea, opium, dyes, salt, cotton and silk.

By the early nineteenth century, at the height of British rule in India, the company employed a private army of over a quarter of a million soldiers, twice as many as Britain's army, with which it ruled most of India. It was a complete monopoly.

After the 1857 rebellion, the Crown took over control and eventually the company dissolved. Wealthy individuals like Victor Trevor's father bought large tracts of land to cultivate and tea plantations dotted the fertile jungles.

As I slid under the bubbles, I pictured Victor in my mind, sitting on his wide verandah, writing letters, reconciling accounts, discussing the daily chores of the plantation with his *Mohurirs*—the supervisors of the estate. Perhaps he would chat with the night watchers, the *Chonkeydars* before retiring for the night. I imagined him slipping into bed, pulling a mosquito curtain around him and falling asleep to the strange sounds of his adopted home.

The magazine contained many articles about what it was like for women who travelled to India. Thousands of British women had found husbands in India. The men welcomed girls from home—well-bred young ladies who hoped to marry businessmen, lawyers, doctors, teachers, engineers or squires and planters like Victor, all of whom thought they could help India benefit from the progress Great Britain could offer her. Some of the young women were bored at home and sought adventure; some were tired of country life or simply wanted more independence. In India, no one would chide them that the Empire would fall if they failed to go to church one Sunday. So some were not unlike what Sherlock had been saying about the ladies who now surrounded me—they simply did not wish to conform. They simply wanted more freedom. And oh, I could understand that!

As I lingered in the hot, scented water, I closed my eyes and imagined the unfamiliar scents and odors of Victor's new home. Garlic and cooking oil, pungent tobaccos, and tangy spices like ginger and clove and turmeric. And the floral scents—jasmine and sandalwood. And the less appealing ones, like the burning cow dung that Victor had mentioned in a letter to Michael. I turned to the page in Sarah's magazine that listed what a woman should plan to pack for her journey to the Indian Empire. The article recommended calico nightgowns, cotton slip bodices, Lisle thread stockings, petticoats in silk and flannel. Winter morning dresses, winter afternoon dresses, evening dresses, riding habit, ulster, handsome wrap, umbrella and sunshades, Mackintosh—a full-length waterproof coat— walking shoes and boots, evening shoes, the new sanitary napkins—not so easy to obtain in India, the author said. It appeared that the *memsahibs*—the British ladies who went to India—were expected to dress well and to keep up with the fashions of home. It was their duty to keep up appearances of prestige in the Raj. It seemed important that British women not be seen as 'going native.'

"Ridiculous," I said aloud. *I wouldn't need all that*, I thought. And I certainly would not need to dress to impress anyone. Besides, I thought, what would be so very wrong with going native? With wearing the colorful, beautiful clothes that India's native women wore? Something Effie had written in her journal suddenly popped into my brain—and made me lift up my head with a start. *I see you not in a surgeon's apron, but in a deep-blue sari. I always told you that blue is your colour.*

Unnerved, I closed the magazine and dropped it to the floor.

After soaking for a long time in the tepid water, into which they infused bran once the oils had dissipated, I was tortured with a heavy dose of exfoliation with a wash cloth "to create bright and smooth skin," Sarah said. As she scrubbed, she asked if I did anything to keep my nice complexion. "I've heard that to achieve the fairest skin possible, some women use paint."

"My God," I said. "You should never cover your face with a poisonous cream!"

"What about eating arsenic, chalk, slate, or tea grounds? A bit pricey but—"

"Absolutely not! You don't eat poison, Sarah, for heaven's sake. Get seven to eight hours of sleep each night, take some sun, walk a great deal, and eat a healthy diet. That's all you need to do."

"I will get my fair share of sun when I move to India," Sarah said.

"You're serious, aren't you, Sarah?" Maggie asked, and she nodded.

I scowled. "While you are still here, Sarah, I am going to hold a lecture at the clinic for you and your friends about healthy eating habits *and* healthy regimens for good, clear skin."

"Well, whatever you are doing," she responded, "is what we should all be doing. Your skin is flawless, Pop . . . I mean, Penelope."

They fussed about how to do my hair. I had washed my hair the day before because it took all night to dry; it was halfway down my back. I usually pulled it up into a tight bun. But that was not what they had in mind.

They dampened it and toweled it furiously. Then they shaped it with rollers and clips.

"What about a small coquettish chignon?" asked Ann, the one with brown hair and eyes like an owl's.

"Or this?" asked Sarah, showing Maggie a picture in *Godey's Lady's Book*. "What about this, Miss Mayhew? I think this would work."

Maggie showed it to me. "What do you think, Poppy?"

"Penelope. Remember, this evening I am Penelope Potash."

"Of course. Penelope."

"How would you do that?"

"Do what?"

"All those swirls in the front and then those two—whatever they are in the back. It looks difficult."

Now Maggie laughed uproariously. "You wield your scalpel and stethoscope, Miss Potash, and leave the intricacies of coiffure to us."

"But how—?"

Laughing, she said, "The ends, hopefully, will wave and fall on the shoulder. We comb the front hair back. Above this, we back-comb the hair, arrange it in a butterfly bow on each side of the back of your head and fasten it with an ornamental comb. I have just the thing for it. A comb with a string of pearls. Your hair has natural bend. I just hope it will set in a few hours."

Now I knew why she had wanted me there in the afternoon. This bathing, dressing, hairstyling, face-painting ordeal took hours!

"Men don't go through any of this. It's not fair."

Louisa said, a bit sarcastically, "It doesn't appear you go through any of this either."

I had to laugh. She was entirely honest and entirely correct.

"Never mind. Sherlock is going through his own machinations," Maggie said.

"I don't understand."

"His disguise. I believe he has tried on at least five beards so far."

"A beard? Really? Uncle Ormond says that beards are going out of fashion. He even shaved off his mustache not long ago." He had told me that fashionable men were returning to their barbers for a daily shave because beards and whiskers 'are passé,' and considered the domain of the 'conservative, older generation.' Uncle said they were a health risk in the workplace, particularly where food was prepared.

Maggie laughed and added, "Sherlock insists he must have a disguise. He is wearing tails, you know."

"Tails?" I gasped. "So formal?"

She laughed again. "He wants everyone to believe he is an aspiring actor. He will leave no stone unturned apparently. Very persistent, your Sherlock."

My Sherlock. Hadn't Oscar and Uncle called him that on many occasions? Once, Uncle had said, "I must caution you . . . Darling girl, I was—*am* very much like your Sherlock. Intent on keeping my emotions in check. Dedicated to my work to the exclusion of everything else. I very nearly let life pass me by. I had absolutely no intention of becoming romantically involved. Just like your Sherlock—"

Did people who knew me well still think of him that way? Of course, they did. Even Michael had said, just days ago, "you still run to him if he crooks his little finger."

Perhaps it would be good for me to return to Burleigh Manor. Not that it was good that my father was ill but just to get away from London, from Sherlock, for a bit. It was time to put him behind me altogether. It was well past time.

But my practice, my new clinic . . .

"Why, Miss Mayhew," Sarah said, "When we're done with her, she may just walk out with a husband this evening."

"What?!" I cried.

"Sarah, none of the men who will be present tonight would be suitable husbands for Dr. Stamford except, perhaps, for Mr. Holmes. And you of all people should know that while the one thing most people agree upon is that women should be beautiful and married, and landing a husband is still seen as the primary goal for young women, that goal is not for everyone."

"You won't put too much on my face, will you?" I begged.

"I know, I know. Face paints are only used by performers and prostitutes, so therefore high society views them as deplorable," Maggie said.

"The devil's trickery," Louisa scoffed. "But remember, this evening, you are not a high society lady."

They argued about how much lip gloss, rouge, eye shadow and powder to put on my face. "Beautiful and striking," Maggie said, "But controlled. Do a light dusting of the faintest veil of rouge across her cheeks and finish with a transparent layer of powder. A little lip reddener, a touch of green on her eyelids. A little line of black above her lashes."

"Oh, and a beauty patch!" Ann decided.

"A what?"

"You've never heard of them?" Maggie asked.

I shook my head.

"Women use them to cover up smallpox scars and such. You cut pieces of velvet or silk into the shape of stars, moons, or hearts, and apply them to cover up the scars. There's even a secret language for their use."

"You mean like the silly nonsense with fans for flirting?"

"Exactly. A patch near the mouth means you are flirtatious. One next to the right cheek signals you are married. One on the left cheek announces you are engaged and one at the corner of the eye, like mine, means you are somebody's mistress."

"So you belong to—"

"My friend with the estate where he keeps a horse for me, yes. I am his—for now. The men who come to my establishments can expect no favors from me. Now I'm going to see about preparations upstairs. And Poppy—I'm sorry, Penelope, don't worry too much. The men will be advised that this little opening is for dinner, drinks, conversation and congeniality and nothing more. You needn't worry about anyone crossing lines they should not."

"For if they try to do that," Ann said, "Miss Mayhew will show them proper out the door!"

It was time to finish getting ready, to lace up the corset and slide into the dress like pork stuffed into sausage casing.

Maggie placed the velvet beauty patch near the right corner of my mouth. She tenderly touched my cheek. "I will see you in a bit."

"Now, we're almost done. Stop fidgeting," Louisa said as she plucked my eyebrows for a second time. A painful process I intended never to experience again.

19

Toward six o'clock, the other girls started to change into their evening clothes. Maggie gazed at me, assessing her new creation. "Jewelry. Nothing too fancy. Something tasteful. This must be carefully edited."

I reached into my bag and showed her the diamond necklace and earrings.

"These are beautiful, absolutely beautiful. But I brought some things with me, because I did not know what you had. Seeing your dress, I have these in mind now, but if you want to wear your own—" she frowned.

"No, no, Maggie, that's fine. Show me."

From a small satin pouch, she took a lovely strand of violet amethyst beads, graduated in size and connected at the neck with a silver clasp. She also had a pair of delicate tear-drop amethyst earrings. "These would match your dress."

"They are lovely, Maggie."

"A gift from my sister."

My eyes narrowed. I knew that she did not have a sister. I knew that her sibling in the photo was a brother, the man in the Union uniform. But I said nothing. I took off my cherished locket, the one with the photo of Victor, Effie, Sherlock and me, put it with my diamond necklace and earrings in the velvet pouch and placed it in Mrs. Hudson's desk. Maggie helped me put on her earrings and clasped the amethyst necklace around my neck.

"Now look in the looking glass," she said, turning me around.

I was surprised, amazed actually, that the image reflected was actually me. I'd never imagined what I might look like with perfectly coifed hair and face paint. These made an enormous difference, one I rather liked.

We bid goodnight to Mrs. Hudson, who said she was going to visit a friend for the evening, and ascended the stairs to an anteroom off the main open section of the floor that Mrs. Hudson had not sectioned off into separate suites yet. It was adorned with velvet drapes, comfortable chairs and a long table that groaned with many platters of food, bottles of wine and champagne, dishes and cutlery. As she pinched and twirled strands of my hair into place, she whispered, "The final touches," and then asked, "Where did you tell your uncle you were going this evening?"

"To see Sherlock."

"And that is acceptable to him? Your uncle doesn't require you to have a chaperone?"

"Oh, he hasn't for years. We have an understanding, Uncle and I."

"That you are pig-headed and he helped make you so," Sherlock said as he entered the room. "I fancy that it is an arrangement that suits you both very well."

I turned to face him. He did indeed look like a different person with his wig and faux beard. His physique was entirely suited for his tails and top hat. He looked quite dashing. In the dim light, I could not help remembering Sherlock standing near the window of the moonlit cottage at Holme-Next-the-Sea. Thinking of that night, of our physical sharing, made me tremble. Dissecting our relationship always seemed pointless, but I would still wake in the night, saying his name over and over in the dark.

He stepped slowly toward me and seized my hands. I stood rigid as a statue, my eyes a bit glazed, I believe, by the stark difference in him and his reaction to me. He stammered out, "Poppy, I . . . I—"

Then he opened wide his astonished eyes. In a choked voice, he murmured, "You have never looked lovelier. Absolute perfection."

Instantly consoled that he did not think my appearance too tawdry, I said, "You don't think anyone will recognize me?"

"First of all, no one who is coming knows you, Penelope." He said the name with emphasis and with a mischievous glint in his eyes. "Secondly, people see what they expect to see and are generally blind to what they do not expect to see. While I am trained to examine the face, not the trimmings, most people are not. It is the first quality of an investigator to see through a disguise, but I will be the only detective here. Worry not."

I gave a sigh of relief, but caught my breath as his hand came up to my cheek and he placed his palm against it. "You are exquisite, Poppy. Your trimmings will be difficult for anyone to ignore this evening."

At that precise moment, the flame of three lamps went down and Maggie turned up the wicks. We heard a prolonged gurgle and the lights went out completely.

"Damn," Maggie muttered as she fumbled about for a candle, found one on a table and lit it. "I'll run downstairs. I believe Mrs. Hudson has forgotten to put oil in the lamps."

I could barely make out her figure in the darkness but heard the rustle of her dress as she left the room. We would await her return in total darkness.

It was when I heard her footsteps as she descended the stairs that I realized Sherlock had never taken his hand from my face. My senses spread out from head to toe. Once again my secret longings threatened to gush out despite the very real possibility that my rain-cloud of unrequited affection would be met with utter scorn and dudgeon. Sherlock's feelings were buried deeply; they were never going to burst their bonds. His empty heart would not suddenly fill and sob out his need for me. That was a stone he refused to allow to turn and melt.

Yet I covered his hand with my palm. The sensation of his flesh was almost too much to bear. I could imagine myself unfurling my hair, letting it flow like a dark tent that covered our faces. I had fleetingly tasted the hidden honey of him long ago and still the nectar, the light I felt in those moments, was sweet, a thread that wove us together, whether we liked it or not. Whether it was held by love or just the memory of one, perfect night really did not matter. It would be thrilling to experience it again either way.

I do not know if he could see my enticing smile in the darkness even though our faces were but an inch apart. I actually wondered if he could hear the pulsing of my heart as it pumped blood to every region of my body and my mind raced with erotic thoughts that should have embarrassed me—but didn't. Even a spinster could lust, couldn't she? I believed he could hear the thumping in my chest, for I'm sure it sounded like Kate's lovely mute swans when their wingbeats made a beautiful throbbing sound as they flew. I think my heart must have sounded like that in that moment, and not because I had any shred of optimism that we could be together. We couldn't. It was simply the ferocious sensuality of the moment—him in his tuxedo, me dressed so seductively for the evening, the two of us alone in the darkness. I felt a sharp, searing, twisting pain in my stomach that took my breath away.

We'd been so young and inexperienced the first time—the only time—and slightly intoxicated as well. Alone in that cottage, caught up in the moment, we'd fumbled our way through it. I believed it could be different now. We were so comfortable with each other, knew each other so well—I knew him as well as anyone could know Sherlock, I supposed. And now I had pent-up passion, a purely physical fervor I was rather tired of suppressing, which cried to be released from its bonds. I wanted to feel something wild. I wanted to feel the goosebumps turn to sweat breaking out on my forehead; I wanted to feel the burning, the scorching as my body burst into flames. I wanted to feel the weight and warmth of a lover, the shock and pleasure of exploration by candlelight, the stirring release I'd gone too long without. In that moment, I did not need love or promises or commitments. And afterward we could sink into deep comfortable slumber, feel the soothing warmth of limbs stretched and curled around each other. It would be like an amazing dream with no meaning in it.

What if we could both give in to that? I thought. *Just that, and nothing more.*

"I have never seen you look quite . . . like this," he said softly.

I rubbed my thumb across the back of his hand. "And is it tempting, Mr. Holmes?"

"My work requires me to be cold. Calculating. Impervious to emotions."

"I know."

"Emotions are a barrier to clear thinking. To accuracy. To logic."

"I know," I said again. "I know that is what you think. And you do not trust human beings generally. Even if you occasionally find one charming or alluring."

"That's true. Women are insoluble puzzles. My brain must always govern my heart. I test people's patience, don't I?"

"You do try people's patience. Often," I said laughing lightly. "Daily."

"We're too different, you and I. I focus on the object— solving the case. You see the light and the shade . . . like the pain and grief of the father when he mutilated the swans. The gentle side of Kate despite her prior profession. It's been true in every case we've handled."

I started to protest. He had a tender, compassionate side as well. "It was your idea to ask Uncle to hire Kate as our cook. It—"

"That was logical. I have trained myself to do what is necessary to carry out my duties. You assist me yet you often are the exact opposite of my logic."

I sighed. He had trained himself to become a literal thinker who has no room for art or love or ambiguity, just problems to be solved by any means necessary. It seemed that the barriers he had built for himself were the sort of darkness from which no lightness can emanate. The pretense of being a human being while feeling dead inside would kill anyone.

Then he took a quick breath and said, "You look as if with my leave or without it, you are going to kiss me."

I was caught off guard. "Now it is you who flatters himself, Sherlock Holmes."

129

But he smiled widely, put his arms around my waist and leaned slowly in to accept what I might offer. My eyes half-closed, my lips trembling, my shoulders shaking and my chest aching, I leaned toward him. I kissed him. He tried to easy away but I pulled him back and kissed him yet again. Part of me could not let go of him, of the idea of him, and I thought, just then, part of me never would however much distance I put between us.

Footsteps padded up the steps and the sound struck me to the core like a piercing arrow. Sherlock broke away and a dark melancholy disappointment squeezed the pit of my stomach.

I heard the rustling of Maggie's petticoats and skirt and her voice saying, "I've got the oil," as she entered the room. She held the candle to light her way. I managed to see her tall, graceful figure moving about. The fragile moment had passed and Sherlock broke away.

Silence followed for a few seconds. "What a blessing," she finally said. "It is too late to go out for oil now, but I found some that Mrs. Hudson had stashed away in her pantry."

She turned to us, Sherlock now standing more than a foot away from me. She eyed us curiously but simply said, "The guests will be arriving soon. Shall we go to the party room?"

Sherlock offered his arm to me. I threaded my arm through and placed my hand over his and followed him to the reception.

20

For the next three hours, lights flickered and crystal glasses clinked above the quiet conversation and murmuring and flirting. For most of it, Sherlock sat on the other side of the room, quietly smoking his pipe, wolfing down coffee, shaking hands and taking notes as if he were writing scenes in a play. He looked older somehow, his eyes keenly observing everyone, his lips tight when he spoke. Occasionally he looked my way and forced a smile. A few times I met his stare but could not read this thoughts. Often his expression was of distinct boredom.

My 'assignment' was Littlecode—the Eton and Cambridge alumni, who worked on the London Stock Exchange but was previously in his family's banking business. Michael had explained the Wall Game he'd played in some detail so, after I had made it clear that I had some education and was familiar with literature, plays and the more lofty aspects of life so that he would talk to me about something other than mundane nonsense, I used it.

"I understand, Mr. Littlecode, that you played the Wall Game at Cambridge."

His eyebrows shot up.

"Maggie told me. The most important match of the year is played on St. Andrew's Day, is that right?"

"Yes, absolutely. The Collegers—the King's Scholars— take on the Oppidans, the rest of the school. At the annual St Andrew's Day match, the Oppidans climb over the wall, after throwing their caps over in defiance of the Scholars, while the Collegers march down from the far end of College Field, arm-in-arm, towards the near-end, where they meet the Oppidans. It's quite the spectacle."

"Were you an important player, Mr. Littlecode?" I asked, touching his hand. "I'm sure you were."

He proceeded, of course, to recount his glory days on the team. I frequently had to turn my head to disguise my boredom at his running, tedious, self-aggrandizing commentary. Finally, I was able to coax him to talk about his business ventures. He did, in fact, have a scheme, relating to the building of the new cathedral.

"People are quite gullible, Miss Potash."

"Penelope," I said.

Twirling a stray strand of my hair, he smiled and said, "Penelope, you tell them that their investment will reap mounds of additional money and they believe you. They fall for anything."

"So you are not procuring benefactors for the building of an abbey?"

"They think I am. But actually, there is little need for that so I am not really hurting anyone."

"I don't understand, sir. You take their money and—"

"But you see, the archdiocese will find the money needed for the church. When you start talking to people about a grandiose building dedicated to the Church—and it will be an extraordinary church—neo-Byantine style, a floor area of over five thousand square metres, a spacious and uninterrupted *navea pendentive* type of dome—when you tell people that, all of a sudden they are keen to be benefactors. "

"And the money goes where then?" I asked, now gripping the arm of the chair because I was so furious.

"Into my pocket. Well, for a time, at least. The benefactors provide seed money for my own more prudent investments. I invest and reap a profit, but these people don't really expect a profit, you see. It's the finest gambit. They simply hope to be a part of something big, something dedicated to God. It serves to make them feel they made a down payment on heaven. You know the Stock Exchange does not have a good reputation, so people look elsewhere to place their money.

"All I have to do is remind them that two Parliamentary investigations of the Exchange have taken place and that in the Exchange, the powers of evil are decidedly ascendant. People falsify documents to receive their quotations, for example. Or I remind them of the Eupion Gas Company fraud."

"The what?"

"The Eupion Gas Company fraud of 1874. You have not heard of it?"

I shook my head.

"There were no applications on the part of the public for shares in the company so to secure a quotation, the promoters induced people to make dummy applications. The promoters then used their own money to represent shareholders deposits. This same money was deposited and withdrawn many times over in the company's bank to represent a large volume of applications and deposits. The Exchange Committee was so lax in its examination of company assets and documents, it did not even notice that the deposit money was withdrawn by promoters as soon as it was paid in. The market is rigged by brokers who collude with each other—though they plead ignorance, of course.

"So smart people are a bit shy to deal with the Exchange these days. As for my church scheme, I simply convince people of this worthy cause and, at the right time, I advise them that the Church just hasn't made any solid plans as yet and that it might be a decade away before it does. They walk away satisfied and I'm all the richer for it."

"Have you asked Maggie to invest?"

"Oh no. I would not defraud Maggie. Never! Besides, she hardly seems the type to be worried about heaven, do you imagine? No, I leave Maggie out of my business dealings. I come here for pleasure, not to discuss business or stock portfolios. Speaking of pleasure, Penelope, I definitely want to see you again. In more private surroundings." he said, gripping my hand.

I pulled my hand away but forced a smile. I wanted to know more about his designs to feed his greedy appetites. I wondered if he had pulled in others who frequented Maggie May's houses and perhaps was worried about them going to the authorities. It was such an obstacle that had led to the murder of Cecil Gray, Kate's former lover. He'd withdrawn his support of a mad man's 'scientific' research and paid the ultimate price for it.

"Tell me more about these stock dealings. Perhaps I shall have a bit of savings one day and I don't want to be foolish."

Clearly flattered that I wanted to pick his brain and clearly unable to discern my lies the way my uncle always did, he opened up even more. "I'm more of a stockbroker than a company promoter. That gentleman over there, Mr. Hamilton, is a financier who specializes in bringing new companies to market. And Mr. Epley, the man to his left, has great integrity, in that regard at least," he said with a wink. "But there are those who specialize in over-capitalizing and over-valuing them while skimming off as much as possible from the proceeds."

"Over-capitalizing?"

"It means that a company has more shares in issue than the underlying business is capable of rewarding adequately in its dividends. You skim cash by selling shares which cost the promoters very little to acquire before the company comes to market. It's easy to get away with it."

"It's a lucrative form of chicanery then."

He laughed. "You could say that. I know someone," he said, "who has just returned to England from America. His first career was in America, in the mining business. He plans to use his money to acquire mining interests in Canada. Now, the mines are real but by manipulating the market and juggling finances, he can speculate on new projects."

"But what if the new project doesn't work out?"

"Then, dear girl, investors are ruined and investigators will likely find debts, false balance sheets, fraudulent accounts and a lot of people will go to jail for pillaging cash from other companies. But my friend will leave England if prosecution is threatened. He'll flee to France or America to evade justice. That is what people like us do.

"And it is not as though these things are completely in the shadows. I have a friend, a playwright—perhaps your poet over there, Oscar Wilde or the actor know him. He is writing a play about financial fraud, and not just about one individual's dishonesty but about all of the institutions who contribute to it— banking institutions, economic dynasties, even the government."

"But don't you worry about getting caught? What if someone is keeping track of what you do?"

"Who would do such a thing?"

"Oh, I don't know," I said slyly. "Someone like me? Someone like Maggie?"

He laughed uproariously. "Maggie invests in only the soundest propositions, nothing speculative. She never takes chances. I did not even think to approach her about the abbey. And she is the epitome of discretion. She would never reveal a client's identity or anything she knows about them. I have been in contact with her for years and she has never said a word to anyone."

"I certainly trust her. And you as well?"

"Of course. And you? Girls like you don't worry their pretty heads about such financial matters." Then his eyes narrowed. "Though you do ask a lot of questions."

"How can I ever hope to become a proper mistress to a savvy gentleman like yourself if I do not learn about his business dealings?"

He laughed again and I excused myself and stood up. "I'll be right back," I promised. Then I signaled to Sherlock and he met me outside the room.

"Have you found anything out?" Sherlock asked.

"Nothing concrete that would exonerate him nor be worthy of charging him in our matter. I can't quite get anything out of him that gives him an alibi for the night of the break-in, but he doesn't seem the slightest bit nervous or uncomfortable talking about Maggie. But he is a slimy worm, Sherlock. A genius of fraud and finance, I think. He's fleecing people out of money, promising them he's investing funds in the abbey, just as we talked about. But I truly do not get the feeling he is after Maggie or her list in any way."

I related to Sherlock the details of my conversation with Littlecode and he said, "We have but one mystery to solve—who broke in to Maggie May's establishment and why."

"Are you declining to look into these financial dealings?" I asked.

"I did not say that. I am saying that I cannot immediately investigate this. Two cases arising out of this evening is confusing."

I was greatly disturbed. These men were ruining people's lives. "But, Sherlock—"

"But, while I cannot commit myself to it at the moment," he added hastily, "rest assured I will not let these cunning devils escape unscathed. Once we have determined who broke into Maggie's place and why, I shall interrogate both of them and analyze all of their financial dealings. After Oscar's reading, a few men left," Sherlock said. "They were clearly interested in enjoying a paramour more than poetry and conversation. But Arthur Barclay, the gambler and alleged manager of the sisal plantation in the Bahamas . . . he mentioned being in on this scheme with Littlecode to procure benefactors for the building of an abbey as well. He tried to entice me and Oscar to invest. So given Littlecode's admissions and his own, he is clearly the stock exchange promoter's accomplice. But like you, I do not believe that either he or Littlecode ransacked Maggie's office. Apparently, on the night of the break-in, he was at that gathering Maggie mentioned at St. Giles. She must have forgotten. When I managed to get round to talking about it, he seemed very perturbed about the burglary. He is clearly fond of Maggie."

"And what of Gerard Hamilton, the gambler?"

"Polly has spent most of the evening with him. She says he has an alibi. On the night in question, he was in another city promoting a new company."

"So other than new spider webs to untangle, we have come up with nothing."

Sherlock disagreed. "I wouldn't say that. I spent some time with Mr. Epley."

"Littlecode said he is very honest in his business dealings."

"I agree but he had some interesting tidbits to say about the Savoy."

"What about it?"

"Epley's family specializes in hollowware, mostly kitchenware, and in all sorts of other odd things. Bell pulls, door knobs, knockers, cast iron nails and most recently, smoothing irons. The business has grown exponentially and he is worth a fortune. His family has been interested in expanding into the hotel business. He has become acquainted with Cezar Ritz, the manager, and Georges Auguste Escoffier, the French chef. He believes they are taking bribes and fiddling with the books."

"Really?"

He nodded. "Something to pass on to Lestrade so he can delve into it at once. And as to our friends Littlecode and Barclay, the information on those blackguards shall be turned over to the Royal Commission and the Archdiocese. The truth is that Littlecode in particular . . . his fortune has dried up, evaporated, and his fraudulent activity is connected to shares of companies brought to the market illegally and Barclay is his accomplice. I think all of them are pathologically incapable of straight dealing. They are surrounded by a harem of chorus girls, back theatrical schemes, own racehorses, and are devoted to the pleasures of the boudoir. Next thing we know, they'll be running for Parliament."

I turned and hid my smile.

"All of these men would like to wash down their breakfast kippers with champagne and a young lady on their arm but nothing I have heard this evening leads me to believe they are after Maggie's list."

"Do you think Maggie knows about any of these schemes?"

"I believe Maggie knows a great deal about a great many things, Poppy. But her three suspects, while scoundrels, do not seem distrustful of her or the least bit afraid of her. I do not like to go on intuition, of course. I believe we will prevail on this case from a different angle."

"And what is that angle?"

"I have not quite determined that. I think we should try to bring this evening to a close and speak with Maggie."

I agreed but then sighed with disappointment. "All of this . . . disturbing Mrs. Hudson, the disguises, all of it seems for naught as to Maggie's break-in."

His grey eyes were stern and his jaw set when he next spoke. "No, no. We must be pertinacious in our endeavors, Poppy, and always look beyond what others see. Remember, they see but they do not observe."

The expression on his face softened momentarily. "For example, looking at you now, one would not necessarily remember what your normal daily fare is. But I would."

"You would?"

"The first time we met, you wore a pale blue skirt with ruffles, a white blouse with wide lace, a coat with long sleeves and wide cuffs and scalloped edges at the lapel. Your gloves and parasol matched, I believe. And I seem to recall the hem of your skirt was thick with mud. You told me later you had waded near the water during the rowing race."

"You remember that? How could you remember that . . . what I was wearing? I don't remember it!"

"Precisely. But it is because I—" He stopped and looked away.

I guided his face back to me by nudging his chin. "Because?"

"Because I *do* observe, Dr. Stamford. All things at all times." He took in a breath. "Now, this evening," he continued, "we have discovered an on-going scheme of two men to enrich themselves at the expense of others—the church scheme. We have acquired information about possible malfeasance and misfeasance by Mr. Ritz and the French cook. In good time, we shall pursue both of these nefarious plots, but I must give this some thought. There may still be some clue here that we have missed. But it will not take long for these cases to be complete and rounded off.

"And in addition, it occurs to me that a woman can have a distinct advantage in navigating a complicated investigation by encouraging a man to reveal secrets he might otherwise keep close to his vest. Littlecode clearly wanted to impress you. Feminine wiles certainly can be the key to unlocking a treasure trove of otherwise elusive information. *And* I have had the distinct pleasure of observing you in a totally different light. You have shown yourself to be an excellent spy and I have never seen you more—"

He hesitated a moment, then finished his sentence in true Holmes fashion. "More satisfyingly altered."

"Sherlock, you certainly know how to turn a woman's head," I laughed.

A short time later, though it was a much earlier evening than the men expected, Maggie ushered all of them out and gathered up her girls.

Except one was missing.

"She's the youngest," Maggie said. "Polly. Where could she have gone?"

21

All of us picked up trash and started to put the three rooms back into some semblance of order while Maggie looked about for Polly. She could not find her anywhere.

"Perhaps she went off with Hamilton. She spent most of the evening with him," Louisa said. "She's always with him."

Maggie frowned. "No, I don't remember seeing her with him for the last half an hour and I bid him goodbye not long ago. Maybe she did not feel well and went back to The Pink Flamingo," she shrugged. But she looked uneasy.

Louisa nodded and Maggie said, "Sherlock, will you come back with me and have a port? And discuss what we've learned, which apparently isn't much."

Looking bored, Sherlock lit his pipe and said, "Hmm, yes."

"I'm going to go and change, Sherlock." I went down the steps to Mrs. Hudson's flat. The door was ajar and I was certain she had locked it. I hesitated a moment, then pushed the door open. The second I saw the open drawer of Mrs. Hudson's desk, my heart sank. I ran to it and picked up the empty velvet pouch.

My locket, my diamond lavalier and the matching earrings were gone.

I ran back up the steps and told Maggie and Sherlock.

"You are certain you put them in the drawer?" Maggie asked.

"Yes, certain. And where did you put the other jewelry you brought with you?"

Her face flushed. "In Mrs. Hudson's bedroom."

We flew back down the stairs.

Sherlock followed and pushed us aside as he looked quickly around the room. He dashed into the bedroom which was in total disarray. He turned to Maggie. "The jewels. Where did you leave them?"

"On the night stand, next to the bed."

The stand had been overturned. Handkerchiefs, a clock, books were strewn next to it. Sherlock rummaged through the mess. "No jewels," he said.

He knocked out the ashes from his pipe into a tray on the floor and slowly refilled it. "Maggie, tell me everything you can about this Polly, as quickly as you can. She's the one with long auburn curls and piercing blue eyes, yes? She wore a dark blue velvet dress which revealed an ample bust, an exceptional figure, as I recall."

"Sherlock," I hissed but he ignored me.

"Maggie, what can you tell us? How did you meet her?"

Wringing her hands, Maggie paced back and forth. "I was shopping. My friend, Lord—" She paused. "My friend, the one who owns the horse farm, told me to buy something for myself for my birthday. It was in early October. So I went to Emmanuel's in Hanover Square. I noticed this young girl, seventeen or so, standing near the counter. She was nicely dressed. Quiet. At first, it didn't occur to me that she was a problem or that she was stalking me. I thought she'd simply been separated from her mother. As I look back on it, of course she took notice. I was dressed in fashionable clothes, wearing a mink hand muff and jewels. I'd alighted from a brougham. Anyway, as I was examining several diamond bracelets, I realized that she slyly slid one of them under the hand muff that I'd placed on the counter and was about to place the muff on herself and turn to walk away.

"I took her aside and confronted her. Then the clerk said he thought he recognized her. He said that she had come in with a slightly older woman a few weeks before. They were accompanied by two men. Apparently, the men had engaged the clerk in conversation while the women made off with two diamond bracelets.

"I told the clerk he was mistaken, that she was my niece, and excused myself from the shop, took the girl by the wrist and dragged her out to the carriage. She told me several stories about her past but one did seem plausible. She that she had nowhere to go, that the woman she had been with at the store before was her aunt, her aunt Lizzie. That this aunt was involved with a man and they ran a scam at the aunt's house at Pimlico. She begged me not to turn her into the police because a couple of years ago, she had been picked up in Westminster for stealing from shops and if she were arrested, she would go to jail."

"Why did you take her in when you knew she was already into sordid schemes?"

"That's precisely why, Sherlock. She's young."

I couldn't quite wrap my head around the fact that Maggie had been kind to her and kept her from being arrested for stealing, yet brought her into a brothel and a life of prostitution. How could that have been any better?

"We need to get in touch with Lestrade," Sherlock said. "We need to find out if this girl is still involved with others or working on her own and we need to determine where she might have gone."

"But Sherlock," I said, shaking because I was so furious that my jewelry had been stolen, from right under my nose, "shouldn't we go back to Maggie's first? Isn't it possible that she did just go back there?"

"You mean you think someone else stole the jewelry?"

"I don't know. I have no idea. But we also have no idea where else to start."

"Right. Change and gather your things and I shall hail a hansom. Hurry."

When we arrived at Maggie's, we rushed into the house. "Polly! Polly!" Maggie called out.

As we ran down the hall toward Maggie's office, we heard a thump. Sherlock pushed open the door. Maggie's office was torn apart and there was Wiggins, badly beaten and bloody, laying on the floor.

"Archie!" I screamed as I ran to him. I sat on the floor and gently turned his blood-streaked face toward me. It looked like he had been raked with a jagged knife. I let his head rest on my lap. I checked his pulse. "He's alive. Thank God, he's alive."

But then I saw the spreading stain on his shirt and I snaked my hand around to open his shirt. There was a deep gash across his stomach. The wound seeped blood. I bit my lip and glanced at Sherlock. "Damn it, I need my medical bag. I—"

"Here," he said, kneeling next to Wiggins and handing it to me. "I picked it up while you were changing your clothes."

I quickly opened it and took out bandages.

Sherlock knelt next to Wiggins. "Who did this to you?" he asked.

Wiggins groaned. "I'm bleedin' like a pig," he whispered.

Maggie gasped when she looked at the wall. Her portrait was missing and the frame was in shatters on the floor. The safe that the portrait had concealed was wide open.

"Someone broke into the safe," Maggie said. She ran over to the safe and looked inside. "Cash is missing," she said, "and another painting. And some jewels that I took from my safe deposit box earlier today when I was trying to decide what Poppy might like to wear."

Sherlock ran over to the empty wall where the painting had hung. He examined the broken frame, bent to the floor, took a piece of the broken frame between two fingers and lifted it to smell it. "He cut the picture from the frame, lubricated the back so as not to damage the painting, rolled it up and hid it beneath his coat."

Maggie stared at him. "Just the way that—"

"That what?"

"Nothing, Sherlock. See to the young man."

"Who did this, Wiggins?" Sherlock asked.

At this point, we heard groaning and Maggie went behind her desk. She shrieked and we turned to look at her.

"It's Polly," she said. "Over here, Dr. Stamford. Polly's hurt, too."

Sherlock scrambled to his feet and went round the desk. But in a split second, I heard a guttural sound, a primal grunt. Sherlock flew backward as Polly roared from behind the desk, a knife in her hand. She ran toward the door. Sherlock found his footing, ran after her and lunged. He tackled her and pinned her down. She fought. She tried to raise the knife, but Sherlock slapped her hard and disarmed her.

I saw hands and fists and I heard him screech as she raked his neck with the sharp, serrated rings she wore on her fingers. She tried to pull a razor from her hair, but he finally pounded her head into the floor until she almost passed out and succumbed.

"Wiggins is losing blood too quickly," I shouted. "His pulse is racing. We need to get him to the hospital."

Maggie ran to the door and yelled to the other girls who were just coming in. "Sarah! Louisa! Hurry, find a policeman or a hansom. Ann, run to the Yard. Get someone here quickly!"

She ran back to me and said, "What can I do?"

"Keep pressure on the wound," I said as I fished in my bag for something to ease his pain. "Put something under his head. There, that pillow."

She grabbed it from the couch and gently placed it beneath the back of his head. I took laudanum from my bag and offered it to him.

"What's that?" he said with a grimace.

"It's laudanum—a tincture of opium and morphine. It will ease the pain until we can get you to the hospital."

"I don't like pills."

"It will make you feel much better Wiggins," Sherlock insisted. "Believe me."

I winced, knowing Sherlock's propensity to such things. Maggie poured some water from a carafe into a glass and handed it to me.

"Sherlock is right, Archie. Now swallow it down."

He popped the pill into his mouth and I helped him drink some water. I examined him again, looking for more than one slash. "He is bleeding badly but nothing is spurting. If an artery were hit, it would be gushing like a geyser.

"Now talk to him, Maggie. Keep him calm."

I applied a bandage as best I could, checked his airway and pulse again, and then pulled an afghan from the other couch and draped it over him. A few minutes later, Sarah ran in, followed by three Metropolitan policemen.

"Can you hear me, Wiggins?" Sherlock asked. "Wiggins, you're going to the hospital now. You'll be fine, lad."

Wiggins groaned and waved to Sherlock to bend down. Sherlock knelt next to him and said, "You need to go to the hospital, Wiggins."

"The girl. She caught me . . . off guard."

"It's all right, Wiggins."

"Men. Three men was with her. They took the picture and—" His next few words were unintelligible.

Two cops picked Wiggins up and carried him out to their hansom. We followed and I said, "Bart's. Take him to Bart's. Ask for Dr. Sacker. Please."

The third policeman stayed behind to manage Polly and we watched helplessly as the Black Maria screamed off into the night.

22

Sherlock went back into Maggie's office and yanked Polly to her feet. She pressed her palm to her eye where Sherlock had struck her. It would soon be black and blue and swollen, but that made no difference to him. The way he looked at her—I saw an expression of anger and loathing I did not see very often on his face.

But she was indignant. On her face was only defiance.

"What is your real name, girl?" He asked, giving her a shake.

"Polly," she mumbled.

He shook her again and shouted, "Your real name."

Sheet white, shivering and straining to get away, she finally yanked her arm from his grip. Teeth clenched, she choked out, "Mary Carr."

"How old are you?"

"Seventeen."

He pushed her back into the chair. "Where are the jewels?"

She smiled at him and he returned the smile with a look of furious anger. "Where are the jewels you stole?"

Maggie stepped forward. "I believe one or two may be hidden in that ample bosom you mentioned earlier. They do not look quite so smooth and inviting now. Hold her."

Sherlock pulled Polly's arms behind her and Maggie reached between her breasts. She retrieved my diamond necklace and held it up. "Lift your skirts," she demanded.

"Hard to do when you're yankin' my arms off," Polly said.

She struggled as Maggie pushed up her skirts and petticoats. Several secret compartments were sewn into her dress and bloomers. One by one, Maggie retrieved my earrings, several pieces of jewelry that belonged to Maggie, and finally my locket.

"My locket!" I cried and snatched it from Maggie's hands. I hastily put it back on.

"Seventeen and already a jewel thief," Sherlock muttered.

Maggie May touched his arm. "But she is a child, Sherlock. A child and—"

"I'm no child. And it's you who will pay. I'm part of the Forty Thieves," she yelled, bolts of hate hurling from her eyes. "I'll be the Queen of Thieves one day, you'll see," she spat.

Puzzled, I looked at Sherlock as he stood, staring at the girl's head-turning face. I realized then how beautiful she really was with her long auburn curls and perfect face. But Maggie was right. She was a child.

While Sherlock kept her occupied, I quickly changed and then we jumped into a hansom to follow the police cab that had arrived to take Polly to the Yard.

Inspector Lestrade met us at the door. Polly, aka Mary Carr, was swiftly put in a cell and Sherlock started to relate to Lestrade what she had said about the Forty Thieves. Wordlessly, Lestrade went straight back to the cell and we followed. He stepped inside and pulled Carr's hand toward him and examined it closely.

"What? What is it?" Sherlock asked.

"She's one of them all right. You see the dots on her hand here? Five?"

Sherlock nodded.

"It's a gang tattoo. We've seen it before. The tattoo between thumb and forefinger distinguishes her as one of the Forty Thieves."

"That's exactly what she said earlier."

"Mr. Holmes, as soon as one of Maggie's girls described the thorny rings on the girl's fingers, I suspected she was with the Forty Thieves. They also call themselves the Forty Elephants. Now that I've seen the tattoos, I'm certain of it."

"Elephants?" I gasped. I thought of Effie's warning. "Did you say elephants?"

Lestrade nodded. "Come with me," Lestrade commanded. As we walked to his office, he said, "The women—just young girls really—they are the female branch of a crime syndicate. We have been trying to break them up for years. Decades! They live near Elephant and Castle." He paused. "Hence the female gang's name, the Elephant Gang. They're thieves, bookmakers. A violent bunch. They'll pull the rings right off your finger, or take the finger itself if the ring is too tight. And from what I understand, some of the men protect this motley crew of women."

I swallowed hard.

He pulled out file after file. Searching through one of them, he finally took out an old newspaper article. It was in the *Morning Post* and dated September 1828. Sherlock read it out loud.

"– The Forty Thieves. Two
little urchins, about twelve years

of age, were brought up by one of the parish constables, who stated that he saw them loitering about Covent-Garden market and suspecting they were after no good, took them into custody. On examining their hands, he found the private mark of the Forty Thieves, and they were numbered respectively on the palm, 5 and 8. These marks were made by first pricking with a pin and afterwards, rubbing the part over with gunpowder. They were both committed."

"You see," Lestrade said, "the gang's notoriety is displayed by the 'five dots tattoo.' It's how members recognise each other. Its meaning is not clear. But we think it may be connected to the Five Points in New York."

"New York? America?" I asked.

"Correct. That's where the gang started. They were just as famous there as the Plug Uglies, the Shirt Tails and the Dead Rabbits. Mostly Irish immigrants. The Forty Thieves—some kind of *homage* to the Arabian Nights—they prowled the Five Points area of the city."

"Five Points?" I asked.

"A violent, infested slum. Worse than the worst we have here," Sherlock said.

"Here's another article," Lestrade said.

He handed it to me and I read it quickly. It was dated November 1829 and detailed the arrest of thirteen-year-old Thomas Robert Linchin, who was charged by his grandmother with 'repeated acts of thieving, endeavouring to set fire to her house, and threatening to take away her life.' The tattoo between thumb and forefinger distinguished him as one of the Forty Thieves.

"Back around the time of these articles, our newspapers described them as a 'youthful gang of depredators,' Lestrade said. "They were based on the Surrey side of the Thames, in Lambeth. Terrorised the neighbourhood.

"They committed the most daring exploits. Even back then, several girls were connected with them, and they adopted the tattoo."

"They became well established," Lestrade went on. "And the female side of it has grown."

"Back in the day, August 1828, I think it was, a young man named Edward Greyson was one of the first of the gang to be brought before Surrey magistrates. He was spotted rifling through passengers' pockets on a London-bound coach. When he made off with a handkerchief, he was arrested. He was fifteen. In October, more boys were arrested. The magistrate sent him to Brixton for six months, one month of that time in solitary confinement, and he was publicly whipped 150 yards from where the robbery was committed. That was a light sentence back then. But the public was tired of the street crime and the law wanted it nipped in the bud. When four other members of the Forty were caught stealing, they were each sentenced to seven years overseas for stealing cheese.

"Where overseas?" Sherlock asked.

"Australia. When the boat they were on, the *Elizabeth,* docked, the magistrates were warned about them. England didn't hear much from the gang again for ten years or so. Just one thief, John Hall was arrested around 1852 and the papers said the Forty Thieves were dead. Not so," he said, nodding toward the cell where Carr was screaming and banging on the bars. "They are not even close to dead.

"By the 1850s," Lestrade continued, "the New York gang had broken up. But in London? Oh, they're active. We've had regular cases involving boys and young men—they're in Islington, Camden, Covent Garden, Spitalfields, Clerkenwell, Limehouse, Greenwich, Chelsea and Woolwich. And also south of the river in Southwark.

"So here's the thing," Lestrade said. "This isn't just about a burglary at Maggie's place or the assault on young Wiggins. If that girl knows anything about the gang, anything at all, we have to get it out of her. It's not just about the jewelry she stole, or even the painting. She could lead us to the ring leaders. They are petrifying half of London. You caught her red-handed with the stolen goods. She obviously injured young Wiggins. We can charge her. Make her talk. We know they are based in Lambeth near the Elephant and Castle. But we need to know more. And we might need some help."

"Help?"

"I know someone who has dealt with these criminals for decades. I'm going to send young Hopkins to fetch him. You want some tea?"

"Actually, I'd like to get to the hospital, Inspector Lestrade," I said. "I want to see how Wiggins is doing. The jewelry is recovered. There's no reason for me to stay, is there?"

"That's up to you, Dr. Stamford."

I turned to leave and realized that Maggie was nowhere to be seen. I hurried to Carr's cell and found her there. She was pacing and tearing up.

"What is it, Maggie?"

"She's so young, Poppy. I'm just trying to get her to talk to me." She turned back to Polly.

"Where are your parents?" Maggie asked.

"My mother is dead. She died when I was nine."

"And your father?" Sherlock asked. He had suddenly appeared behind us with Lestrade in tow. "Where is your father?"

"Jail."

"His name?"

"John Carr."

"John Carr, I know that name," Lestrade said in a whisper behind me. He and Sherlock had followed us to the cell. I turned and looked at him. I could almost hear the gears and wheels in his brain working. "John Carr? The forger and thief? The *international* thief? That is your father?"

She nodded. She actually smiled with pride.

Sherlock turned to me. "Mycroft told me about him. He's part of an international scheme—thievery and forging bonds. He and his gang intercepted ten thousand pounds in bonds aboard a ship bound for Harwich from Rotterdam. The bonds were supposed to end up with a banker here in London but never arrived. Carr and another man, Joseph Wilson, were caught with them. They were sentenced to jail for five years."

"So her mother is dead and her father is in jail. She was left to fend for herself," Maggie said. "I know how that feels."

"Were you abandoned, Maggie?" I asked.

"Just like her. Mother dead. Father in jail. We . . . I had to fend for myself and Liverpool is not a friendly city. Many gangs. If we'd stayed there, my brother—"

She stopped, realizing that she had slipped. She gave out a sigh. "I have a brother. I was very worried that he would get caught up in the High Rip gang."

"Ah, I've heard of them," Lestrade said, nodding his head. "Liverpool, yes?"

She nodded.

"The gang is known for vicious street robberies and revenge attacks," Lestrade told us. "They're in a bitter turf war with the Logwood Gang."

"They operate mostly around Portland Street," Maggie said, "and in the dock area. They target lone dock workers on their way home from work. I was always worried that my brother would be attacked, or worse yet, fall in with them."

While we waited for Hopkins to return with the mystery person whom Lestrade seemed so eager to consult, Maggie, Sherlock, Lestrade and I huddled in a corner and discussed what Polly had done and what to do with her.

"What will become of her, Inspector Lestrade?" I asked.

"Don't worry about me," Polly said. "I can take care of myself."

Sherlock glared at her. "She stole your diamonds, Poppy. She broke into Maggie's house. I should think they will go harsh on her."

"And the painting?" Maggie asked. "She obviously does not have that." Maggie turned to Polly. "Who was with you? Wiggins said there were three men with you. You took the jewels and they took the painting, didn't they?"

Polly shrugged. Maggie looked at Sherlock. "She wouldn't know the value of my portrait. She does not have the background nor a trained eye."

"And what is the value of it, Maggie?" Sherlock asked.

"It was painted by Poynter when I was an artist's model," she replied.

"And?"

"The painting—the one of Georgiana Cavendish, Duchess of Devonshire, that was stolen four years ago. Have you heard of it?"

"Yes, it was taken from the Thomas Agnew Gallery." I said.

"Where?" Sherlock asked.

"Do you know nothing of contemporary artists, Sherlock?" Maggie asked impatiently.

"Indeed I do," he scoffed. "My grandmother was sister to the French artist Vernet."

"She was? You never told me that," I said.

"Oh, I am certain I've mentioned it, Poppy. Now Maggie, what do you estimate the worth of your portrait is?"

"The painting that was stolen from the Agnew—and in a manner similar to the one that is missing from my safe—is estimated to have a value of ten thousand guineas. Anyone in the world of art knows that Poynter's paintings will soon be of similar value. He is now principal of the National Art Training School."

"And was the thief who took the Duchess painting ever caught?"

She shook her head. "But it is highly likely that it was Adam Worth. Scotland Yard learned of the escapade from a police informant but they couldn't prove anything. Detective John Shore believes that Worth had the help of two associates, Junka Phillips and Little Joe Elliott."

"John Shore?" Sherlock asked. "He was with the Bristol police for a while and now he is with the Yard. The C. I. D."

"Yes," Maggie said. "That John Shore."

"Little Joe—he's one of the Forty Thieves," Lestrade said.

"And Junka Phillips?" Sherlock asked.

"A thug. Barrel chested, a drooping mustache. A towering, imposing man who acts as Worth's bodyguard. He's also a safecracker. They call him Junka because of his habit of keeping his pockets leaden down with random junk," Lestrade explained.

"And what does this Worth look like?" Sherlock asked.

"Small, five foot five or thereabouts. Thin. Wiry. Always elegantly dressed down to his pearl buttons and gold watch," said Lestrade. "Goes by a number of aliases. According to Detective Shore at least."

Maggie glanced toward Polly and back at Lestrade. "Neither one fits the description of the man that Wiggins described as his assailant. From what he said, it's one of my clients, Mr. Hamilton." She paused a moment and paced. Then she stopped and turned sharply to look at Lestrade. "What if we can get Polly to talk? Would you be lenient if she cooperates and helps you find the leaders? Couldn't you send her to a home for rehabilitation? Someplace like St. Mary the Virgin."

"The Female Penitentiary in Stone?" Lestrade asked.

Maggie nodded. "It's strict and punishment is swift for even the smallest transgressions. The girls are taught by Anglican nuns—reading, writing, and scripture. The one in Stone is for wayward girls, fallen women and prostitutes and girls with no place to go. They have homes for orphans and the disabled as well. Unmarried mothers are taught to care for their babies. All the girls are trained for employment."

"And how do you know about this place, Maggie?" I asked.

She paused a moment. "I've donated to it."

I suspected that was a lie by omission. I suspected that Maggie had been there herself.

"The goal is to rehabilitate," Maggie added. "To turn sinner into penitent."

Sherlock turned to Lestrade who shrugged. "It's not up to me, Holmes."

"But you could suggest it," Maggie urged. "You could request leniency. She's stolen nothing from me."

"Only because she was caught!" Sherlock cried. "She took your jewels and Poppy's. She and her associates attacked Wiggins and took the painting."

"But she's like a caged animal, Sherlock. Fighting back. She has no one. Perhaps she can lead us to the man who stole the painting. She did not concoct that scheme, I'm sure of it."

"I have family," Polly yelled. "I have my brother John and my sisters Ellie and Annie."

"And just where are they?" Lestrade shouted back.

She slumped in the chair and looked away.

"I guess I better send someone to fetch Shore as well," he sighed.

"He is off duty?" Maggie asked.

Lestrade nodded.

"Send someone to Nellie Coffey's Rising Sun on Fleet Street. When he's not at my place, Shore is there. He likes his whores." She turned to Sherlock and said, "What do you think will happen to Polly?" Maggie asked.

He shrugged. "Polly . . . Mary Carr will either become a nun or do exactly what she seems determined to do—become the Queen of Britain's first female crime syndicate."

23

Lestrade sent Hopkins to bring back Shore and the mysterious person who had dealt with these criminal gangs before and, out of nowhere, Rattle showed up at the station.

"Rattle, what have you learned?" Sherlock asked.

"Sherlock, when did you . . . how did he—?"

"Poppy, there is little that goes on amongst the street arabs that doesn't travel at lightning speed. I am certain Wiggins had someone keeping watch outside of Maggie's place for intruders. For all the good it did Wiggins. I suppose none of the urchins would have thought anything about one of Maggie's ladies returning to the house with escorts."

He turned back to Rattle. "Well?"

"Wiggins is gonna be fine. Your uncle, Miss," he said to me, "'e said t' tell yer that there was no in . . . inter . . . ."

He was obviously groping for the right word. "Internal?"

"Yeah, that's it. Internal. No internal problem."

"Thank God," I whispered.

"Mr. 'olmes," Rattle said, "Wiggins knows the bitch who did it. 'e's seen 'er before."

I was a bit taken aback by such language from a child but shouldn't have been. Rattle and most of the others had lived on the streets all their lives. "'e's seen 'er round. 'e knows 'er."

"Is he stable enough to talk to us?"

Rattle nodded.

Within minutes Sherlock and I were in a hansom bumping its way to Bart's to speak with Wiggins.

We were advised that Wiggins was in an out-patient room and that "all arrangements for his care had been taken care of by Dr. Sacker."

God Bless Uncle.

A short time later, Uncle came out of surgery. Taking off his bloody apron and handing it to his dresser, he looked tired and worn out. "Come along," he said. "I'll take you to Wiggins." He spoke to Sherlock. "But he needed a dozen stitches and he's very tired. He needs rest."

When we got to Wiggins' bed, I hesitated. His face was pale. His eyes were closed. "We should not be disturbing him," I told Sherlock.

"We must see what he knows. He would not want it any other way, Poppy."

I sat down next to him and gently took his hand. A large bandage covere4d the sutures in his torso and he had several stitches on his cheek where Polly's diamond-ring knuckle-duster had cut deeply into his face. "Archie. Archie, how are you feeling?"

"Awright. Been better."

Sherlock pressed him for details. The gist of it was that Wiggins knew Polly and further that he had been approached by members of the Forty Thieves but he always turned them down. He'd seen them hanging around the Elephant and Castle pub in Southwark. They often looted stores like Selfridges on Oxford Street and Gamages in Holburn Circus. Their clothes were designed for theft. Slits in the outer garments fed into pockets cunningly sewn in into the layers beneath. They easily concealed loot in their coats and muffs and skirts and bloomers. Some had sidelines—blackmail and looting homes. They used false letters of reference to get hired as maids and then robbed the houses. They seduced men into brief affairs and then blackmailed them with threats of ruining the men's reputations. As Maggie had described her first encounter with Polly, they often laid down a muff or a coat on the counter and scooped up the goods they wished to steal. They also employed a decoy approach—while staff waited on one person, an accomplice stuffed armfuls of clothing or jewels beneath her dress. They also used something that Wiggins called a 'crush.' A crowd of women would press around the counter demanding to be shown make-up or jewelry. They would hand the goods to each other until the goods ended up with a girl at the back of the crowd who left the store while the others, who had no goods on their person, cried out their innocence and were let go.

"They're crazy," Wiggins said.

"And clever," Sherlock added.

"Yeah. And wicked. One of the girls got in trouble with a bloke who ain't from Southwark. She defied the others and married him. A while back, the gang got t'gether at Lambeth's New Cut Market. All of 'em was drunk and felt like fightin'. They marched over to the pregnant girl's place, smashed their way in, held her down with a pistol to her head and beat the husband with bottles and stones and lumps of concrete. They wanted us to fence what they stole. Heard of one of 'em who stashed things at a shop at Red Lion Market. The cupboards are doors to rooms where they hold things."

Sherlock shook his head. "Why have you never told me of any of this?"

"They's all poor, like me. They's all come from Lambeth Workhouse and the like, just like me. One of the gals told me once that there's four choices. Be a servant or get married and have a bunch of babies and stay poor. Or be a street woman or be a thief.

"I know the one who did this to me," Wiggins said, touching his cheek. "A painter lady wanders about doin' drawings of us. Of me and Rattle and all of us. She wants to do a book of her paintings. I sees her all the time. Her name is Dorothy. Dorothy Tennant. And I 'member seeing the girl who attacked me with her. She was sittin' on a stoop and the lady, Dorothy, was paintin' her."

"I know that name," I said. "How do I know that name?"

I rose and paced a moment. "Now I remember. Aunt Susan met Miss Tennant when she and Uncle were on holiday on the Isle of Wright. They leased a home near the one owned by George Frederic Watts, the painter and a sculptor," I explained. "And Mr. Watts's next door neighbors were the Tennants and they had two daughters, one of whom was Dorothy, a talented young artist. She paints portraits. Mr. Watts apparently has helped her get her work into galleries."

"This woman, would you think she would have any idea where the others in the gang are?" Sherlock asked. "Perhaps she has attempted to paint them as well?"

Wiggins shrugged. "Don't know. I just know the girl got paid a few shillings for sittin' for her. For bein' a model. But mostly she likes to paint little beggars. That's what she calls us."

"Wiggins, the men she was with. Can you describe them?"

"Only the one. Heavy set, full beard. 'e had strange eyes."

"Perhaps we should talk to this painter," Sherlock said. "She may have some knowledge of where Polly Carr was living before she came to Maggie's. And Hamilton. We must find out more about this man Hamilton."

"Sherlock, he needs to rest."

"Yes, right. We should get back to the station. Perhaps Maggie and this person Lestrade is so keen to talk to will shed more light on things."

24

"Are you tired?" Sherlock asked as we bumped along in the hansom.

Fatigue had fallen away. "I should be. It's so late. Yet somehow I am not."

"It's the adrenalin. It is what moves us forward in the game."

"It's not a game, Sherlock. Wiggins could have died. And these people you want to hunt down. They are violent. Ruthless."

"It is much larger than this female gang or even these Forty Thieves. This is all part of an international scheme, one that I am sure Mycroft has been keen to get to the bottom of. I need to speak to him."

We did not speak again until we arrived at the station.

We told Lestrade about Miss Tennant and her sketches of Polly, and Maggie suddenly excused herself.

Seated in Lestrade's office was an older man. He looked to be in his late sixties, with pure white hair and long bushy sideburns. His eyes were tired, propped up by puffs of sagging flesh beneath and crowned by dark bushy eyebrows above. His face was creased and worn, the folds so downtrodden that even if he smiled, no mirth could be detected. He was dressed in a dark jacket with a bow tie slightly askew. He sat erect, like a military man who even years after separation from the service continues to take pride in his posture and stride. His head swiveled like an owl's as his eyes darted around the room, very like Sherlock's always did at the beginning of an investigation. The way they swept over everything, it appeared that he was cataloguing every inch of his surroundings in moments.

"This is John Whicher. He is a retired inspector. He was one of Scotland Yard's first eight detectives."

"I know who you are," Sherlock said. "You were the best on the force! An amazing detective."

"Thank you," Whicher whispered but looked away. His eyes reflected dim and difficult memories of a distant past, one that was not, as Sherlock said, amazing.

"The Forty Thieves. I know this lot," Whicher said. "One of my first brushes with the Forty Thieves was over twenty years ago. The Constance Brown case.

"And then there was the case of James Pearce and Emily Laurence. They went to Hunt & Roskell and made off with diamond bracelets. Early the next year, she and Pearce went to Emmanuel's in Hanover. She was dressed to the nines . . . mink hand muff, jewels, expensive clothes. She rested her muff on the counter while looking at jewelry. The Elephant Gang firls still use that ploy. Pearce wrote a fake address down for the clerk. Next day, they realized that a locket worth sixteen hundred pounds was missing. And Pearce had the temerity to go back to the store with loose gems and try to sell them!

"They were reported to the police and arrested at a home in Stoke Newington by me and Inspector Fields. Pearce came after me with a poker but Fields got it away from him. We found diamond rings, expensive dresses, gold watches and chains . . . a long list of stolen goods. At the prison, when Pearce was ordered to remove his shirt, they even found a diamond sewn into it.

"He was a cunning son of a—" Whicher paused and looked at me. "He was clever. He went to prison but feigned insanity and he got out! So did Laurence a few years later.

167

Within months, they were in Sussex, stealing again. Laurence went back to jail in Lewes Prison, tried several times to escape, and eventually got sent to Millbank in Clerkenwell. She escaped again and we haven't seen her since 1875. We think she's connected to a den of thieves, your Forty Thieves."

He took a sip of coffee and looked at Lestrade and then at Sherlock and me. "The Forty Thieves have been around for at least a century. The women took their name from the Elephant and Castle Tavern, a coaching inn back in the day. It had an emblem of an elephant with a castle on its back. It was taken from, let me see, oh yes . . . the coat of arms of the Worshipful Company of Curers, a livery company.

"The tavern stood at 1 Newington and it was a good resting stop for travelers. Early on, the original Forty Thieves gang often assaulted travelers, stripped them of bags and purses as they left their coaches or robbed them while they were asleep in the pub. Then they graduated to robbing warehouses and stores and they mostly lived around William Street in Lambeth and some in Southwark on Bridge Road. The girls were raised to be loyal to the Forty. They went into dance halls and pubs and put on quite a show for the boys. But none of them would put up with being knocked around. These girls were—*are* tough. They fight cops, shop keepers, whoever they need to. They have favorite tools, too. Hat pins, a cut-throat razor, diamond knucklers."

Sherlock touched the scrapes on his neck. "I can attest to that."

"They plan their shoplifting meticulously. Every detail. The present gang operation started with the Pitts family and then the Gormans. Now I hear that John Carr has pretty much taken the lead."

"John Carr?" Lestrade asked. "That's the girl's father. But she said he's in jail."

The wry smile again and then a shadow crossed Whicher's face. "Is he?"

25

Sherlock took his leave and disappeared for more than two hours. I knew where he went. He was going to consult with his brother Mycroft who could get his hands on almost anything from anyone about anyone in record time.

While he was gone, I had tea with Lestrade and Whicher and then gratefully accepted Lestrade's invitation to nap on the divan in his office. When I awoke, it was obvious that Lestrade had been gathering as much information on recent gang activity as he could so he and his men could start searching for Mr. Hamilton—or John Carr?—who Lestrade had deduced was coaching Polly Carr and who perhaps had much more in mind than getting a few jewels.

I accompanied Whicher to Polly's cell. He proceeded to interrogate her but she was stubborn, resolute. When he asked, "How did you get into Miss Mayhew's safe?" she smiled widely. "You all think we're so stupid."

Whicher shook his head. "Stupid? No, never. Lawless, immoral, yes. But never stupid. Where is your father?"

"I told you. He's in jail."

"No, he's not," Sherlock said. He had appeared again, out of breath, flushed, but his eyes twinkling as they always did when he was on to something. "Poppy, Detective Whicher, if you'll join me."

We went back to Lestrade's office and sat down. "Mycroft heard that Carr and his American counterparts were living somewhere in England, possibly near Pimlico," Sherlock said. "His informants say the gang intends to intercept some bonds that are scheduled to be on a ship bound for Harwich. Mycroft's people have been watching for them."

"Who are these American counterparts?" I asked.

"Charlie "The Scratch" Becker and a bond fraudster, Adam Worth," Sherlock replied.

"Becker," Whicher said. "He's been described as one of the greatest forgers of all time. The Yard has compared him to Michelangelo, Rembrandt and Whistler in artistic talent. He's been, I am told, trying to invent a forgery-proof paper and ink which he thinks he can sell to the very banks he robs!"

"And Adam Worth?" I asked.

"A master thief. The head of a vast crime syndicate."

"The Napoleon of Crime," Whicher said. "Your friend Inspector Anderson calls him that."

"As do I," a man said and we turned toward the doorway.

Lestrade rose to shake the man's hand; he was dressed in a dark suit, white shirt and bowler hat. His face was full, flushed from the cold, and his eyes were narrowly set like a bird's. He removed his gloves as Lestrade reached out to him. "Detective Shore, good of you to come."

Lestrade introduced us and Shore asked, "So what has he done this time?"

"Worth, you mean? Well, we don't know, of course, if it's Worth. But a painting is missing. An expensive one."

"It's Worth. He's damnable taunting me."

"Why is he called the Napoleon of Crime?" Sherlock asked.

"Because he's so grand at it, and because he's small. Five feet five or so. Last time I saw him was at the Criterion Bar. You never forget Worth once you've seen him. Dark, almost black eyes. Eyes like a volcano crater, devoid of emotion. Shaggy eyebrows above them, like an arch of primeval trees in a forest.

Short thick hair that he always parts to the right and combs to the side. A long mustache that curls up his cheeks and meets thick side-whiskers. He marks his own deck, Worth does. He is intelligent and determined. Ambitious. Always wanted to better himself and triumph over his adversaries. Hates me. Hates me through and through. He tried to set me up once at Nellie's."

"How so?"

"He tried—" He stopped and looked straight at Lestrade.

"It's all right, John. I've heard the story and Dr. Stamford is quite familiar with the criminal world and completely trustworthy."

"He tried to engineer a police raid at Nellie's when I was there," Shore said. "Intended to catch me out in the raid. But Worth relied on an old drunk to tell police so I'd be caught in a brothel but the drunk wandered off at a key moment and I wasn't there. What Worth didn't know was that I'd caught wind of the plot from the drunk.

"I often find it necessary to receive information from thieves and drunks and street people, people of the lowest grade. Much like you from what I hear, Mr. Holmes. If no information is forthcoming, we ignore it and the authorities aren't in the habit of asking names. And it's well known that Adam Worth and I have been playing cat and mouse for years. Ask Chief Inspector Cruise or Lestrade here."

"Assuming Worth orchestrated the plot to steal Maggie's portrait, do you have any idea where he might be?" Sherlock asked.

"If he's running with John Carr again, I'd start there. His sister has a place in Pimlico, I believe. Last we heard, Carr was in business with Charlie 'The Scratch' Becker, Little Joe Elliott, Henry Wade Wilkes and, of course, Adam Worth," Shore said.

"Adam Worth? Did you say Adam Worth is here?"

We all turned our heads toward the door at the sound of Maggie's voice.

"Yes, Adam Worth—the bane of my existence," he grumbled.

"We thought you went back to your place, Maggie."

Her face was beet red, her eyes like dry ice. "No, I went to see Dorothy Tennant. The artist that sketched Polly—Mary, whatever her name is. Mrs. Tennant is a student at the Slade under Poynter, who drew me when I was an artist's model. She recognized Polly—and she said that she often saw her with a man who fits Hamilton's description."

"We have reason to believe that the girl's father is not in jail, that he is living here in London. Mr. Hamilton could actually be Carr," Lestrade said.

"Polly was always with him. Only him," Maggie said. "She hasn't been with me very long so I thought little of it. I thought she might even be trying to get him to take her in or marry her. Perhaps he was not a client at all. I believe that Hamilton may be her father."

She started to pace, her face still flushed, her fists tightly coiled like she was about to punch something.

"It all leads back to Worth. Elliott, Becker and Joe Chapman and Carr . . . the Pinkertons and the Yard have been after them for years. Most recently they've been involved in fictitious bonds, French certificates of income, Russian bonds. They travel back and forth to New York and Paris and

Constantinople and Amsterdam the way you and I hail a hansom to Trafalgar Square. They could be anywhere."

"I agree," said Lestrade. "We've heard that they've thrown in with Wilkes, who goes by several aliases."

"This Wilkes, who is he?" Sherlock asked.

"The chief of an international board of bond forgers and counterfeiters. Last we heard they were in Florence.

"About a year ago, they forged some French certificates. Then they went to Paris and then Madrid. And then they went on to Naples and Rome and nine or ten other places, disposing of the forged certificates."

"This is incredible," I said.

Lestrade shook his head and was about to say something but Whicher interrupted.   "Carr has a sister. Lizzie. Shore, you say she's in Pimlico? I had heard she was in Islington."

"No one is sure. If he's running with Worth, there was a rumour that Worth had an apartment in Mayfair but he was reportedly seen in Wooten, too."

Wootton was in an area of horrible housing and itinerant street vendors. Recently released prisoners and thieves inhabited every household.

"Wootten makes no sense," Lestrade said. "It's one of the streets where the Yard looks first for robbers and burglars."

"Nevertheless," Whicher said, "you need to send your men there, as well as to Pimlico, Islington and Mayfair. If we find Hamilton—who likely is Carr—we may find the others and maybe the rest of the Forty Thieves."

We all returned to Polly's cell and Shore banged on the bars. "Your aunt . . . your Aunt Lizzie. Where does she live?"

"Do you know where your father is?" Lestrade demanded. "Do you know where these fraudsters may be?"

She turned to face the wall.

"Miss Carr, if you tell us where your aunt lives, things might go a bit easier for you. Instead of jail, perhaps a short sentence in a home for wayward girls. A few months at best. Or you can look forward to hard labour at Wormwood Scrubs."

She refused to answer. We turned and started to walk away.

"I won't go to jail?"

"Not this time," Sherlock turned an said, "You can go back to the streets or sell flowers at Covent Gardens, I don't care. But an address. I need an address."

"She's in Pimlico. We've had quite a bit of fun there."

"What?"

"We trap gentlemen like you. I pretend to faint, the gentleman escorts me home, and I lay down on the couch and while he's comforting me, my Aunt Lizzie comes in and I start screaming. I've earned as much as four hundred pounds from some blokes in Parliament who don't want their names in the papers. I had planned to do even better with Maggie's list."

She laughed, a low, menacing laugh.

"An address," Sherlock growled. "Now."

"I don't know the number. But it's a blue house. Now will you let me out of here? You got your pretty little trinkets back."

"And you think on balance that you are deserving of your freedom? I think not," Sherlock said.

"But you said if I told you—"

She spoke rapidly, almost too fast to be understood, and she could hardly catch her breath. Sherlock and I were already halfway down the hall as she shouted in protest.

Once again in Lestrade's office, Shore said, "Becker is an infamous forger in his own right, but he is really only a tool of Wilkes. And all of them are tools of Adam Worth. All of them. And we do think that Worth may still be in London. We had leads to two hotels on the Strand and a house on Tottenham Court Road but they never panned out."

"But I can tell you this," Shore said. "Anyone who wants to fence bonds or certificates eventually ends up connected to Adam Worth."

"This is massive," Sherlock said in a whisper. "This must be stopped."

"We've been trying, Mr. Holmes," Shore said. "About ten years ago, he and his coalition of thieves robbed the Ocean Bank, then the New York Central Railway. They broke out of the White Plains jail and hit the vaults of Boyston Bank in Boston. Honestly, the history is too long to even recount to you. But we are talking about the top echelon of international criminals assembled right here in London."

"So Worth really *is* here then . . . here in London." Maggie said.

"Maggie, what is it?" I asked. She looked so distraught, as though every nerve ending in her body was on fire.

"Nothing. It's nothing."

Sherlock stared at Maggie. "Maggie, stop. Whatever you are thinking—"

But Maggie had already turned on her heels and was running toward the door.

I grabbed my cape and ran after her but she had already alighted into her brougham.

I went back and Lestrade was scrambling his men, barking orders and preparing to go out with them. "You two stay here," he said, pointing to me and Sherlock.

"Of course," Sherlock agreed.

But the minute Lestrade was out the door, he turned to me and said, "The game's afoot."

"Sherlock, there is more to it than this for Maggie. We must find her. The way she looked, the way she reacted. She knows where Hamilton lived, I'm sure of it. She could lead us to him. Call it instinct but this feels more personal than just the fact that Hamilton or Carr or whoever he is might have been involved in the break-ins at The Pink Flamingo."

"You are quite right. It is more personal for Maggie. Mycroft filled me in on a great many things."

"About Worth? About Maggie?"

Sherlock nodded and looked at me. "Are you ready to go home?"

"No, absolutely not. I'm ready to go with you."

26

Sherlock gave directions to the cabbie that had nothing to do with Pimlico or Islington, nor Wootton or Mayfair.

"Where are we going?"

"I believe we will find Adam Worth—and Maggie—in Clapham Common."

"That was never mentioned."

"Mycroft said he had heard that Worth bought a lodge at Clapham Common. It has a bowling green, tennis courts, and a shooting gallery. Posh furnishings. He's been masquerading in high society as he builds his criminal network. I found notes in Maggie's safe, also in code, which confirm this. She mentioned Carr and a few of the others and all the areas where Lestrade sent his men. But she also made note of what Mycroft told her just a few weeks ago. The very last reference in her notes was Worth's name and an address at Clapham Common. I am certain she was working to confirm his suspicions and follow up."

"Her code? You broke it then."

"I tried the Rosicrucian Cipher, in which two letters are put into each section of one grid and one X. When the second letter in a section is used, it is accompanied by a dot. Confederate agents operating in New York City used the cipher to communicate with government officials in Richmond. You remember Maggie mentioned Elizabeth Van Lew from Richmond?"

"Yes, of course."

"Well, her code was ingenious. But it didn't work with Maggie's notes. So then I tried one used by a famous female Rebel spy, Rose O'Neal Greenhow. You know I study ciphers.

She used a cipher in 1861 when she warned General Beauregard that the Union Army was advancing toward Bull Run. When Pinkerton detectives arrested Greenhow, they found that she had made a critical mistake by not destroying some encrypted and deciphered messages. As a result, the Pinkertons were able to break the cipher she used.

"The most common method of Confederate encryption was a variation of the 16th- century, the Vigenère Cipher. It uses a table consisting of 26 alphabetized letters across and 27 letters down. Messages were encrypted by using the first line of horizontal letters to match the letters of a key phrase, for example, 'Manchester Bluff,' and the first line of vertical letters to match the message.

"For example, if one wanted to encrypt the word "Jackson" he would find the first letter of the key phrase—M— in the first horizontal line and then the first letter of the desired word, J, in the first vertical line. Where these lines intersected gave the first letter of the encrypted word: V. By following this process, the word 'Jackson' would read as 'VAPMZSF.'"

Sherlock took a piece of paper from his pocket and showed me the table. Of course, it made no sense to me. I was pathetic at such mental gymnastics.

```
A B C D E F G H I J K L M N O P Q R S T U V W X Y Z
B C D E F G H I J K L M N O P Q R S T U V W X Y Z A
C D E F G H I J K L M N O P Q R S T U V W X Y Z A B
D E F G H I J K L M N O P Q R S T U V W X Y Z A B C
E F G H I J K L M N O P Q R S T U V W X Y Z A B C D
F G H I J K L M N O P Q R S T U V W X Y Z A B C D E
G H I J K L M N O P Q R S T U V W X Y Z A B C D E F
H I J K L M N O P Q R S T U V W X Y Z A B C D E F G
I J K L M N O P Q R S T U V W X Y Z A B C D E F G H
J K L M N O P Q R S T U V W X Y Z A B C D E F G H I
K L M N O P Q R S T U V W X Y Z A B C D E F G H I J
L M N O P Q R S T U V W X Y Z A B C D E F G H I J K
M N O P Q R S T U V W X Y Z A B C D E F G H I J K L
N O P Q R S T U V W X Y Z A B C D E F G H I J K L M
O P Q R S T U V W X Y Z A B C D E F G H I J K L M N
P Q R S T U V W X Y Z A B C D E F G H I J K L M N O
Q R S T U V W X Y Z A B C D E F G H I J K L M N O P
R S T U V W X Y Z A B C D E F G H I J K L M N O P Q
S T U V W X Y Z A B C D E F G H I J K L M N O P Q R
T U V W X Y Z A B C D E F G H I J K L M N O P Q R S
U V W X Y Z A B C D E F G H I J K L M N O P Q R S T
V W X Y Z A B C D E F G H I J K L M N O P Q R S T U
W X Y Z A B C D E F G H I J K L M N O P Q R S T U V
X Y Z A B C D E F G H I J K L M N O P Q R S T U V W
Y Z A B C D E F G H I J K L M N O P Q R S T U V W X
Z A B C D E F G H I J K L M N O P Q R S T
```

"A Vigènere cipher table was found among John Wilkes Booth's possessions after he assassinated President Lincoln, you know. And also in the office of the Confederate secretary of state, Judah P. Benjamin, after Richmond was evacuated. Some think that that the Confederate government was involved in the assassination.

"Once I broke some of it down, I realized there was mention of Clapham Common but it made no sense until Mycroft mentioned the area to me. That is where we are going. I believe we will find our thieves, and perhaps this Mr. Worth who seemed to upset Maggie so, will be there also."

"Adam Worth. What did Mycroft tell you about him?

"He told me why Maggie is so interested in Worth. It relates to what you discovered in Maggie's office. Maggie knew someone who crossed paths with Worth during the Civil War."

"It was at the sound of his name that Maggie seemed to implode."

"And he is the one Mycroft is most interested in. The head of the snake, so to speak. The Napoleon of Crime—it would appear that is an accurate characterization. Mycroft wants this crime syndicate eliminated. And Maggie was working with him to do so."

"Maggie was working with Mycroft?"

"Poppy, there is much more to Maggie Mayhew than meets the eye. Maggie was a spy for the Union Army during the Civil War."

27

I recalled what she had said to me in her office. *It will be like spying, and Dr. Stamford, I assure you, the spy game is thrilling.*

"What? What are you talking about?"

"Nineteen or twenty years ago, her brother Malcom—the one in the photo in Maggie's office—met a wealthy young woman from New York. She was here in Europe travelling with a guardian. They fell in love and eloped. When they returned to America, Malcolm felt some compulsion to enlist in the Union Army. And so he did. Second Cavalry, Company F, I believe. Then he discovered that his young bride was pregnant. He wanted to get out of the military. And Worth showed him a way to do it."

"Which was?"

"Worth was an accomplished bounty jumper."

"Sherlock, I don't understand."

"Worth served in the 2nd New York Heavy Artillery. He is extremely intelligent and was promoted to sergeant in two months. He was wounded in the Second Battle of Bull Run in August of 1862 and shipped to a Georgetown Hospital in Washington D. C. In the hospital, he learned he had been listed as killed in action and left. And then he embarked on a career of bounty jumping. He made an art of it, actually.

"He enlisted in various regiments under assumed names, receiving his bounty each time and then deserting. You see, bounty jumpers were men who enlisted in the Union or Confederate army only to collect a bounty and then leave. Bounty jumpers commonly enlisted numerous times in the army, collecting many bounties in the process. Worth convinced

Maggie's brother Malcolm to desert and enlist in the Confederate Army, collect his bounty and then jump again. Worth promised him and several others that he would instruct them when it would be easy and safe to escape. He said he had a plan.

"Instead, Worth collected a very large sum of money in exchange for turning them in to the Confederate Army. All of his victims ended up in Andersonville Prison. Worth was last in uniform at the Battle of the Wilderness. I'm not sure if Maggie's brother was captured there or before."

I tried to imagine Maggie's young brother. Of course, it was wrong to desert, to shirk his duty. But being so young, having a young wife with child . . . .

"My God. Oh, my God. How she must hate Adam Worth for what happened to her brother."

"Quite so."

"But, Sherlock, that does not explain this spying."

"Maggie was already interested in supporting the North, even before her brother was captured. She had read the newspapers. By then, she had met Mycroft. When one of her clients turned out to be a Confederate spy who had traveled to Britain for the sole purpose of seeking recognition by the British government of the South, Maggie pounced on it.

"When Malcom was imprisoned at Andersonville, she decided that she could avenge him by helping the Union Army win the war. There were many, many spies coming to Britain because Britain was engaged in helping the Confederates."

I remembered the newspaper article in Maggie's office that revealed the sympathy of some British citizens for the Confederacy.

"Maggie was very young, but beautiful, intelligent, charming and cunning. She—with the help of some people high in government, including my brother Mycroft—was able to lure many Confederate spies who were in London into her lair, garner information and get it to the Union Army through letters sent to Elizabeth Van Lew and to her sister-in-law. They forwarded the information to the Union authorities."

"But wait, Sherlock—Mycroft was only fifteen or so during the Civil War."

"Fifteen in 1862, yes."

"If we were siding with the Confederates, why would he—?"

"I'll get to that, Poppy. Patience." He took a breath and continued.

"Maggie still works with Mycroft to glean information from her clients. Anything that might be of interest to Her Majesty. Mycroft needed her talents—her ability to cloak herself in secrecy, her discretion, her trustworthiness, her raw intelligence and cunning and her prodigious memory.

"Maggie wanted more information about Worth and she got some information from her sister-in-law, whose family was very involved in war espionage. She got more information from Elizabeth Van Lew for whom her sister-in-law worked in a spy ring that reached as far north as New York and Boston where the sister and their son settled. Admirable, Poppy. And her personal war on Adam Worth, her mission, then expanded and fundamentally changed to focus upon ferreting out wrongdoing even if it occurred inside her own government."

This piqued my interest. I had long felt that Her Majesty was not always on the right side of things. The Irish immigrants had been treated badly. The India and American colonies were subjugated to British rule, to our wants and needs. And women's rights were suppressed. Even our queen only ruled because she'd inherited the throne at the age of 18 after her father and his three brothers had all died, leaving no surviving legitimate children except Victoria.

"Tell me more about these Confederates who courted Britain's favor, Sherlock."

"Before the war, Prime Minister Viscount Palmerston urged Britain to keep a policy of neutrality. But shipments of cotton to Europe ceased in the spring of 1861and Britain's shortage of cotton was only partially made up by imports from India and Egypt. The North provided us with over forty percent of its wheat imports during the war years and had Britain intervened on the South's behalf, suspension would have caused a severe disruption to our food supply. Also, British banks and financial institutions in London had financed many projects such as railways in America. There were fears that war would result in enormous financial losses as investments were lost and loans defaulted on. And then Lincoln issued the Emancipation Proclamation.

"You know, of course, that we had already abolished slavery. But Gladstone, who was the Chancellor of the Exchequer and a senior Liberal leader, was friendly toward slavery; his family had grown wealthy through the ownership of slaves in the West Indies. So he strongly spoke out for Confederate independence. When the Emancipation Proclamation was announced, he argued that an independent Confederacy would do a better job of freeing the slaves than an invading northern army would. He warned that a race war was imminent that would justify British intervention. Emancipation also alarmed the British Foreign Secretary, Lord John Russell, who expected a bloody slave uprising.

"Well, there was no slave uprising. There was no race war. And based upon the tide of British public opinion, he convinced the cabinet to take no action."

"But I always thought that we remained neutral throughout the war."

"Not so. The elite supported the Confederacy because of slavery sentiments and the whole cotton fiasco and the Confederacy sought Britain's help in securing independence by getting us to intervene with our military. And many in government hoped that the civil war would leave the United States weakened as a mercantile power.

"That is where Maggie's knack for soliciting information and for codes, her own deviations especially, became useful. There was no guarantee that the information could be safely received because it went through naval officers and purchasing agents through blockades. So agents used an array of disguises and codes.

"Maggie used her body and her brains to get information from Confederate spies in London and sent dispatches to the Union Army, either using code or her artistic talent. She could sketch those she suspected of Confederate spy activity and send those sketches to America for definite identification without raising many eyebrows.

"She also enlisted people in the workhouses, hospitals, the people on the ships on the river, and the homeless sleeping under railway arches and in doorways."

I thought of Wiggins and Rattle and Ollie and Ivy and the others—Sherlock's little army of street urchins who helped him gather information for cases.

Sherlock gazed out the window for a long moment. "She had been an artist's model for some time and that gave her a foot in the door to galleries where tourists went. She had also earned money in the tourist business by passing out maps and guidebooks to newcomers, like those that are mounted on linen with a street index. Railway station maps, Omnibus routes, cab fares. The larger ones like Weller's *Environs of London and* Stanford's *Library Map*. Very useful and particularly during our foggy winters."

I nodded, remembering last year's catastrophic fog that had endangered and taken so many lives. One could walk down the street and be unable to see any numbers on shops or houses. People moved like ghostly figures through the black mist. One felt like a breathing chimney at times.

"You realize, Poppy, to the unfamiliar visitor to London the city is a vast labyrinth. A giant puzzle. How confusing it must be for them to find their way." He rattled off street names like a child recites the alphabet. "37 King Streets, 27 Queens Streets, 22 Princess Streets, 17 Duke Streets, 35 Charles, 29 John, 15 James, 21 George, 24 New, 16 York, 14 Cross, 16 Union and 10 Gloucester."

He paused to catch his breath and I gasped. I'd lived here for half of my life and never realized this. Then again, statistics were one of Sherlock's fortés.

"According to Mycroft, Maggie, at the rather tender age of twenty or so, knew every inch and where every sort resided. She knew the artists and authors of Camden Town, the musicians and actors of Brompton, the doctors on Savile Row, the publishers of Fleet, Guy's Hospital medical students in Southwark. Stockbrokers of Baywater and Brixton. Clerks in Islington. When she started her spy ring, she had her own agents everywhere, from the homeless to the high born—whom she often blackmailed into getting information."

I closed my eyes, imagining a younger and even more beautiful Maggie Mayhew, seducing and enticing silk and velvet wearers in Bethnol Green, tanners in Bermondsey and tailors in Burlington Gardens into giving her the beautiful clothes she needed to operate this grand scheme. What a cadre of helpers she must have assembled in her London spy ring.

"Mycroft said she had a lover down in Hoxton who even made toys for the children she employed. She left no stone unturned.

"She had her own cabal of helpers who scouted out hotels where the Confederates were known to stay . . . places like the Burlington where her customers could leave undetected through the door in the back that opened onto Old Burlington. Maggie had agents posted at the railway stations and on boats on the Thames, too.

"She and like-minded people who were well-placed in government had spies in shops as well . . . haberdashers, shawl shops, music shops. Apparently one of her most rewarding and fruitful places was the Burlington Arcade in Piccadilly. It's renowned, as you know, for luxury goods, and escorts of a better sort like Maggie's friends paraded there each day and often were able to connect with Confederate spies who were seeking gifts to take home. They employed street entertainers and street vendors. Think of it, the astonishing advantage of having a vendor of oysters or hot eels or roasted chestnuts who might overhear a conversation between these Confederate spies and their London contacts.

"And of course, her friends in entertainment. She connected the Confederates to the gentlemen's clubs of Pall Mall and procured tickets for them for half price at theaters like Theater Royal or the Adephi. These were highly sought after by the Americans."

"Sherlock, you speak of Maggie and Mycroft as if they were working closely together. How did they—I mean how, did he meet her? He was very young and he doesn't seem—"

Sherlock laughed. "Inclined to visit brothels? No, he is not. But he loves art and he met her at one of the galleries." He laughed to himself. "He was there with our mother, actually."

"Oh. Oh, I see." I thought a moment. "Sherlock, you are describing a vast network. Why is it that Kate never mentioned any of this?"

"Kate came into Maggie's life long after the war, Poppy. By then Maggie had infiltrated brothels to help the Yard apprehend criminals. With the help of some government subsidies, she bought The Pink Flamingo to try to bring down people like Littlecode and Barclay. But she never stopped hunting for Adam Worth. "

"Putting Maggie aside, Sherlock, why did Mycroft so deeply feel a need to help the Union if it ran opposite to the British government? That doesn't sound like him. And he wasn't working for the government at that age. I don't understand."

"Once Mycroft felt the diplomatic presence of Jefferson Davis's emissaries, he knew that people in high places had to make a choice. Poppy, you have to remember that though

Mycroft was only fifteen years old, he was brilliant and already at university. He was anxious even then to become an integral part of the government. When he was not in school, he worked as a parliamentary page. He stayed with your Uncle, in fact."

"With Uncle?"

"Your uncle befriended him when he was young."

It was then I recalled a brief conversation with Aunt Susan about how Uncle and Mycroft had become friends. *Uncle Ormond was on a visit to see a friend of his from university who was teaching at Mycroft's boarding school. His friend told Ormond that there was an awkward boy in his class who needed help.*

Mycroft was—is brilliant, of course," Aunt Susan had continued. *"A bit lazy. But always focused, intent even then to be of service to Her Majesty. He was odd, not like the other boys. Ormond talked to him, shared stories of his own unhappy childhood because he, too, had always been odd and friendless. He would visit Mycroft from time to time and they corresponded. By the time Mycroft graduated from Cambridge, Ormond had ingratiated himself to many in the House of Lords. With his influence and Mycroft's impeccable scholastic record, it was a good fit."*

"As a page, Mycroft had to deliver and receive messages to and from Lord Wharncliffe who had a manor on Curzon Street in Mayfair. It was the perfect entrance for Mycroft into government."

"Who?"

"Lord Wharncliffe was the president of the Southern Independent Association of London, a group of very highly placed British men who favored independence for the South and intervention by Britain to achieve it. Mycroft was young but excellent at reading the minds of the people. Trade unions, workers. *They* did not favor the South at all. Not to mention, and this is most worthy of mention, your uncle had a huge influence on Mycroft then. Think of how your uncle would have felt about the concept of slavery or the idea of the British government siding with the South."

I nodded. Of course, Uncle Ormond would have a favored the North. He'd often cited England's Slavery Abolition Act of 1833 as a "milestone of evolution." Had he been American, he would have been an abolitionist.

"Even at that tender age, Mycroft read between the lines," Sherlock continued. "He brilliantly deduced what was actually in Britain's best interest even before most of her people had. He knew that recognizing the Confederacy might guarantee long term enmity of the United States. He read the tea leaves, as it were. Though the newspapers were sympathetic to the South at first, tides of public opinion changed and working people did not support the Rebel cause."

"And you knew nothing of Mycroft's involvement until this evening?"

"I was but what? Eight or so? Mycroft never told me or our parents of his anti-government activities. Father would have disowned him. After all, he disowned me simply because I would not attend the college of his choice or go into engineering as he wished. You are well aware of Mycroft's ability to manipulate people. Like he did with you in our Baby Farmer Case."

"So with Mycroft's help, Maggie's quest to avenge her brother—"

"Turned into one of the most productive pro-North spy rings in the history of England. But always, Poppy, her true mission was to find Adam Worth and destroy him. And Mycroft has helped with that behind the scenes because he wants Worth's syndicate, the Forty Thieves, all of it eradicated. He has in many ways been subsidising her—helping her buy The Pink Flamingo, for example, and supplying new contacts she might exploit. Maggie has been helping Shore and Mycroft and others in attempting to find Worth for years.

"After the war, Adam Worth founded his own gang of pickpockets, and then began to organize robberies and heists and gangs like the Forty Thieves. When he was caught stealing the cash box of an Adams Express wagon, he was sentenced to three years in Sing Sing prison but he escaped. He and Charley Bullard robbed the Boylston National Bank, and the Pinkerton Agency and John Shore—and Mycroft—have been tracking them ever since. Worth decided to move to Europe with Bullard. Mycroft believes it was Bullard who blew Maggie's safe."

"So not the person Maggie knew as Hamilton? The one we think is John Carr, Polly's . . . Mary's father?"

"Certainly Carr is involved in all this. He likely came up with the scheme to capitalise on Mary Carr's presence in Maggie's establishment. But safe-cracking—that is Bullard's expertise. Shore knows that Bullard and Worth were in Liverpool for a while. Maggie has been trying to find them since they left. Liverpool is where Maggie is from and her contacts there filled her in. Mycroft's spies heard that Worth bought a lodge at Clapham Common. As I said, he has penetrated high society. Junka Phillips, Bullard, Little Joe Elliott—they are all working with Worth. From what Mycroft told me, there are all sorts of rumours about him, about his background, I mean. Some say he was a professor. Some say he was high-born; some say a businessman. But who can say? He is a master of the masquerade.

"Mycroft didn't tell Maggie that Worth was here at first. He knew she would go after him alone if she found him. He never should have told her," he spat. "I am guessing that if we locate Worth, we shall retrieve the painting. But more importantly, if Maggie has gone looking for Worth, she is in grave danger."

"Yes, Sherlock, this could be very dangerous. Have you your—"

"Gun? Of course," he stated as he turned to look out the misty window.

It took just a little over thirty minutes to get to the north side of Clapham Common. "The address I have is just around the corner," he said. Sherlock tapped on the side of the cab for the driver to stop at the corner and we got out about half a metre from the house.

Clapham Common was a large triangular urban park in south London. Originally common land for the parishes of Battersea and Clapham, it was converted to parkland just two years earlier and large Georgian and Victorian homes overlooked the park area. Grand mansions were built around the village, especially fronting the Common. Many of its residents were famous . . . Granville Sharp, one of the first English campaigners for the abolition of the slave trade, and William Wilberforce, the English politician, philanthropist, and also leader of the anti-slavery movement. Zachary Macauley, a Scottish statistician, one of the founders of London University and also an antislavery activist, was a neighbor. Ironically, these social reformers so eager to abolish the slave trade rubbed shoulders with their opponents, for many of the substantial estates nearby and around the fringes of Surrey and Kent were financed on plantation wealth.

When we got to the house, Sherlock started to pick the lock but then realized there was no need. He took out his pistol and opened the door. We entered the large entrance hall. The house reeked of alcohol and smoke.

We took the steps two at a time up the beautiful curving staircase and checked each room. There were eleven bedrooms, three dressing rooms, a domestic office, and a housekeeper's room upstairs. Finding nothing, we ran downstairs and checked the huge dining room and breakfast room. It was then that we saw several lights go out in the drawing room. Just one lamp flickered.

We heard a scurry of footsteps and a tinkling, a jingling. I tugged on Sherlock's sleeve. "You remember what Lestrade said about Junka Phillips?" I whispered. "He mentioned that he keeps his **pockets** leaden down with random junk."

Sherlock nodded. "He did say that, didn't he?" Then he whispered, "Stay here."

"I won't. You know I won't."

"I said stay here," he insisted. As he took a step, so did I.

"You are stubborn," he hissed. "Brilliant. Observant. But stubborn."

Then we quickly made our way toward the faint light. As we reached the drawing room, a gargantuan man with an untidy handlebar mustache attacked Sherlock, knocking the gun from Sherlock's grip. His eyes were full of fury. I realized it must be the man Lestrade had talked about, Worth's bodyguard Junka Phillips, a goliath of a man who relished in violence and gore. The man did Worth's dirty work for him so he wouldn't get his own hands dirty.

I felt my mouth freeze and a silent scream caught in my throat as the giant picked Sherlock up and tossed him side to side. He was like a fish thrashing and flapping on the deck of a boat. Sherlock tried to grab and punch but his peculiar form of self-defense seemed useless.

I grabbed one of the lanterns that had been snuffed out, ran toward Junka and smashed it against the side of his head. Blood trickled down the right side of his forehead as he whirled around. With a grunt, he put his hands around my waist and hurled me across the room. He turned and started toward the door. I caught a glimpse of Sherlock as he stood up with the gun once more in his hand, but Junka lunged for him and tossed Sherlock into the air as if he were a rag doll. Sherlock landed on me, knocking the wind out of me and the gun from his hand. He picked up the gun, but Junka landed a kick to Sherlock's chest, sending the gun across the floor again. Sherlock scrambled to retrieve it, but Junka kicked him squarely in the back. Sherlock groaned and curled up into a fetal position. He let out a ragged, convulsive breath. He didn't move for a moment. But then in the flickering light, I saw the glinting blade of a large hunting knife. Sherlock scrambled over to it and picked it up. I caught Sherlock's determined expression. He was mentally marking the spot on the man's chest where he would plunge it.

His teeth clenched, his eyes focused, his fingers tightly curled around the handle of the knife, Sherlock rose and wheeled to attack.

Junka was quicker than his enormous size would have suggested. He side-stepped Sherlock as he grabbed Sherlock's wrist and twisted his arm backward. Sherlock squirmed away and drove the pointed end of the knife into Junka's side.

He gave out an agonized shriek and shoved Sherlock halfway across the room again. Terror washed over me as I contemplated Junka's next move. With a deep growl, he clutched his bloody side, gave Sherlock one last, heavy kick and limped with a hitch to the door. We heard him open the door and slip away in to the night.

Sherlock moaned in pain and I reached out to him and stroked his hand. "Are you all right?" I asked, the words barely forming from my constricted throat. He nodded. "Are you?"

"Yes, yes. Go!"

He withdrew, swore under his breath and rose. He searched in the darkness for his gun, his face, milky white in the dim light. He seemed a tangle of emotions he would never admit. Defeated in combat. Defeated in his quest to apprehend the criminal, at least for now. It must have felt like an axe had splintered him in half.

But as he looked at me, his eyes unblinking, he summoned his inner strength and resolve. There was absolute silence and then it was like electricity pulsed through his face. The vein in his temple bulged and pulsed. He grabbed the gun and gave chase.

I grabbed the knife and followed Sherlock.

We embarked on a wild chase across an extensive lawn, through the fields, the kitchen and flower gardens and between shrubs, past the brew house, two greenhouses and a grapery. We saw Junka duck behind the shrubbery that wrapped round the whole summer-house and then he skirted through the farm yard of barns and piggeries.

We caught up to him at the stable.

"Sherlock, that's Maggie's brougham."

We ran to it and the driver was slumped over. I took a breath and checked his pulse. "He's dead, Sherlock."

We crept inside the stable. Junka was there, making his way to the other doors at the back and Sherlock charged him, trying to tackle him. But Junka had already reeled around. He pushed Sherlock's chin back and clouted his throat. The heavy blow to Sherlock's windpipe knocked him off balance. He stumbled backwards, grabbing at his throat and coughing. He had trouble regaining his footing and as he tried to rise, Junka rushed forward and pummeled Sherlock's face with three or four hard blows and several backhanded strikes that threw Sherlock off balance yet again. Sherlock rasped with great, heaving breaths for a moment.

Junka ran out the back of the stable, hollering and yelling as Sherlock, weak-kneed and wobbly, pushed himself to straighten up. Two horses banged against their stalls, lifting their front hoofs up high. Sherlock ducked and ran after Junka. When we got to the cart stable, Sherlock struck Junka behind the knee with a great forceful kick. This thrust Junka forward. Junka fell, but he rolled and popped back up, grinning. Sherlock bent over and then came up strong, bringing the heel of his hand up into the wound in Junka's side. This time Junka reeled back, screaming. He looked down at his bloody shirt. As he hesitated, Sherlock lifted his gun and pointed it at Junka. But a figure came out of the shadows. He was short and dressed in evening clothes.

"Worth," I said, thinking out loud.

A shot rang out. Sherlock cried out and tumbled to the ground, losing the grip on his gun yet again. In an instant, he reclaimed the pistol and was trying to get up but by the time he could stand, Junka and the shadowy figure had already disappeared.

I ran to Sherlock and touched the bloody spot on his hand but breathed out a long breath when I determined he had only been grazed. I helped him steady himself but he bent over, still having trouble breathing from the chop to his windpipe.

Hands trembling, I lit a lantern that was on a stool in a corner of the cart stable. Then we ran after them, but we saw no one. We heard the thunder of hooves and wheels as the cart that must have been waiting for them disappeared into the mist.

Sherlock finally let his arm drop to his side in defeat and bent forward, gasping for breath. Quietly, evenly, he whispered, "That shall never happen again." His voice never quavered. There was only the faintest hitch in his tone and delivery. "I will find them and next time, I will end them."

"We need to get back to the station and tell them what happened, Sherlock."

We turned and walked back to the stable. We heard a groan coming from one of the stalls. I shone the lamp in the direction of the sound. That's when I saw Maggie lying in the straw in an empty stall, her dress covered in blood.

29

"Maggie, sweet Jesus, Maggie!" I yelled as I ran to her and dropped to my knees next to her. She was covered in so much blood that I couldn't tell the color of her dress. The front of it was awash in a red stain spreading from the gunshot wound to her abdomen.

Sherlock dropped to his knees beside me and said, "Maggie, why didn't you tell us? Why didn't you wait for us?"

I pulled away the bodice of her dress and ripped a strip of the hem to put over the gaping hole. I ripped another piece off and handed it to Sherlock. He wrapped it around his hand and then knelt next to her and we worked together side-by-side, trying in vain to put pressure on the wound. I gently pushed her over to check her back for an exit wound. I found none. The bullet was still inside her and she still bled heavily.

"Sherlock, we must get her to the hospital," I said after I took her faint pulse. "If the bullet has hit the liver—"

"What?" he whispered. "What if it has?"

There was no time to give him an anatomy lesson. The liver is close to many large blood vessels. If the bullet hit one or more of them, she'd bleed to death quickly. Even if a major vessel hadn't been severed, the liver oozes blood very quickly." She'll bleed to death," I said hoarsely.

"Where can we take her? What hospital is close by?"

I bit my lip, trying to remember.

"Think, Poppy!"

"Bolingbroke. The Bolingbroke Hospital on Five Houses Lane near the Wandsworth Common just opened this year. It's small, but it has an Accident and Emergency Department. They may have an ambulance."

The hospital was nothing more than a converted eighteenth-century house but it would have to do.

"Sherlock, hurry. Ride there quickly and get an ambulance back here. Hurry!"

But as Sherlock started to rise, Maggie reached out to him and pulled him closer so he could hear her. She was visibly failing and all I wanted was to get her to the hospital as quickly as possible, but Sherlock cradled her head in his lap and strained to hear her.

"Sherlock, she has only minutes."

"Maggie, who did this to you?" Sherlock asked.

"I don't know. I don't which—" She coughed up blood.

I wiped it away from her lips and cheek and said, "Don't talk, Maggie. Just hang on," I said, squeezing her hand. She beckoned me to bend down to her lips. I leaned close and she gripped my hand tightly. "This is important, Dr. Stamford. There were three," she said. She shifted her eyes back to Sherlock's face. "Sherlock, one of them was Adam Worth. He goes by other names, Sherlock. Many names. The Professor. Henry Raymond. Morrie Art or something like that. Detective Shore will know more."

"Maggie, stop now. Stop talking," Sherlock said.

"He took the painting, Sherlock."

"We know, Maggie," Sherlock said.

"The other one, from my safe. A nude painting of me by Poynter. They took it from my safe."

Her voice was raspy now, her breathing shallow.

"I'm going to get help, Maggie," Sherlock whispered. "Stay with us."

"Sherlock, in my safe. There's a diary. My brother's diary. Read it so you will understand. Promise me. Promise me you will find Worth. And promise me you won't let them send Polly to jail. She is—" Her eyes rolled back and she strained to speak. "She is young
and—"

She could not finish the sentence.

"Yes, Maggie. I promise," Sherlock whispered. "Now I'm going to go get help for you."

Then Sherlock rose, jumped on one of the horses and galloped away.

I kept pressure on the bullet wound and tore more strips of fabric to replace the bandage as blood soaked through. But when I checked her pulse, it was barely there. She was dying. I could almost see what was happening inside of her. Time was of the essence and the scale was tipping in death's favor.

It was like walking through a dream, a bad dream.

The average human can lose about a liter of blood before going into hypovolemic shock, and a little over two before having insufficient volume to perfuse adequately through the brain. Up until that point, the body will systematically shut off blood flow to the extremities, concentrating the remaining volume in the abdomen and head. We were taught in medical school that since there's so much space in the abdomen for blood to pool, it's often extremely difficult to identify just how bad the bleeding is. The larger blood vessels in the abdomen run along the inside of the spine for most of their journey through the body. You won't see any spurting or pulsating that would usually indicate a laceration if they have been ruptured. In short, my instructors had said, assume the worst. Slap a large trauma pad on there, apply direct pressure and transport to hospital immediately.

Maggie groaned in pain and I ripped more of her dress away to change the bandage. The bandage was sopping wet with blood. Her blood.

Her lips parted and she said a few unintelligible words. I gripped her hand and she curled her fingers around my wrist. "I'm sorry I won't see the clinic open."

"You will, Maggie."

But her grip loosened and she had almost no color in her face.

When I was faced with death, I always tried to be calm and distant, as Uncle had told me. He said that it was the only way to survive in our profession. But I felt like I was swimming in a swirl of blood and it was our fault. Our fault for this stupid scheme, this stupid charade. If we had kept watch. If we had protected her . . .

I felt the tears slip down my cheeks and onto Maggie's face as I bent over her. She was unconscious now, the inferno, the fierce battle of life and death raging inside her. I tried to become that stranger on the outside looking in, a detached, physician . . . observant, logical. It wasn't working. Not this time.

Once again I descended into that murky heaviness of hell where death resides.

Minutes went by but it seemed like hours. I wasn't even sure the little hospital would have an ambulance. Most hospitals in London would not have ambulances for many years to come.

"Maggie," I croaked, my voice sounding scratchy. "Maggie, I am so sorry."

Sherlock ran in, his face flushed. Two policemen were right behind him.

"We have an ambulance wagon, Poppy. They'll take her to the hospital now."

I felt her pulse again. I found none.

Beautiful Maggie. The life was leaving her supple body. The strong, elegant limbs still, the full lips unable to speak. The chest beneath the plunging neckline motionless, the expressive, elegant hands that ended in blood-red nails now still. As her heartbeat had slowed, I had a remarkable epiphany. Working with Sherlock always led to death. First adventure, then death. If not for me, for others. The revelation slammed through me. The instability, the alternate reality he created in my life was intolerable, unbearable.

My brain seemed to detach from my feelings. I felt wooden, numb as I looked up at him. An icy burn in my throat, I could not speak. I shook my head.

Finally, I was able to murmur, "We're too late. She's gone."

30

Three days after Maggie's death, I was sitting in my aunt's morning room, wrapped in my old cape from nursing school with its tattered hem and frayed collar. I had barely moved from that spot. I had not left the house. I'd get washed and dressed and be ready to leave for my office or the clinic and then dissolve into such despair that I felt paralyzed.

I had slept little. I dreamed about Effie, about her wedding, about our many wonderful moments of friendship. I dreamed about the life she might have had with my brother Michael and their son. I dreamed about my many adventures with Sherlock—the highs and lows, the dangers and suspense of our baby farmers case, of the sinking of the *Princess Alice* and the train wrecks. Of the British Museum murders and Uncle in that awful prison cell when he was falsely accused. Of the mutilation of the Queen's swans and of Kate Dew witnessing the murder of her lover.

And I dreamed of Maggie. Her breathless beauty, her effervescence, her clandestine career as a spy. But—perhaps because my mind simply refused to accept her violent death—in my dreams, she lived. She took care of her ladies like a mother protecting the last of her puppies. She rode her horse at her gentleman friend's mansion in the country and, eventually became Lady … Someone . . . of the manor. She wore her beautiful gowns. She flitted in and out of my clinic, always smiling, so happy that she had been able to open it, that she had been able to do something so selfless, so good.

I sat staring through the window at the sprouts and potted plants in my aunt's arboretum. My head throbbing, droplets wetting my cheeks. I cried silently, but inside was a deep rage that welled up and caught in my throat. I felt sometimes that I should lock myself up in a room and beat my hands against the wall until they bled. Perhaps I could push away the feelings of despair if I hurt myself and distracted myself with physical pain. But I was lost in an internal fury, in a dark wedge. My psyche was like a black and blue bruise, mottled in purple, a fugue of hate and love.

It was during such an inert episode that Sherlock came to see me. He brought with him the diary, Maggie's brother's diary to which Maggie had referred as she was dying.

He sat down on the piano bench but did not speak at first. Then he removed his cape and said, "You did not attend Maggie's funeral. Well, the mourners' gathering, such as it was. Tell me why. Tell me what you are thinking."

I turned my head back to the greenery just beyond the glass. I turned to try to concentrate on life.

"Poppy, what is it?"

I shook my head, still unable to speak to him. In some perverse way, I think I blamed him—and myself—for Maggie's death.

"Your aunt says you have not left the house. The ladies at the clinic have wondered where you are. And why you did not go to Maggie's wake."

I did not acknowledge that fact.

"I was surprised you did not attend. Do you want me to tell you about it?"

I think I must have raised my eyebrows. Sherlock? At a funeral? Impossible.

Finally, I found my voice. "I'm surprised that you did."

He ignored my sarcasm. "I was there to make sure her instructions were followed after the viewing . . . the wake. Maggie left specific instructions. They were in her safe with her brother's diaries and other papers. In the event of her death, she had made arrangements at a facility in Woking, Surrey."

"Surrey?"

"I felt I should be there, at the visitation, to demand that her instructions were followed."

"So she is buried in Surrey?"

"No. I saw to it that she was cremated as she wished. At the first working crematorium in all of England. It is near her lover's country estate. You remember, he keeps . . . kept a horse for her there?"

"Maggie was cremated?"

He nodded.

No grave to visit. No gravestone upon which to lay a bouquet of flowers.

My heart hammered in my chest. I felt as if I were crawling toward a wall, a wall to use as a brace so I could rise up, but the wall kept moving.

"It is not so odd, really. Maggie was a progressive thinking woman. And it is not as if this is a new way to dispose of the deceased. After all, the practice of burning bodies is ancient. And it is certainly no stranger to the poor. According to Wiggins, he actually observed cremations when he was participating in his grave-digging schemes. He told me that at night, he often saw the diggers burning the bones of 'commonses,' as he called them. He's been released, by the way. Wiggins. In case you were wondering."

Then he continued to drone on about funerary practices. Truly, all I could think was that the perpetual fog that clouded his emotions would never lift an inch. If anything, it was becoming ever more impenetrable.

"It is only Christianity that curtailed the practice here."

"What?"

"I gather that the Bible commands that the dead be buried, that Christ's entombment was seen as essential to his resurrection for if his body had been destroyed he could not have risen up. Belief in the dead's eventual resurrection on Judgment Day, with the body reassembled with the soul is fundamental to Christianity, is it not? It's scientifically impossible, of course, but were I an apologist, I would argue that it should be no easier for an omnipotent God to reassemble a decomposed body with its soul than a cremated one."

I couldn't believe he was saying this . . . that he was talking about this. "Sherlock, I don't care to—"

But he interrupted. "This issue has been hotly debated in the medical journal *The Lancet*. Maggie was a member of the British Cremation Society."

"The what?" I said, trying very hard to hold back more tears.

"Maggie and like-minded individuals first determined whether cremation could be legally performed in this country and a case was drawn up and submitted to eminent counsel. As opinion was favourable, a building for cremation was proposed. A piece of ground was offered to the Society in the Great Northern Cemetery of London but the Bishop of Rochester said that the establishment of a crematorium on consecrated land must be prohibited. So then the Society found an alternative site at Woking. That city's inhabitants were likewise rather hostile to the idea and a zealous vicar appealed to Sir Richard, the Home Secretary, to prohibit the use of the building. He espoused that cremation might be used to prevent the detection of death following violence or poison, which is ridiculous. Ultimately, the Woking Crematorium went forward when Parliament authorized it, but he forbade the Society from spreading information and trying to change public opinion."

"Maggie's body was burned then," I whispered. "It does not seem appropriate somehow."

"Why not? She requested that her ashes be sent to America to be buried with her brother, according to her instructions. You see, after the war, after the Andersonville prison was closed, a nurse, Clara Barton, set about trying to identify soldiers who had been incarcerated there. She received thousands of letters from relatives of the missing and the dead once her mission became known. Malcolm's body was identified and the remains were sent to his wife."

I nodded. I could not think of any reply.

"So about this gathering in Maggie's honor at The Pink Flamingo. A very short wake. That was in her instructions as well. She detested the usual formalities, the delays in interment, and the prolonged keeping of dead bodies in the rooms of their living kindred."

He rose and went to the glass partition, now staring himself at the greenery. "Think of it, Poppy. At least among the poor, the deceased is soldered in his wooden coffin and this is all that divides the decomposition of the dead from the respiration of the living because it is tenanted night and day by the family of mourners. For some days the corpse just lies there amid the living—beside them in their sleep; before them at their meals."

I started to feel ill. I wanted him to stop. But I could barely breathe, let alone roil against him.

"It is a pernicious custom. One would think that the educated classes of the community would adopt the usage of earlier burial or cremation."

"Please, Sherlock, I can stand to hear no more."

He ignored me. Completely.

"Maggie's mourners assembled the very day after she died . . . We were led down into the back-kitchen to view the coffin and the corpse. I mention the coffin first because in everyone's view, this was the main point of interest. Could Maggie have been shown in an orange-crate, she would gladly have done so to save the expense, but her ladies and friends dealt a handsome sum to the undertaker. Her coffin would be the talk of London if she were not . . . well, if she were not who she was. The coffin was inspected inside and out, admired and appraised. At the same time every detail of her life and death was discussed and mused over."

I stood up. I turned on him in a red rage. Truly I saw every shade of vermillion.

I went mad for a moment, lost my mind at the thought of it, of yet another death in which Sherlock and I had been involved and not of some stranger, some criminal we had apprehended. It was Maggie who died because we did not prevent it.

I dropped to my knees, gagging at the thought of it, and pounded my fists into the floor. As I managed to wipe tears from my face, Sherlock's arms came around me, pressing his palms to my hair, soothing me. I struggled to pull away from him and stood up, gulping for air. I screamed, "Enough! Damn you, Sherlock, enough! Get out!"

He moved away. He looked taken aback. I do believe, in retrospect, he started to tell me about the funeral simply so I would feel a part of something I'd forgone for a reason he could not fathom. I believe he did want to comfort me.

But in that moment I hated him.

"Poppy, I—"

Just then Uncle Ormond entered the room. He touched Sherlock on the shoulder and said quietly, "Sherlock, I think it's best you take your leave."

Sherlock reached out to me with a journal in his hand. "I've read this. The whole of it. It was her brother's diary that he kept from after his capture until he died in the prison. I fully understand why she wished to help defeat the Confederacy and why she hated Adam Worth, so I shall not rest until he no longer walks among the living."

He handed me the diary, put on his cape and left.

31

I ordered myself to stop thinking, to breathe in and out, to stop shaking and trembling. My legs rocky, I had to brace myself against the wall for a moment. But as soon as Sherlock had cleared the room, I burst into tears. I could hold them back no longer. Uncle walked over to me and cradled me in his arms. "There, there. Let it out, Poppy."

As I huddled in his embrace, I felt myself shudder and go limp in his arms. After a time, I slumped into a chair. Uncle left the room for a moment and returned with two brandy snifters filled to the brim.

"Uncle, it's only mid-day," I said.

"Does it matter?"

I shook my head and eagerly took the glass from him and swallowed several gulps.

"Do tell me what you are thinking, sweet girl. What you are feeling? Because we are very worried about you."

I choked back more tears and shook my head.

"You lost your dearest friend and did not retreat so. When Victor's father died, you were not this upset and you knew him all your life. You've seen many deaths—at the train accidents, after the sinking of the *Princess Anne*. What is it this time that has made you turn so inward? You barely knew Miss Mayhew. I realize that she was most kind in setting up the medical clinic and asking you to take charge of it but . . . but this is quite abnormal for you, Poppy."

I took several deep breaths before I could speak. "I don't know. Truly, Uncle, I do not know. It feels . . . I feel guilt. Like I should have done something more. And I feel like Sherlock leads me down a darker path every single day. I have . . . I have tired of it."

He sighed. "Poppy, it was Maggie's choice to go to that house. Sherlock told me about her background and why she was obsessed with Adam Worth. The Napoleon of Crime, he called him."

"Yes, that's what the Yard calls him."

I took another sip of brandy. "Uncle, I understand you went to Maggie's funeral, too. To the gathering, whatever you want to call it. Why?"

"To pay my respects. I did not know her well but, as I said, she arranged for the clinic and for you to have the opportunity to really use your skills as a physician. That meant a great deal to me."

"Was it nice? The gathering?"

"Yes, but you know my opinion on those things. I overheard what Sherlock started to tell you about cremation and so on. I concur. It was prudent of Maggie to plan her earthly exit in advance. Our current practice is upheld by no law of necessity whatsoever, only out of habit. We used to have to wait for relatives to arrive from outside of England or fears of premature interment, which are now seldom spoken of but with a smirk. The longer interval, once rightly insisted upon as necessary for the gathering of distant friends has now, because of progress, has become absurdly excessive."

I felt my breathing shudder. I couldn't bear the thought of seeing Maggie dead. Of seeing her dead *again.* That was why I had eschewed the wake. Once was enough. I'd felt the same way with Effie but because of our relationship and because I was Michael's sister, I'd had no choice in the matter. I had to attend.

I had to help with preparations and be congenial to the mourners. I'd hated it.

"But the gathering for her—"

"Was well attended and tasteful, as these things go."

"Tell me, Uncle."

"Poppy . . . ."

"No, I want to know. Were there a lot of people?"

"There were. Her ladies. Clients, I assume. And people from government, which surprised me."

It did not surprise me. She had been, after all, a valuable asset.

"Upon arriving, we were conducted first of all into the front-room on the ground-floor, the parlour. There were refreshments and desserts on the sideboard. A low cupboard in a recess was surmounted by a frosted model of St. Paul's; it was quite lovely."

"St. Paul's? Really?"

"It's where she worshipped."

"Maggie was religious?"

"I was told she was very conscientious and reliable about attending church. And dutiful in tithing."

"I must admit that astounds me."

"I suspect Maggie was far more complicated than anyone realized. At any rate, behind the model was an oval tray painted with flowers with tiny desserts. Petit-fours, I think they are called. She'd painted the tray, I was told. Sherlock told me about the portraits that were stolen. There was one of Maggie in the parlour and also a portrait of Queen Victoria in her early reign. We all took a glass of wine and went down into the back-kitchen to view the coffin.

"One gentleman stood off to the side for quite some time. He briefly went over to the casket and placed a white rose inside. I asked the ladies about him but they said nothing. If they knew him, they did not let on. He was tall and light haired. He wore a dark suit and black gloves. I overheard him speaking to one of the ladies. He seemed a kindly fellow, conciliatory, and he had a soothing voice. Someone did say that he had a mansion at Trent Park and a country estate. Did Maggie have a paramour?"

I nodded.

"Well, then." He paused. "Poppy, I am leaving tomorrow—going to the Broads to see how your father is doing. I want you to stay here and work at the clinic but perhaps you should come with me after all. You don't seem to be yourself. Maybe a change of scenery, some fresh air and visiting with your parents would do you some good."

"I shall think about it, Uncle. Thank you for asking. And I am sorry if I've worried you or Aunt Susan."

"You are like our own daughter, you know. Of course we are concerned. And for what it is worth, even though Sherlock can be completed disconnected from propriety or social graces and is often devoid of any recognition of someone's emotions or suffering, he is also quite worried about you. Whatever his flaws or shortcomings, I have no doubt that he wants only what is best for you."

"Sherlock Holmes wants only what serves his own whim," I spat. "He is an inconsiderate malcontent. I have finally realized that he is reclusive and eccentric and not a good companion on any level."

"He is Bohemian."

"He shuns society, friendship, even rules. He is callous, arrogant, and bad tempered."

"He is at his core a scientist in a world obsessed with science," Uncle said. "He is introverted and solitary yes, but also imaginative and brilliant. Don't you see, Poppy? I tried to tell you early on. Where there is a thread that runs through a case, he feels it is his duty to unravel it, to isolate it, to expose it, and he does this to the exclusion of all else."

"He is reckless and cruel and obsessive and sometimes inhuman."

"Harsh words, girl."

"Are they? Have you not warned me a hundred times that he is too self-centered and self-absorbed to have a relationship?"

Uncle smiled. "And I would warn you a thousand more. Poppy, Sherlock knows himself. He knows that if her were encumbered with a romantic interest, or even the prospect of one, it would spell disaster for his career. If you were ever to leave your partnership with him, if you were to put your feelings for him aside and marry and move on with your life, as you certainly should, he would put your relationship aside. It would be a sealed book and he could not allow it to affect his life. But does he not treat women with respect and courtesy? Has he not proven that he realises that, in certain circumstances, the impression of a woman may be more valuable than the conclusion of an analytical reasoned man? Look how he treated Maggie's ladies. Look at what he just did—attending her funeral. He may say he did it to ensure that her instructions were followed but—"

"You heard that?" I blinked in surprise.

"Yes, I heard him say that just now. In truth, he went out of respect. As for being reckless and cruel, yes, he can be those things. But this is what makes him tick. However baffling a mystery, there is a solution to be found, and Sherlock is almost always capable of finding it. But it is his concentration of thought and his precision that leads him to the solution. I find it reassuring that Sherlock uses his logic, his imagination, his brilliant mind . . . and occasionally a street urchin or a young female physician to solve problems."

"No. No, he has an aversion to women. He thinks we are never to be trusted."

Uncle smiled. "Does he think that a woman's heart and mind are insoluble puzzles to the male? Indeed he does. As do I, much of the time. But that does not mean that he doesn't recognize a brilliant woman like you. Or a courageous patriot, like Maggie.

"Does he not fill you with apprehension, Uncle? I am never sure how far he might go in pursuit of the truth or a solution."

"Often Sherlock appraises and seizes the destiny of the moment. But that does not mean he does not care for your well-being. Nor does it mean he doesn't love you."

"What?" I gulped and felt the color drain from my face.

"I think that Sherlock made a vow long ago to avoid any kind of strong emotion or affection, any kind of close human relationship, not just romantic love, and that it was only by accident that he ended up with Victor Trevor as a friend and with you as something so much more than that. I think he found Maggie May to be a beautiful, challenging and interesting individual. These are hard things for him. He wishes to be free from any deep attachment. You must realize that when he allows himself to be capable, even in the abstract, to love deeply, he becomes vulnerable. Do you have any doubt that he would kill anyone who harmed you? And that would always be in the way of his detective work. For Sherlock, the idea that he could even conceive to kill a person who harmed someone he had allowed himself to love—this is the hardest thing in the world for him to manage. Do you know what he told me once? It was when he asked me how to get a copy of the photograph you have in that locket you hold so dear. I expressed my surprise and asked him what his intentions were toward you. He didn't answer but he did say, 'She is a complete and remarkable young woman. No young man could cross her path unscathed.'

"He said that?"

"It doesn't change anything. You cannot have what I know you really want with him. You must remember that. But also remember, Poppy, a person does not play one note. People can be chancers and scoundrels yet still display empathy. They can have a streak of meanness yet be pillars of society. I think every soul has a dew-drop of God and a tear drop of Satan."

He kissed my forehead and hugged me. "The Soul selects her own society – then – shuts the door."

"What?"

"Emily Dickinson. Don't shut the door on the world for too much longer, Poppy. Find a new path if you must, but don't retreat from us or from life."

Then he left me to my silence and solitude.

I was about to go up to my room to lie down but instead opened Maggie's brother's diary. I skimmed it and then read every entry. Just a few would make a grown man sick to his stomach.

May 6, 1864. *Captured on Plank Road. Gordon's attack made good progress against us. We'd spent most of the war manning the artillery defenses of Washington, D.C. We were inexperienced. I thought—Worth told us—that the darkness and dense foliage would give us cover for our escape. Instead, Sedgwick's line was extended overnight to the Germanna Plank Road and early in the morning, the Union line collapsed and we were discovered trying to make our way out of their reach.*

...

May 21, 1984. *Hot and damp. Two men shot. Still lying where they dropped.*

...

May 21, 1864. *A thousand new prisoners. Camp already overcrowded. Not built for this many prisoners. Killed some swallows for food. Ate raw.*

...

May 29, 1864. *Another thousand prisoners. Thousand. We are in ragged tents. No shelter from the rain. Feeling sick to my stomach all the time.*

...

June 4, 1864. *No rations at all. Scurvy setting in. Symptoms of dropsy. A sea of faces and skeletons.*

...

June 8, 1864. *More new prisoners. 25,000 here I understand. Getting sicker. Full of lice.*

...

219

June 11, 1864. A break out was attempted but failed. Raining all the time. A giant mudhole we sleep in. Many sores. Afraid of gangrene. Slept next to a man with a hole in his head. Saw the maggots.

...

June 16, 1864. Losing teeth every day. Mouth is very sore and bleeding. Try to exercise but my legs are so swollen I cannot stand. We are forgotten by the Union. Will soon be forgotten by our friends and relatives. Will never see my child. Wonder if it is a boy?

...

June 25, 1864. Vermin, lice, flies, maggots. Scurvy, sores, dropsy. No shelter. No water fit to drink. The air is foul. The stream is poison. The sun broils the skin. Cannot laugh. Cannot talk.

...

June 30, 1864. 150 to 250 die a day. Sure I will be one of them soon.

...

July 7, 1864. Too tired to go on. Pencil is a stub and have no strength to write. Exchange rumors float about. I won't make it. Won't make it to sunrise.

...

That was his last entry. He died on my birthday. My eighth birthday.

32

I sat there for another thirty minutes or so, sipping my brandy and thinking. Thinking of what Uncle had said about Sherlock. Thinking about Malcolm Mayhew and the horror he had lived through. His suffering. His death.

Thinking of Maggie. Her loss. Her courage. Her sacrifices.

What right did I have to despair? *What right, Poppy Stamford!* I screamed in my mind. I slammed my fist down on the piano keys, sending discordant notes screeching thru the house.

My cat Sappho wandered in and jumped on my lap. I petted her head, amazed that at the ripe age of twelve she could still be so spry. A few moments later, Kate popped her head in. "I'm taking Little Elihu for a walk, Poppy. Can I get you anything before we leave?"

"Stop treating me like you are a servant, Kate. You are no longer. You are the apple of my brother's eye and the healer of his heart."

She blushed. "Poppy, I—I don't know what to say to that."

I plopped Sappho on the floor, swallowed down the rest of my brandy and said, "You should say, 'Poppy, you are stupid and self-absorbed and ungrateful and unappreciative of all you have. It is time you put these events behind you and stop lingering on them and get to work saving every person you can.'"

Shocked, she made a face and said, "I'd never. I couldn't."

I laughed then. "I am talking to *myself*, Kate. What you should tell me is to get up and walk with you, that you have a sympathetic ear I can bend. Perhaps then I can pull myself together and get back to work."

"Well, we have all been worried. And wondering if you were still going to work at the clinic."

"Indeed I am, just as soon as you and I give Elihu his proper exercise."

She smiled and Elihu pulled on his leash, panting in anticipation.

I did go back to work that afternoon. I went to my medical office where several messages for me had been left at the door. I'd begun using little Rattle on and off as a page and fortunately found him round the corner from my office playing marbles near the British Museum. I gave him the notes and some coins to track down the patients and to tell them I had been 'away' for a few days and to please come back to my office the next day. Then, with new adrenalin in my belly, I went to the clinic. The sign was up over the door. *Mayhew Clinic*.

I went into an open examination room where a young boy was on the examination table. Dr. Olivia Robertson, the young doctor my uncle had brought into the clinic, was patching up a deep cut on his hand.

"Dr. Robertson?"

She turned. "Dr. Stamford. You're here!"

Now I took a better look at her than when we had met. She was petite and thin and flat-chested as a young boy. Behind glasses were glacier-blue eyes. She had a narrow nose and high cheekbones and the cheeks were peachy with robust health. Her thick, black hair was in a tight bun. She wore a dark blue wool skirt and a white, tailored blouse. I smiled to myself thinking that she could be a considerable beauty with a little help from Maggie's ladies—a touch of pink on her lips, a bit of color to accent her eyes.

She grasped my hand and shook it firmly. "I am so glad you are here. It's been very busy. But I know with Miss Mayhew's—"

"Let's not talk about that. Just tell me what to do."

"Me? Tell you what to do? It's your clinic!"

I glanced out at the swarm of people waiting in what had once been a front parlour to a whorehouse. "No, Olivia. It's *their* clinic."

We worked late into the evening and as we sent the final patient on her way, Sarah, the tall brunette who wanted to go to India to find a husband, and who had appointed herself the clinic's official receptionist, appeared in the doorway with three glasses and a decanter of blue-coloured liquid.

"What is that?" Olivia asked.

"Blue Curaçao. It's a liqueur."

Rainbow liqueurs were all the rage but I had never tried one.

She poured some into each glass. "I understand the Royals are partial to purple, but I like the blue."

"What makes it blue?" Olivia asked.

Sarah laughed. "You don't want to know."

"No, I do."

"The blue is created out of coal tar," she explained. "I suppose not particularly pleasant and not good for you."

"Well, it's better than all those things you told me you considered using to make your skin pretty," I said.

Sarah laughed again and, naturally, Olivia looked puzzled.

I swallowed some of the drink, nearly gagged, but drank some more. After a few more sips, feeling quite daring, feeling quite happy to be alive, I took Olivia's glasses from her face and said, "Sarah, how do you think Olivia would look with a bit of face paint?"

I heard Maggie's voice ringing in my ears and said, "Nothing too fancy. Something tasteful. This must be carefully edited."

33

The next few weeks were dizzying and frenetic—not in the way that solving mysteries and cases with Sherlock always were but just as adrenalin-inducing. It was like a switch had been flipped. Effie had wanted me to be happy and enjoy life. Maggie did as well. The best way to honor them was to do so.

Each day, I spent several hours in my medical office but many more at the clinic. Dr. Olivia, as people were calling her, and I worked well together and separately. Things were humming.

The only contact I had with Sherlock was a note he'd sent with Rattle to my office. He advised that Polly Carr had been 'sentenced' to St. Mary the Virgin Female Penitentiary, just as Maggie had hoped. Adam Worth and the others still eluded the authorities.

We heard from Uncle sporadically and his telegrams were cryptic. I was worried about my father but, perhaps in self-defence, convinced myself that Uncle Ormond would hide nothing from me and that things would be fine. Aunt Susan was busy packing clothes and household goods she was taking to Scotland. I had great freedom and indulged it.

Many nights a week after working at the clinic, several of the ladies and I would go out to social halls to listen to music and dance. In many of the thoroughfares of London, there were shops which had been converted into a kind of temporary theatre . . . admission one penny . . . where dancing and singing took place every night. Much to my surprise, within a circuit of five miles of St. Paul's, at least twenty dens of amusement were found. My parents would have been horrified but I had decided I was going to do what I wanted to do and live life to the fullest.

I would borrow a gown from Maggie's extensive wardrobe; the ladies would delicately and lightly paint my face, and off we would go to music halls or public houses to enjoy the penny gaffs—short, theatrical presentations. We'd find a place in the hall where we could buy something basic to eat or to drink. Sarah McBride brought me magazines and books to read about India and each day brought me closer to a decision to leave London and make a new life elsewhere.

Sometimes the lyrics of the songs were so smutty that I was embarrassed but most of Maggie's ladies just laughed—both at the songs and at my naiveté. One could even describe the proceedings as indecent and disgusting. But I did enjoy the dancing. I knew few of the newer dance steps, but I could keep up with a good dancing partner who led me in the Mazurka, the Schottische, or a Polka. Sometimes the music was so loud, we could hardly think, but Sarah and I managed to talk a great deal about India.

"It will be so different for me there, Poppy," she said. "Not like here. No one will know me and I can be a gardener or a seamstress. I can sew, you know. My mother taught me. And you! Think of all the people you can help."

"If I go, I would hope so, Sarah. I do hope so."

"And I'll find a husband. At least Maggie taught me how to make a man want me. That's something."

I cupped her hand. "Yes, Sarah, that's something."

"Think of it! There will be flowers everywhere—buds and blossoms."

"You may just wake to the sound of a tiger's roar."

"I don't care. And think of it, no fog."

"Sarah, I hate to disappoint you. I've read about the weather in India and the hallmark of their winter season is the notorious fog, thick enough that you can't see a foot in front of you."

Her face fell for a moment but then she smiled. "I don't care! I can't wait."

One of our favorite spots was Wilstons Music Hall at the East End, in Whitechapel at Wellclose Square. It was a large, attractive hall in easy walking distance of The Tower of London and the river. A much-loved artist named George Fredericks had taken over the licence in April of 1873. In between the comedy songs he performed with his wife Carrie Julienne, George would launch into a sad or sentimental song and be rapturously encored.

Wilton's was notorious for drunkenness, prostitution and violent crime. Keeping an orderly house was challenging, and probably not a high priority.

The coster lads and lasses who made up the bulk of the crowds were amongst the roughest in London; always ready for a fight or a frolic. But the ladies protected me. Maggie's Girls, as I came to think of them, hovered over me like a flock of starlings in open combat defending their nests and assaulted anyone whose advances seemed untoward.

There was one young man I willingly danced with, however. His name was Sam and he was thin and short and unattractive but he sought me out to dance every time we went to Wiltons. The right side of his body was under-developed, his arm and hand much smaller than on the left side. He always seemed surprised that I would dance with him but he was a wonderful partner and easy to follow. He told me that his mates called him 'Clock' and I must have looked puzzled.

"You know, Miss, big hand, little hand?"

I was appalled. "Do not let them bully you in such a way. It must be very hurtful."

He just shrugged. "I'm used to it. And you felt sorry enough to dance with me."

"That's not true, Sam. I dance with you because you dance so well and I can follow you and you make me look good."

He beamed and after that I sought him out to dance every time.

This pattern continued until mid-December. It was then that Uncle sent word to Michael, me and Aunt Susan that we should get to the Broads as soon as possible. This message was ominous, frightening.

Upon arrival at Burleigh Manor, Uncle immediately took me aside. We were seated in the parlour, the room to which I always went first on a visit. This was where my favourite things welcomed me. . . . the angel wings depicted in the heraldic glass over the mantle of the stone fireplace and the comfortable raised seating area in the bay window that contained stained glass depicting our coat of arms. The alcoves with oak paneling on either side of the fireplace, the mirrored walls and built-in glazed display cupboards. I loved the warm glow of the decorative woodwork and the richness of the walls lined with rare and valuable seventeenth-century embossed Spanish leather. I always admired my mother's collection of stained glass items that dated back to the thirteenth century.

"What is it, Uncle? I need to go see Papa."

"I need a moment with you, Poppy. I want to prepare you. I am counting on you to be stalwart for your mother."

Fear, the strong grip of it, washed over me. I looked down at my lap.

"Look at me, Poppy. Just look at me."

Lifting myself up a little, pulling back my shoulders, I braced myself. His next words stung like whiskey poured into an open wound.

"Robert—your father has stomach cancer. He needs to have a gastrectomy."

I had seen illness, death, crime, treachery, rejection. Effie's death and Maggie's had affected me deeply. Sherlock's rebukes had as well. But I'm not sure I'd experienced a moment quite so heart-wrenching in all my life since Effie's death. I was certainly not prepared for the cavernous depth of grief I suddenly felt. Slightly dazed and clutching the arms of the chair, I whispered, "What?"

"Your father is at Norfolk and Norwich Hospital."

"He is not here? He's—"

"We did many tests there. Those are completed now. It's not Bart's, which I would far prefer, but travel is not an option. Robert has lost a great deal of weight and is quite frail."

I took a moment to soak in a long look at Uncle's face. The lines seemed deeper. The wrinkles on his forehead were more pronounced. He had lost the easy cheer that he could usually summon when he was trying to reassure me.

"I cannot perform the surgery for I have no privileges here, but Dr. William Crosse is a fine physician and I have been granted a consulting surgeon status. We have been studying Dr. Billroth's procedures—you remember him, don't you? He is in Vienna."

How could I not know of Dr. Billroth? He had performed the first esophagectomy in 1871, the first laryngectomy two years later. But his attempts at gastrectomy had been ill-fated, utter failures. In fact, after his first attempt at gastrectomy surgery during which the patient died, he'd almost been stoned to death in the streets of Vienna.

I had a million questions. This was my father's life at stake.

"Uncle, Dr. Billroth has never been able to succeed at excising a cancerous pylorus."

"But he and his assistants have discovered that in more than a third of the patients with stomach cancer, the tumor is localized at the lower end of the stomach, at the pylorus, and it can be resected. When he first explored the possibility of this procedure, he was successful in gastrectomies in two of seven dogs. And since applying Lister's antiseptic procedures, the operation was a success in fourteen dogs."

"Dogs," I said flatly. "Papa is not a dog, Uncle."

"It is a fine hospital," Uncle said. "A special nurse has been assigned to duty in the Surgery Department. Miss Adam, the Superintendent of Nurses, says she is the best surgical nurse she's ever seen. The Operating Theater was recently renovated to the most aseptic views. I believe that gastric resection for carcinoma of the stomach is possible if Lister's methods are applied."

I remembered many conversations with my brother and Sherlock about Lister, the pioneer of antiseptic surgery. He promoted the idea of sterile surgery while working at the Glasgow Royal Infirmary and introduced carbolic acid to sterilise surgical instruments and to clean wounds.

"Dr. Crosse has practiced the surgical technique on cadavers," he added.

I took a breath, looked into Uncle's eyes. "Papa is not a cadaver either, Uncle Ormond."

"We will perform the surgery tomorrow morning, Poppy. There are adjoining cottages in Crook's Place where you and your mother may stay for a few days so you do not have to travel back and forth."

I sat there, numb. "Can he survive this?" I asked. My voice broke.

"I hope so, Poppy," he said adding, "but I caution you to remember that even if he does, we are only buying him a few months, perhaps a year. You know that."

There was no confidence in his voice. No ego, no arrogance that is part of a surgeon's genetic makeup. I was more frightened than ever by this. I gripped the arms of the chair tighter and stiffened.

"Now, go see your mother. She is . . . she is a bit frantic, Poppy. Even Susan seems unable to comfort her."

I rose and brushed past him. Uncle, my beloved Uncle, seemed suddenly alien. He had delivered unbearable news and he was unable to give me any reassurance that my father would live.

"And Poppy," he called out.

I stopped at the doorway and turned.

"Victor Trevor is back. He was here last night. He wanted to see if there was anything he could do."

Anger surged from deep inside. "If a great surgeon cannot save my father, there is nothing a tea planter can do," I said in a sharp voice. "I—"

He put up a hand to quell further outburst. He came over to me and laid his hands upon my shoulders. "You remember I said that every soul has a dew-drop of God? Victor Trevor has a waterfall of them."

35

After we went to visit my father, who had lost at least two stone and who was sedated to ease his pain, Aunt Susan, Michael and I spent much of the day trying to comfort and support my mother but no amount of succor would alleviate her fears. She and my father had been married for thirty years. During that time, they had never spent a night apart.

Early that evening, I wrapped myself up to brave the cold and wandered in the withered garden behind the house. I was lost in thought, in despair, when I heard footsteps and then, almost inaudibly, my name— my first name by which Victor Trevor had always called me instead of my nickname.

"Hello, Priscilla."

I looked back and saw Victor Trevor.

The change in Victor was dramatic. He was still tall and lean, his blue eyes intense and soft at the same time. But now he was browned from the sun and muscular from hard labor.

"Victor. It is good to see you."

He strode over me and we awkwardly embraced. He ran his palm over my hair as I leaned my head for a moment against his chest. "I am so sorry that your father is so ill. What can I do?"

I pulled away and looked up at him. There was nothing he, or anyone else could do. My father was in the hands of God and surgeons . . . and medicine had advanced considerably but not far enough.

"Walk with me," I said.

And so we did, for hours. He told me about India, about his tea plantation. He told me about the other British inhabitants who 'longed to be amused and spent their days in endless visits and parties.' His voice dripped with sarcasm and disdain. He seemed to set himself apart from his contemporaries, at least in this regard.

"Your plantation . . . Mrs. Hudson read me one of your letters about it. It sounds beautiful, Victor."

"It is. I think you would love it there. There is a dearth of modern conveniences but we have servants. But their caste system . . . it makes it imperative that a plantation owner recognize this. They are strict about it themselves. Gardeners garden, cooks cook. There is no overlap. I have tried to think of them more as friends than servants.

"I detest some of my neighbors. Watching the servants pull off the sahib's boots, comb the memsahib's hair—"

"Memsahbib? Sahib? The lady of the house and the master?"

He nodded. "And the endless balls to prepare and the daily picnics. Forcing the servants to drag stoves and food hampers and rugs and everything else their masters demand just to stage a picnic. The country is under British rule, of course, but why must we behave like we think rulers must diminish the people they rule? Always struggling to keep British ways and society alive."

He laughed. "Including our rather antiquated view of anything bordering on erotic."

I felt my cheeks flush as they always did when Wiggins drooled over the naked statue of Tara at the British Museum.

"Oh, I am sorry!"

Then I laughed. "Victor, I am a physician. I am accustomed to all aspects of human anatomy. So, do go on. I am not ignorant of the symbols in the culture."

"Human anatomy in all its glory is prominently displayed in their religion, in their temples. What is hilarious is that my acquaintances there *claim* to find it revolting, but in fact they are completely intrigued by it!

"What I find so unfathomable is that to continue to treat these people this way is to invite another uprising. It has been only twenty years and yet it's as if we do not remember what happened. It is as if we have forgotten The Mutiny, forgotten the children hacked to pieces, the bodies left in the well."

I was only a year old when the Indian Rebellion began but when I was older, my father, always interested in politics and particularly in The Raj, the Crown Rule of India, told me one of the most tragic stories when I was older. It was almost unbearable to listen to Papa's account of what happened during the rebellion against British rule that sparked many uprisings throughout India. Amongst these, none had such horrifyingly tragic results as the June 1857 uprising in the town of Cawnpore.

After a three-week siege, the British agreed to surrender on the condition that the garrison and their women and children would be given safe passage out of the city. But at Sati Chaura Ghat, as the British were about to board the boats that would take them to safety in Allahabad, they were attacked by rebel Sepoys. Their boats were burned and most of the men were killed. When the men had been put to the sword, the women and children, many wounded and bloody, were brought to the bank of river. They were ordered to give up their personal possessions—jewelry and the like—and then they were taken to a building called the Bibighar, "The House of the Ladies," a small, villa-like residence in the cantonment magistrate's compound. It had a courtyard and a well. With two hundred women and children in residence, illness was quick to strike. Several died from cholera and dysentery as a result of the unsanitary conditions.

At first the captives were used as a bargaining chip with the British. But when news arrived in Cawnpore that General Henry Havelock was nearing the city with relief troops, an order was issued that all of the British women and children at the Bibighar were to be killed.

Two days before the retaking of Cawnpore, the rebel soldiers in charge of the hostages were ordered to kill them by firing their rifles through the windows of the Bibighar but the guards only fired one volley and refused to do more. So a local execution squad killed all the prisoners with their swords and dumped the stripped and mutilated bodies of the women and children in a well.

"And you think that it could happen again, Victor? Another rebellion?"

"Of course," he answered. "The people of India do not like feeling like they are enslaved. And while we have not forgotten the massacre at Cawnpore, they have not forgotten General Neill's retribution either."

I nodded, remembering the rest of the story.

When Brigadier General Neill arrived to take command at Cawnpore, he exacted a brutal vengeance against those deemed responsible for the massacre. He arrested rebels, lashed their backs with a whips, tortured anyone in the town who had known of the British hostages' plight but had done nothing to stop it. A set of nooses was set up next to the well at the Bibighar, so that they could die within sight of the massacre. Some rebels were tied across the mouths of cannons that were then fired— an execution method initially used by the rebels, and the earlier Indian powers, such as the Marathas and the Mughals.

"But that is one reason I endeavor to be kind to those who work for me," Victor said. "To lift them up rather than abuse them. For the most part, my life there has been very tranquil. Lonely," he added, "but serene."

"Mrs. Hudson told me that you have had some problems, Victor."

"Did she?"

"In the letter she read to me, you said that your labourers from Nepal and Chota Nagpur blame illness or a bad harvest on witchcraft, a curse. And a witch doctor has convinced some of his people that the poor harvest was a curse because . . . well, because you are British."

"There are instigators. And there are people with strange thinking like this witch doctor, yes. India is a big country with many people and many gods and a past that can't be ignored. There is much that is hard to comprehend on both sides. They fear losing their culture, the British fear losing ours. So that can be a danger."

"For you, Victor?"

"I have tried to teach the people who work for me about the good things the British bring and I have tried to learn from them the many good things they have to share. That is not to say there are no dangers. I would not want to mislead you, Priscilla. There are."

Later that evening, after I had given my mother a sedative and talked more with Uncle about the imminent operation, I found Victor waiting for me in the parlour of my parent's home. Over a cup of Fry's Cocoa and my favourite macaroons, he told me more about his experiments with the soil on the plantation and about Jalpaiguri, the nearest town, already famous for its tea cultivation.

"I am surrounded by Bengal tigers and one-horned rhinos, hog deer and barking deer, elephants, wild pigs and bisons. It's a fantastic place, Poppy, like something out of a dream."

I took note of the fact that he lapsed and called me Poppy. It was so uncharacteristic that it startled me.

"You called me Poppy."

"It occurred to me earlier that so much has changed. I know you prefer it, so it's time for that to change as well. So what do you think about a place with tigers and snakes and such?"

"I don't know, Victor. Honestly, being surrounded by Bengal tigers sounds a little more like a nightmare than a dream."

"I think you would have the adventure of your life there, Poppy. I assume that is part of the reason you have cultivated your relationship with Sherlock . . . to seek out adventure?"

"There is excitement in what he does, what we do, yes."

He stared off as if he were looking at something far in the distance. "Well, just think of this. India's starlight and low moon can lift anyone from brooding over the loss of even the dearest companions and loved ones."

I took in a deep breath. I knew he was thinking that I might soon lose my father. But if I went to India, I would be leaving everything. My medical practice. The clinic. My new friends. Michael and my nephew and my mother. And Sherlock.

"Right outside my bedroom are mango blooms so rich in fragrance, they smell like heaven. And the people—they are exciting, Poppy. Different from us, of course, in their religious beliefs, especially. Hinduism. But it's quite interesting."

I almost told him that I found Hinduism and Buddhism and other religions very interesting indeed and that Sherlock and I had talked about them often.

"Poppy, have you seen Sherlock recently?"

"I contacted him to inquire about the problem with Loke at your estate. You are aware of that situation, aren't you?"

"I am. We will get to the bottom of it. Is Sherlock still on Montague Street?"

"He still lives there, but Michael said that he may be moving soon," I told Victor, hoping he did not inquire further. "And no, I have not seen him recently," I lied, telling myself that I hadn't seen him in several weeks so it wasn't entirely an untruth.

Victor sipped his cocoa and said, "This is good. I needed a Proustian taste of home, something to remind me of all the richness and goodness of the distant past here in England."

He proceeded to tell me more about his life in India— about the pigs he slaughtered for breakfast bacon, the bread that was baked daily, about the women in saris, the men in skirts with their long, tangled locks beneath brilliantly coloured turbans.

Victor was also so much more vibrant and confident than I remembered, like a character out of a lost world novel.

To me, a place like Terai-Duar, a place nestled in the savanna and the narrow grasslands at the base of the Himalayas, sounded as exotic and mythical as the jungle-shrouded pyramids of Maya or the mythical golden kingdom of El Dorado.

"Poppy," he said, as he rose to leave and ride home, "I have to tell you that I am somewhat surprised."

"Surprised at what?" I thought he must mean that I had actually finished medical school and was still living in London.

"That you are still unmarried. Surprised, but very happy," he said.

36

The next day my family and I went to the hospital. I held my father's hand. I told him I looked forward to hearing him play the piano again and promised I would try harder to improve my own pathetic performance on the ivories. He actually smiled and squeezed my hand.

"You need make no such promises, my sweet girl. You are a physician and those hands were meant to heal patients. I cannot tell you how proud I am of you. I am so proud."

I kissed his forehead, told him I loved him, and, over my uncle's objections, Michael and I sat in the gallery to watch the operation while Aunt Susan, Mum and Victor waited in the nearby cottage.

Uncle had warned that it was quite possible that performing the gastrectomy would be hindered if the cancer had spread, for example, to the pancreas. He said the operation had to be done; my father could not take enough food and was rapidly becoming emaciated. Of course, the surgery might not stop the progress of the disease but it could inhibit what was called "ichorous decomposition," caused by food remaining in the affected area. As a result of the operation, the carcinoma might grow less rapidly. If a gastrectomy is performed at the proper time, the life of the patient may be prolonged for many months, even more than a year. Uncle was worried that they had decided upon the operation too late, but admitted he had delayed in part because of my mother's misgivings. I understood. And I understood that he could make no promise other than that he would try.

241

The field of operation was prepared as in every abdominal operation; Uncle took great care to make sure the theater was as aseptic as possible. Dr. Crosse made an incision about three inches in length through the outer edge of the left rectus abdominis. As soon as the abdomen was opened, a portion of the anterior wall of the stomach was drawn into the wound and two purse-string stitches of fine silk or linen were applied. These stitches grasped all of the layers of the stomach down to the mucous membrane. He punctured the space within the inner circle with a trocar, and inserted a rubber tube. This would produce an infolding of the stomach wall. Then Dr. Crosse applied several rows of Lembert sutures to each side of the tube. The end of the tube in the stomach would be closed with a cork so that no stomach contents could be expelled during the course of the operation. The next step was the attachment of the stomach to the abdominal wall by inserting silk-worm gut sutures, then out through all of the layers of the abdominal wall on the opposite side and then to the peritoneum and transversalis fascia by a number of interrupted sutures.

I watched Dr. Crosse and Uncle carefully. Things appeared to be going well and I expected the next step to be suturing the stomach wall to the peritoneum, then closure of the stomach incision and application of sterile gauze through which a feeding tube would pass. But Dr. Crosse stopped before the closing procedures.

Uncle looked up at us and motioned to the door.

My heart hammered in my chest. Something had gone wrong.

Michael and I met Uncle outside the operating theater. "What is it, Uncle Ormond?" my brother demanded.

"Michael, the growth has infiltrated the pancreas."

"So what are you going to do?" Michael asked.

"We must attempt a gastrojejunostomy and resect the tumor."

This procedure had never been done. It would involve making a connection between adjacent blood vessels of the stomach and the proximal loop of part of the small intestine.

"It is difficult," Uncle said. "I must speak to your mother."

"No! No there is no time!" I yelled. "Do it! Just do it, Uncle."

"He could die on the table, Poppy. Or if the stomach isn't draining . . . . "

"He's dying anyway," I said. "Do it, Uncle."

Uncle Ormond turned to Michael who nodded in agreement and Uncle went back to the operating room. During the remainder of the surgery, Michael and I held each other's hands so tight, it hurt.

That evening, all of us paced the floors of the little cottage, wondering what would happen next. Wondering if the surgery had indeed been successful and even if it was, given the fact that the cancer was obviously spreading, how long Papa would live.

By midnight, Uncle assured us that Papa was resting comfortably. He told us to go home but my mother refused.

"You go, Poppy," Michael said. "I shall stay with her tonight. We can take turns."

And so, over the next several days we watched and waited and prayed. During this time, I spent every waking minute with my father or walking the grounds with Victor.

Much of the wounds Victor and I had inflicted upon each other before he left for India were put aside. His sweetness and great kindness, mixed with his new confidence is all that got me through that horrible time. I knew my father's days were numbered no matter how successful the surgery was and life would seem unbearable to me without his presence in the world. I had not seen my parents often in the last several years because I had been so busy with nursing school, then medical school, and then with my practice and my cases with Sherlock. I regretted this. Victor helped me to fight off those feelings to some extent and when I could not, he entertained me with more stories of his new country. Though it was very cold outdoors, we strolled the snow-laden grounds around his home, and I often felt it was Victor's warmth that kept my heart from growing cold with bitterness and guilt.

Our prayers were not answered. For the next several days, Papa suffered from continuous vomiting.

Two days before Christmas and just ten days after the surgery, my father died.

My mother did not want an autopsy, but Michael and I insisted. Dr. Crosse and Uncle had fought valiantly and we had to know what had happened. The post-mortem exam revealed there was a small narrow opening of the belly wall to the outward loop. It was kinked at the site of the reconnection of the blood vessels and did not drain the stomach.

We were devastated. Despite knowing that Papa had a terminal disease, we had hoped for a little longer with him. But worst of all, when Michael tried to explain what had happened, my mother blamed me. I'd given permission for the alternate surgery. I hadn't consulted her. It was my fault in her mind that my father was dead.

37

The next night, I went to the parlour and found Uncle Ormond sitting in the dark, nursing a brandy.

"Join me, Poppy."

Wordlessly, I sat down on the divan next to him.

He squeezed my hand, then rose to pour me a brandy. He sat back down, handed my glass to me and lifted his glass.

"To Robert."

I clinked his glass and choked back tears.

"Uncle, Mum is so angry with me. She—"

"She will come round, Poppy. Give it time."

"But it isn't just for the surgery. Her words were scathing earlier. She chastised me for continuing to live with you all these years. For not visiting more often. For missing last Christmas when Michael and I stayed in London to treat people affected by the fog. No explanation satisfied her. She said I didn't care about her or Papa."

"You know that is not true. She knows it isn't true. Your parents sent you to live with us so that you could attend a private girls' school, so that you could live in the city and explore its shops and museums and theaters and all that London has to offer. They did not disapprove of you going to nursing school. I remember on your birthday when they gave you the diamond necklace. I remember what your father said. Do you?"

I shook my head.

"He said, 'It's not just for your birthday, Priscilla. It is also a graduation gift. We know how much it meant to you to finish your nurse's training, but we aren't sure we ever showed it.'

"And they were just as proud when you finished medical school and started your practice. Your mother's feelings are raw, like an open, seeping wound. She lashed out at me as well. And even at Susan. It will pass, Poppy."

"I hope so. But I have been thinking. Perhaps I should move back here to be with Mum. She has never been alone."

"You should do no such thing. Your brother has already offered to have her move in with him. And as to that, we also talked about him moving into our house. I suspect he intends to marry Kate. I don't know how she'll get along with Endelyn, but more importantly, is it going to be too crowded for you there? You are used to living just with us and we have tried not to interfere with your life. We have never hovered."

"No, Uncle, you have not. But if I do not move back here, I have been thinking about striking out on my own."

"You mean your own place? You don't have to do that. I can tell Michael he can't move into our house, Poppy."

"No, no. That's not what I mean. It's not that I want to live alone there or that there is not enough room. I have—well, Victor and I have been talking a great deal."

"I see. So he has asked you to marry him then? And you've accepted?" His smile seemed forced. "Victor is a fine young man and—"

"Sorry to interrupt you, Uncle," I began, "but no, he has not asked me. He has not even asked me to come back to India with him but I am giving it serious thought."

"Moving to India? But what of your practice? The clinic?"

"My practice has greatly diminished since the fog cases have ceased. And Olivia—Dr. Robertson is very capable."

"Maggie opened the clinic for you."

"No, she opened it for her ladies, of whom I am very fond. And for the community. The clinic will thrive whether I am there or not. I have been thinking about it a lot, Uncle."

He finished his brandy, then said, "If you really feel you must leave London, then come to Scotland with us. The house in London will be waiting for you if you decide to return."

"Uncle, you should just deed the house to Michael. I shall have no need of it if I am going to India."

"But what if you wish to come back?"

"Then I'll come here to Burleigh Manor. Or I'll rent a place wherever I decide to settle down."

"Settle down," he repeated. "I am not sure you can do that. You have always been restless. Always looking for the next challenge. And speaking of challenges, what about Sherlock, Poppy?"

I gave his hand a squeeze. "Did you not say yourself we have no future? I have come to terms with that. And didn't you also tell me that he wants me to be happy?"

We sat for a long time without speaking, the words sticking to my numb tongue, "Uncle, it's too cold to bury Papa."

"Endelyn made the same observation, Poppy." He turned to gaze out the window as snowflakes clung to the pane of glass and the cold air formed intricate lacy-like etchings upon it.

"You are right. We have had an unusually cold winter and right now the frost layer is about three feet. It is not possible to dig the grave," he added. "But have you never noticed what looks like a small tomb at the edge of your family cemetery?"

I thought for a moment. I had not been there in years. Not since shortly after I'd met Sherlock. The last time I had gone there was to visit my grandmother's grave. I used to like to ride out to the West and wander, looking at all the old headstones. Many were tilted by the shifting of the ground over hundreds of years. I'd wonder what kind of lives the departed had lived, what they had dreamt of or wished for.

My grandmother was buried in the middle of the cemetery next to my grandfather. The inscription on her grave said: *Olympia Anne Price—born 1800, died 1851. Beloved Wife and Mother.* I had never known my mother's parents, but I was often told I was following in my grandmother's footsteps. As the local midwife, she'd been heralded for her knowledge of healing herbs.

"I suppose I have seen the small tomb. Why?"

"It's actually not a tomb at all. It's a holding vault, Poppy. You see them in many cemeteries, especially old family cemeteries. You see, when someone dies during these cold months, there are three choices. Try to hack through the frozen ground. Try to warm it somehow. Or wait until the spring thaw. Perhaps in a few weeks, if it warms up, they can dig the grave. Or they could try a grave warmer."

"A what?"

"Sometimes a piece of equipment is fashioned out of bronze or the like. It looks like half a storage barrel or half of a canon. It's filled with charcoal, lit and surrounded with sand to make sure the fire stays in the unit. It is left at the grave for a day or two and then removed."

"And it heats up the ground and the diggers can get through the ground just as they would in warm weather?"

"That's right. I proffered that to Endelyn and she is mulling it over. Relatives like us are here from London, friends and colleagues of your father are coming from other places to pay their respects. But if the grave cannot be dug now, there can be no interment and everyone will have to come back for a graveside service. For now, the pallbearers could take the casket to the little vault building in the cemetery. He would stay there until spring."

"The holding vault. I guess I always thought it was a tomb."

"They are not unlike tombs. Often there are spaces for ten or more bodies. They are made of limestone. On one side is a small brick inset with a ventilation pipe. And the door is made of steel. Like the one in your family's cemetery, these vaults are usually tucked into a small hill. Incorporating hills and valleys when you place the vault helps to maintain a consistent, cool ground temperature to slow—"

He paused and I finished the sentence. "Decay."

"Yes."

I took a sip of brandy. "Of course, I will defer to whatever my mother wishes. But Maggie's decision to be cremated is starting to make a great deal of sense."

"Indeed," Uncle agreed.

I looked down at the glass I was holding. It was larger than those I usually sipped my wine from. It was from one of my mother's beautiful crystal collections. A tall goblet engraved with scrolls and leaf-like festoons above the band. I was glad it was a large glass. I needed more alcohol than usual.

I looked at the grandfather clock in the corner. It was stopped, as were all of the clocks throughout the house. All the curtains had been drawn and all the mirrors had been covered with black cloth.

"Aunt Susan is trying to help Mum decide what to wear for the next several days. She has always hated black. I think she has just one black dress."

Uncle grunted. "We've already had an argument about that. Endelyn wishes to wear the traditional garments."

I nodded. He meant the mourning 'uniform.' Black crepe dress and white crepe collar and a crepe veil that's very unhealthy.

"Silly trappings of grieving," he added. "And unhealthy. This fashion can cause diseases of the eye."

"Yes, Uncle, it is a thousand pities that fashion dictates the crepe veil, but so it is. It is the very banner of woe, and no one has the courage to go without it."

"You should. Tell me you do, Poppy."

I took another sip of wine. I did not answer.

I remembered seeing a young widow in St. Paul's several years before. As I knew my mother would, the young woman paid close attention to the rigorous demands of mourning. She was my age and wore a black dress, a crepe bonnet, and a veil that covered her hair with streamers to mask the sides of her face. My mother called this attire *widow's weeds.*

The rules were very strict at that time for family members and mourners. For the first six months, the dress should be of crepe or Henrietta cloth collar and cuffs of white crepe, a crepe bonnet with a long crepe veil, and a widow's cap. Dull black kid gloves were worn in first mourning; after that Gants de suède or silk gloves were proper. After six months' mourning, the crepe could be removed, and grenadine, copeau fringe, and dead trimmings used. After a year, the widow's cap could be left off and the veil exchanged for a lighter one. Dresses were made of silk grenadine, plain black gros-grain, or crepe-trimmed cashmere with crepe lissé about the neck and sleeves. Because it was so cold, Mum could pull out a black fur or something in seal skin.

I would also be mourning my father, so I would be expected to wear a dress of Henrietta cloth with black tulle at the wrists and neck. I'd don a deep veil at the back of my bonnet. Jet ornaments alone were dictated for over a year. No diamonds whatsoever. And then in the second year, I'd be required to wear black mourning flowers at my hands and wrists and then flowers of grey and mauve after that. *How shall I work with these?* I thought in passing.

"What about Aunt Susan, Uncle? Ladies of the family wear their deepest mourning. Will she—?"

"Not if I have anything to say about it," he said. "Nor will we be absent from dinners or restaurants or the opera or any of that. And neither should you, Poppy. Life is for the living."

My mother entered the room, followed by Aunt Susan. She was very thin and I swear her hair had started turning white almost overnight. I placed my glass on a table, rose and embraced Mum. She stiffened. She was clearly still angry with me.

"I should like your opinion, Ormond," she said, breaking away from me. She bit her lip as it quivered. "I've chosen a coffin lined with satin. Black cloth on the outside with a silver plate for his name. Robert Michael Stamford. And he'll wear his favorite dark grey frockcoat, his Kingsley vest—the claret one—and a neat white shirt. A black silk puff tie and a pearl tie tack. The one you gave him for his last birthday, Poppy. What do you think? Will that be . . . will he look—?"

She broke down and Aunt Susan draped an arm around her. "Endelyn, we'll take care of everything. You need to rest now. You really must lie down."

Uncle rose and whispered to me, "I'll be right back. I think she needs a sedative."

I nodded and pulled a deep breath. I wanted to run. To be anywhere but here.

But because of family, because of protocol, because of societal morés, I was trapped.

38

On Christmas day, my mother announced that the next day, on Boxing Day, instead of passing out Christmas boxes to the servants, as was traditional, my father would be 'temporarily interred' at the family cemetery early in the morning and she invited everyone to join the family there and for refreshments at the house afterword. She also announced that she would be leaving within a few days to stay with Michael in London for a while. The mood was glum and solemn. There was no mirth and the unopened presents beneath the tree seemed to mock us. I was glad Michael had left my nephew back in London with Kate.

Victor came shortly after breakfast—a meal that went virtually untouched by all of us. I went into the library to have tea with him and he let out a long sigh. "I have missed many of our customs," he said. "Like what should have happened today. Before I left, I told everyone on the plantation about it—about how servants usually had to wait on their masters on Christmas Day but were given a box to take home the next day with gifts and money and food. I said I would make up for missing their special day when I got back." He laughed a little and added, "I don't think most of them knew what I was talking about anyway."

I looked down at my lap. "I suppose none of us gave much thought to traditions or customs this year."

"You never did."

"What?"

"You never gave much thought to traditions. I remember you telling me all about two doctors who married in a small ceremony, without even a cake. Hoggan, I think was the name.

You said instead of a honeymoon, they simply went to Richmond for dinner."

I thought a moment and then remembered. It was the day I met Sherlock. Victor and I were walking the grounds of Oxford and he had, once again, brought up the subject of marriage. Back then I thought it a fascinating concept to marry without all the pomp and circumstance. No rich white silk, no spray of flowers, no tulle, no bridesmaids parading in silly pink dresses with lace flounces. But after taking part in Michael and Effie's lovely ceremony and reception, after seeing her float down the aisle in her exquisite dress, I'd had second thoughts about how to commemorate such a day.

I sipped my tea and stared out the window.

"Penny for your thoughts, Poppy?"

"Oh, just everything. How Mum is going to manage with Papa gone. About how lonely she will be."

"You aren't thinking of moving back to The Broads, are you? I know you are concerned about your mother, but you would not be happy here. You must continue your practice. You must—"

I interrupted him quickly. "Victor, no, I believe Mum is going to move into Uncle's house with Michael . . . and with Kate, his . . . well, she is—"

"His new love? He spoke very fondly of her. I am glad he has found someone."

"As am I. Uncle and Aunt Susan will be leaving for Scotland shortly. I have been thinking very seriously of moving to India, Victor."

"You have?"

"Yes. I have read so much about it and you have . . . well, your descriptions are so intriguing and exciting. My practice has not done well here and I believe you have convinced me that medical practitioners are much needed in India."

"You do have the clinic, but I would say nothing to dissuade you . . . for you coming to India with me—I want that very much. I thought of begging you to do so, but I do not want to force you into anything."

"I do have the clinic now, but somehow that constantly reminds me of what led up to its opening and those are painful memories, Victor." I took a breath and said, "Your support and comfort mean the world to me. But—"

"Are you torn?" he interjected. "Do you not wish to leave Sherlock Holmes?"

I was shocked he was so blunt and hoped we were not heading into an argument for our short time together had been so serene and such a comfort. But I wanted to be truthful. I wanted to tell him that I had had many adventures with Sherlock, that even after all that had passed between us, for a long time I had indulged in the hope that Sherlock and I would have a future. I realised that this was not at all what Victor needed to hear, so I bit my tongue.

"My decision has nothing to do with Sherlock Holmes," I lied. "And this has nothing to do with marriage. I would not be going to India to marry you or to find any husband. I would go to practice medicine and to experience a new way of life. I would like to just . . . to just live and see where life takes me."

Nodding his head, he said, "I appreciate your candor and I will be honest with you as well. I have never stopped loving you. I would ask you to marry me without a moment's hesitation

256

if—and only if—I thought you would say yes without reservation. But I do not believe you are any more easily persuaded to do so than you were years ago. Nonetheless, if you wish to come to India, you can live in one of the cottages that I've been building near the house on the grounds."

This was so different coming from Victor. Not long before he left for India, he had spoken of marriage many, many times. But I would not bring that up. Not now.

"You are speaking of the little house you described in your letter to Mrs. Hudson? The small house with floors of red limestone and the thatched roof and the ceiling beams of eucalyptus?"

He smiled. "Yes, that it is the one. Or the other one that is painted all white. Both are complete now. I will make all the arrangements for your arrival."

"Well, we can talk more of this later. I should see if Mum needs anything."

I rose and Victor reached out to touch my hand. "I came here today for a specific reason," he said. "Sherlock is at my home. He came last night."

I gulped. "What? Sherlock is here?"

"He is with Loke," Victor said, "and his wife Marie and the constable at my estate. He came to sort out that business . . . and to attend your father's funeral."

"But how does he know? I didn't—"

"I sent him a telegram, Poppy. I asked Michael for his address."

I felt my breath hitch in disbelief.

"You? You sent Sherlock a telegram, Victor?"

257

"Both things required his attention. And there were other things to sort out."

I paced for a moment. Suddenly everything started to swirl. The room began to spin.

"Before you see Sherlock . . . I want you to know that if you are serious about going to India, I will not pressure you into anything. I swear it. But I want you there with me. Do you understand what I am saying?"

"Yes," I whispered, nodding my head. "Yes, that's exactly what I need to hear. But now I should go talk to Loke. I must . . . I must go."

Without another word, I ran through the door to the right that led to a landing and then on to one of the main bedrooms and a dressing room, my sanctuary. I sat on my bed for a moment, then grabbed my cape and gloves and ran back downstairs, out the door and down to the stable.

"Can you still ride as fast as ever, Ladybird?" I asked my horse as I strapped on her saddle. I mounted her and dashed to the Trevor estate.

I dismounted quickly, awkwardly—it had been a long time and I wasn't wearing the bloomers that Effie had made me for my riding habit. I slogged through snow and ankle deep mud; the hem of my dress was soaked and thick with brown sludge. I went straight into the stable and saw a uniformed constable, Loke, Marie and Sherlock. I ran to Marie and hugged her, then Loke. I whirled around to face Sherlock.

"You're here."

"I am. I—I am deeply sorry about your father, Poppy."

I looked down at the straw on the floor, then back up at him. "Thank you, Sherlock. What is going on? Is Loke going back to the jail? Is?—"

"Quite the contrary. We have gotten to the root of the problem. This is Constable Clarke."

I said hello and turned back to Sherlock. "Tell me!"

"Well," said Sherlock, "The injured party, the man accusing Loke of wrongdoing, Mr. Mansell, was hired to take over management of the estate when the gentleman Victor's father hired left to go back to Scotland. Apparently, Fiona here has exhibited very aggressive behavior of late."

"Went crazy, she did," Loke interrupted. "Ya know, I'm good with horses but Fiona, she's been a bit off. Worse than when she's in season. Usually she's a bright, gentle little lady."

"According to Mr. Mansell, she was irrational, more irritable than ever," Constable Clarke said. "He insisted that Loke was deliberately training her to attack him."

"Horses don't do that!" I cried.

"Don't know much about horses, Miss," Clarke admitted.

"She's always playful, Miss," Loke said. "Like when she's with the other horses, she will flash a hoof when she runs by a playmate to try to stir him up. But she was tense all the time, had her tail clamped down and she'd load up. Nostrils flaring, like she was saying, 'I just can't take any more of this!' Mr. Mansell wouldn't let us call in the vet. Said it was too expensive. She was biting and flinching when I tried to groom her.

"Mr. Mansell wouldn't listen to me. He tried to look at her withers and touched her, and she just wheeled around, ears pinned back and bared teeth. She attacked him. Her front legs went up and then she kicked out. She hit the left side of Mansell's leg. They say it shattered his knee.

"He says it was my fault. Hadn't trained her right. He told the police that I wanted him dead. Ain't true, Miss. It was him wanted *me* dead. Or at least out of the way. He was fancyin' my Marie."

"There were so many inconsistences," Clarke said. "That's one reason why Loke was out on bail. We were trying to get to the bottom of it, but Mr. Mansell had authority over this estate, this property. It seems he silenced other servants. I was glad of it when Mr. Trevor came back and we started to be able to explore other possibilities with his permission. And we had the help of Mr. Holmes here."

"It's all right now, Loke. I spoke with the servants, neighbors *and* Mr. Mansell," Sherlock said. He turned to me. "My brother Mycroft does come in handy now and again. Weeks ago, I asked him to tell the magistrate about Mr. Mansell's suspicious background and about our investigation into an international crime ring in which Mr. Mansell might be involved."

"But—"

Sherlock stopped me. "Mycroft told the authorities that I would be coming here soon to investigate this crime syndicate further and that they must hold Mr. Mansell," he said with a wink.

I smiled for the first time in days.

"He wanted Loke gone. Not Loke's wife Marie, mind you, but definitely Loke."

"He was after me, Miss," Marie said. "Bothered me all the time. Loke and I was plannin' on movin' out. Anywhere's but here."

"Oh, Marie. I'm so sorry. I am so thankful that my mother posted bail and that Mr. Holmes interceded." I turned to the Constable. "You didn't believe Loke or Marie?"

"Loke is the trainer, Miss. He is responsible for the horse's behavior. But now that Mr. Holmes has taken statements from some of the other servants and now that he called in a veterinary surgeon, I think we know it had nothing whatsoever to do with Loke's training. The horse is in pain."

"What's wrong with her?"

"On Loke's advice, I sent a telegram to a veterinary surgeon a few weeks ago. He has treated horses at the estate owned by Maggie's lov—" Sherlock stopped in the middle of the word. "Well, a man in Surrey—you know the one? Maggie's friend?"

I nodded. He had to be referring to the country gentleman who kept Maggie's horse.

"Maggie had the veterinary surgeon's name among other things in her safe. With the diary. The one I gave you?"

"Yes, I understand."

"His name is John Rothwell. He's in his early thirties, Mycroft's age. He lived in Rochdale for a time but now he is in Lancashire. Not far from my brother Sherrinford, in fact. He examined the horse a few days ago."

"And?"

"Fiona has a tumor. An ovarian tumor. Six inches long, in fact. One that produces steroids. He explained that with these types of tumors a mare's attitude suddenly changes. For

261

example, she may display stallion attitudes and postures and may become aggressive."

"She actually tried to mount another horse in the field, Miss," Loke said. "I was turnin' her out only with geldings. She's been kicking, refusing to jump, squealing, throwing her head, stomping in her stall, biting. She tries to run through the stall guard, fencing, what or whoever is in front of her."

A tall, lean gentleman entered the stable and said, "It was classic behavior for such a condition," he said.

"Dr. Rothwell?" I asked.

"No, Poppy," Sherlock said, "This is Dr. John McFadyean. An acquaintance of your Uncle Ormond. Dr. Rothwell was called back to Latham. But he recommended Dr. McFadyean, as did your uncle, so we sent him a telegram."

Dr. McFadyean tipped his hat to me.

"This is Dr. Poppy Stamford," Sherlock said.

"A pleasure to meet you, Dr. Stamford."

"You know my uncle?"

"I do. I met him the last time he was in Scotland for a conference of surgeons. Quite unexpectedly, I'd been invited to discuss *my* type of surgery. Cows and horses. Not the usual fare at these things. Your uncle and I discovered we share an interest in pathology."

"Dr. McFadyean's credentials are impeccable," Sherlock said. "He went to Dick Veterinary College in Edinburgh and lectures on Anatomy there. But like he said, he and your uncle share an interest in pathology. His is simply not of human beings. He is going to perform the surgery on Fiona."

"Your uncle said he would like to assist," said Dr. McFadyean.

"How difficult is this surgery, Dr. McFadyean?"

"Horses have a high incidence of ovarian tumors, Dr. Stamford. More than any other domestic animal. So I've done the surgery before. Tumors this large tend to stretch the ligaments and vessels and this lass is lucky that it has not ruptured and hemorrhaged. A vet should have been consulted weeks ago. As I said, her behavior is not abnormal. Some horses respond to pain by lashing out. This may go away once the pain is relieved. Secondly, if people were frightened and panicky around her and tried to touch her or somehow made the pain worse, she might also associate people who don't usually handle her with the feelings of fear and panic.

"There are many reasons for a horse's behavior to change. Some horses panic when their usual routine is disrupted. Horses like a stable environment, and when their usual life goes into upheaval they may react with hysteria. If your mare was used to being on a certain schedule with Loke before her injury and this was disrupted, then she might have been terribly frightened by it. Horses have fears of instability and want their life to be predictable. Loke told me that the man who was injured kept trying to push him out of his job, take care of the horse himself. He moved her and separated her from her daily routine with Loke. That is enough to disturb her greatly. But it is the tumor, I think, that has really thrown her out of kilter."

"When will you perform the surgery?" I asked.

"Tomorrow afternoon."

"Statistically, sir, what are her chances of survival and to again reproduce?" Sherlock asked.

"Sherlock!"

"Poppy, it is a logical question. Statistics are relevant."

263

Dr. McFadyean smiled and said, "It is a fair question. I assure you, statistically Fiona's odds are very good. "

"May I observe?" I asked. "When you do the surgery?"

"Miss!" Marie cried. "Your father—the funeral."

"That will be over in a few hours and my absence tomorrow afternoon will be perfectly acceptable." I was not at all sure that was true. My mother might object but I didn't care. And quite honestly, she was barely speaking to me and might not even notice my absence.

I turned to the constable. "So you do believe Loke now? Are you convinced he did not turn the horse on anyone? The charges will be dropped?"

"I am and they will, Miss. It seems clear from all the evidence that Mr. Mansell brought his injuries on himself and that he was making unsolicited overtures to Loke's missus. Mr. Trevor has dismissed Mansell. Glad young Master Trevor is back," he added. "He can put a lot of things right, I expect."

I looked at Sherlock, suddenly wondering what other things Victor might be trying to put right.

39

The service at the temporary vault was small and quiet and cold. A neighbor, Squire Parker, Effie's father who had traveled from Oxford, Michael, Uncle Ormond, Victor and Sherlock served as pallbearers. It was good to see Professor O'Flahertie, but I wondered how he would feel when he heard that Michael was involved with Kate. Michael had endeavored to visit Effie's parents so they could see their grandson often. How would that change? What else was going to change? It seemed that shifts and turns in life were coming faster than I could ever have imagined.

I watched my Aunt Susan comfort Mum at the cemetery. Aunt Susan, who was standing next to my mother, was just one year older than Mum and they looked almost like twins, both with dark hair and eyes, both tall and thin, though Mum had lost considerable weight during Papa's illness. She looked frail and once again I considered if I should put aside my life and take care of her.

As the group gathered in the dining room for tea and a light meal, I wandered through the house. I noticed that all evidence of Christmas had vanished. I suspected that Christmas Eve and Christmas Day would never be the same.

It occurred to me that if I actually went through on my plan to transform my entire life and head to India, I might never see this house again. I went to sit in Mum's morning room—so different from Aunt Susan's sparsely furnished solace that housed only a loveseat and one chair and her piano. Mum's favourite place to read and embroider was typical of what the magazines called 'romantic disorder'—it was filled with large ferns, birdcages, seashell collections, paintings and Japanese prints.

Burleigh Manor was an old house, a grand house though nowhere near as large as Victor's. It had quite a history. The Third Earl of Oxford and his younger son, the Honorable MP for North Norfolk, had lived there once. It was built of red sand-faced brickwork throughout the lower stories with diapering in dark blue brick. The upper floors were timber framed with exposed studs under a tiled roof, unusual for Norfolk. The house retained the atmosphere of an Elizabethan house enhanced by later additions, which included numerous magnificent fireplaces, oak paneling, and carvings. The impressive façade faced northeast and the terrace at the rear faced south. Large stone-mullioned windows brought in beautiful light in the mornings and evenings.

I stared through one of the windows at the gardens, now withered and waiting for spring. What I loved best was our spectacularly secluded position within bountiful gardens and grounds of over eighteen acres. I could wander there for hours by myself and never run into anything except a bird or a rabbit.

I went into the drawing room and inhaled the warm glow of the fire. I wanted to sit and watch the flames and close my eyes but I forced myself to join the others. I but noted immediately that Victor and Sherlock were missing. "Aunt Susan, where have Victor and Sherlock gone?"

"Back to Victor's," she said. "Just a few minutes ago."

I thought of the last time they had been in the same room, the ballroom at Victor's house. It was during Sherlock's summer visit to Victor's home. Sherlock and I had wandered up there after Victor's father's funeral. He'd found an old music box which intrigued him.

"Victor told me about this music box," he had said, "a Nicole Freres, manufactured in 1855, a six-air cylinder with three switches on the right and a ratchet wind handle, and a tune card."

He had lifted the top, opened the side compartment, and turned a knob to make it start playing. It was then I held out my arms and asked, "Shall we dance?"

As we moved in time to the music, we spoke about Victor's intention to move to India. Sherlock suddenly said, "If Victor is truly going to move to India, that changes things." He added, "I've cabled Mycroft that I will be returning to London in the morning. Come with me. We will delight in all that the city has to offer." He stretched out his arms to look at me. "And in the summer, we will skim the waters of the Broads in our boat, in our Norfolk Hawker. I cannot think because my feelings for you get in the way. It suddenly seems more logical to allow them to flourish and keep you close so that I can teach them to live side by side with logic and deduction. Tell me how you are feeling."

I placed both hands on his cheeks and pulled him close. "You *know* how I feel. How could you not know? I love you, Sherlock."

We did not heard the footsteps. We did not hear the door to the ballroom open.

The first we knew that we were not alone was when we heard Victor bellow in anger.

"What is this? What have you done to her? What spell?" Then he stopped and faltered. Finally he asked, "And what have you done with him? I insist you answer!"

"Victor! I . . . I—"

They fought. And then, after I had screamed and pounded my fists against Victor's back, he whirled around and yelled, "Get out of my house at once, you whore."

At that, at hearing Victor disparage me so, Sherlock had pulled away from me and clenched his fists again. He launched toward Victor, ramming his head into Victor's stomach and rocketing him backward. Victor stumbled into the stand that held the music box. It shattered and the pieces scattered to the floor.

Shattered. Scattered. That is us, I thought. Victor had seen my affection for Sherlock as a betrayal and left soon after for India. As to Sherlock, I had come between him and his only friend and in so doing, I had confirmed his suspicions about the fragility of love. I knew at once that we could not recover from that moment.

That was the last time Victor and I spoke until a few weeks ago when he'd returned from India.

The memories of that horrible dissolution of friendships and commitments and love rushed at me like waves over rocky ledges. Though Victor and I had spent a great deal of time together since his return from India and it was clear that he wanted me to go back with him, I could not help but wonder what Sherlock and Victor might say to each other. What if they had put aside their animosity *only* until the funeral was over for my sake? What if Victor told Sherlock that I was going to move to India and he got angry or upset?

40

When I arrived, I did not even knock on the door. I bolted in and called out to Victor.

Victor emerged by himself from the library. "The doctor is in the stable preparing Fiona," he said quietly. Then to my surprise, he added, "Sherlock is upstairs."

"Victor, when I saw the two of you had left the wake, I was worried. I don't know what I was thinking but—"

"It's all right, Poppy. Go ahead." He smiled and said, "Go talk to him."

I ran upstairs and opened the door. Sherlock glanced over my shoulder, checking, I assume, to see if Victor was behind me.

"Hello," he said as he walked over to take my coat. He put it over an old chair.

"When I realized you and Victor were gone, I came—"

"To see if fists were flying? Poppy, I've stayed here in his house for two nights. Victor and I have talked at length. He was my good friend, my only friend, in college and we have let things fester for far too long."

Before I could say anything else, he asked, "Do you remember this? The old music box? We spent last evening trying to put it back together. To no avail, I might add. Some things, once broken, are irreparable."

I nodded. I felt my face pinch. Though I was not crying, my lips trembled and I put my hand to my mouth to stifle a sob. I sat down on the edge of the chair and stared down at my boots.

"Don't you have a surgery to attend?" he asked.

"Yes, Yes. I'll go in a moment."

"You look a bit shaken, Poppy. A difficult time. Here," he said. "Finish my port wine. Victor remembered how much I enjoyed his family wine cellar the last time I was here."

"Yes, I remember also," I said, my voice leaden, flat. My head was still down and he walked over to me, tipped up my chin and handed me the glass. My teeth chattered as I drank from it.

He stared at me, talking slowly and in a low voice. "How long were your parents together?"

"Almost thirty years."

"My parents were married a long time as well. But I don't think it was like your parents' marriage. I don't think it was a happy union. Not a particularly good example. Perhaps that explains why Mycroft and I see little advantage in the institution of marriage. Though Sherrinford seems happy enough. You seem to think marriage is a good thing, however. What would you need from a marriage, Poppy?"

It seemed he was trying to gauge my reaction.

I ignored the question. "Marriage can be a good thing, Sherlock. If you find the right person."

His eyes met mine. "Siger Holmes wanted things his way, always his way. With my mother. With his sons. Sherrinford, being the first born, would inherit the country estate. Fortunately, he was most content with that role—to follow my father as a country squire. Mycroft as the middle son would go into government. We both know how well he has excelled. I should have been free to do what I wished. I should have been free of any obligation to the estate or government. But

271

my father wanted me to be an engineer. He never understood me."

"I know," I said, reaching out to take his hand. It felt cold to the touch.

"My mother vehemently disagreed. I told you, I believe, that my father died of tuberculosis and, just a few months later, my mother perished in a carriage accident while visiting Mycroft in London."

"Yes, you told me." Sherlock always talked about his mother with an unusual wistfulness and affection. I think he was devoted to her and that her death was a huge blow to him. I'd wondered if he'd made his decision to dedicate his life to logic was partly because he did not ever want to feel such pain again. But his life was full of loneliness.

"Before she died," he continued, "she actually came to see me as well, at University. She wanted me to know that she loved me no matter what I decided to do. Her personality was as violet as her name. You know that the violet is symbolic—it shows the giver's thoughts are occupied with love."

An image popped into my head. An image of the wild violets and other flowers that Sherlock had placed on a chaise the morning after our one night together in a cottage by the sea.

"My father wanted me to go to medical school at first," he said. "He recognized my deep interest in medicine, spurred perhaps by an uncle on my mother's side . . . the French cousins we called that part of the family. I spent many lovely holidays in Montpellier. Like your Uncle Ormond, my uncle was a physician, unparalleled in his ability to observe and deduce. He was something of a phenomenon, called in to consult with the police."

"Yes, you told me that when we first met, Sherlock. And you told me that your father later suggested engineering, which you found quite boring. And you also told me that when you refused your father's wish to decide your future, he practically disowned you."

"I did tell you that, didn't? Did I also mention that my brother Mycroft sided with him?" He sighed. "My brother Sherrinford was a bit more understanding. Early on, at university and in the first years thereafter, I would not have managed at all had Sherrinford not gone to great lengths to make sure I had some money."

"Sherlock, why are we talking about this?"

"You were so fortunate to have a father who loved and respected you, Poppy," he said softly. "And your parents were fortunate to have such a good relationship. They are rare, I think."

It was as if I could read his mind. "And you hope that I shall have such a relationship, is that right?"

"Victor is a good man. We cannot change the past but we have put our disagreements behind us during these last few days." He laughed a little. "I am sure it is only because he sees that you have not married and he is ecstatic about that. He still wants to marry you, Poppy. He will make a fine husband."

I did not say whether Victor had asked for my hand or if I would accept. I simply nodded in agreement.

"What are you going to do, Poppy? Victor told me you really are seriously considering immigrating to India. Are you?"

"Yes. Yes, I am going to go to India. As soon as possible. Very soon."

"It is the dead of winter."

"I asked Uncle about that. The best time to depart England is November so that you can become accustomed to the climate there. Later than that puts you into the hottest months. But cargo ships sail there all year and Uncle he knows the captain of a cargo ship—someone with whom he served when he was a ship's surgeon on a Greenland whaler. Not long before Uncle Ormond came here to care for Papa, he ran into his friend from his days on the whaler. Uncle trusts him so I do as well. His ship departs for India on January sixth."

"January sixth on a cargo ship!" he exclaimed. "That's just days away. How can you possibly prepare for such a journey?"

"I shall be returning to London on the twenty-eighth to pack and get ready to leave. Aunt Susan and I will help Mum get situated. Then Michael and Mum will travel with me from London to Folkestone where I will board the boat and cross the channel . . . they will see me off. Mum is still angry and hurt about Papa and doesn't want me to go, but now is the time."

Now or never, I thought.

"You could wait until next November. You may change your mind once you are not so distracted by all the recent events. If you still want to go, it will be a more safe and pleasant voyage. And if you really decide you are leaving, it will give you time to train a replacement at the clinic."

His logic was impeccable. Even Victor had cautioned me to wait. He said, "It is against my better judgment, Poppy, to say this for I fear you will change your mind. But I'll be returning in February or March and we could travel together. Or you could wait until November when the voyage is optimum and between now and then, you can comfort your mother and get things in order at the clinic."

I don't know . . . to this day I don't know what compelled me to leave England as quickly and as haphazardly as I did, so quickly after my father's death when my mother needed me. The guilt of leaving her never really faded. I was running from Sherlock, surely; I was asserting my independence and made it clear to Victor that he was but a small fraction of the equation rather than a significant determining factor. I was being stubborn. But Victor's cautionary pleas made me all the more determined to do this alone and Sherlock's counsel set off tocsins in my head that I knew I must heed . . . alarm bells as loud as the striking of the 12-change ringing bells of St. Paul's. If I listened to him, if I stayed, I was certain Sherlock and I would be irrevocably yoked together and that was, indeed, a Faustian bargain just as Sherlock had insinuated. I just know that in that moment, I absolutely convinced that my entire future was in peril. If I did not go now, I knew I would never leave.

Sherlock was a noise in my head that I could not live with anymore. Too much noise and too much hurt. I needed to shed him like a snake sheds is skin. I believed—and still believe— that only putting a continent between us would return my worn out soul to me.

"Why don't you wait, Poppy?" Sherlock asked. "You are grieving. I know people do that and it's the wrong time to make rash decisions."

"And how long should I wait? A month? A year? I have made up my mind."

"Wait until spring at least."

"Sherlock, I have done some research. The Suez Canal has made the voyage much shorter, much easier. No longer do the ships go round the Cape. I know that there are several leading companies that offer magnificent ships with every comfort and convenience. The British India Company, for example, has a splendid fleet of vessels and competent crews."

"But?"

"But none leave until months from now. I shall be on a ship with cargo and mail. The voyage is no longer over three months. It takes only about thirty days. I'll take the train on the South Eastern Railway from London to Folkestone where Michael will be sure I get on the ship safely and speak with the captain. And then I cross the channel on board a steam packet to Boulogne, travel by train to Marseilles. We will stop at Brindisi in Italy—there's a railway connection there for passengers and mail. Then to Alexandria, Suez, Aden and on to Calcutta.'

I took a deep breath. "It will be a great adventure. I have made up my mind, Sherlock."

"But still . . . this is not a game, Poppy. This seems a life-altering decision."

I ignored that remark. "I shall pack only what I need for the voyage," I said. "And some medical supplies. Victor said I can buy anything else I need at the Great Eastern Hotel in Calcutta. There is a vast store beneath the hotel with supplies from the constant stream of ships. I may even explore the city for a few days."

"But Poppy, you—alone on a cargo ship with sailors. Poppy!"

"I shan't be alone."

"Oh," he said, sounding relieved. "You *are* returning with Victor then."

"No, actually he has not yet settled his affairs with the sale of his estate here. He will return to India when that has been completed. He sent a telegram ahead that his servants are to expect me and ready a small house separate from his bungalow on his plantation. I will arrive before the worst heat and have some time to settle in. And I have sent a telegram to Sarah McBride and she is coming with me."

"Who?"

"Sarah. One of Maggie's ladies. The tall brunette. She has been wanting to go there for a very long time. She has loaned me magazines and books about it." I swallowed hard. "I'm very excited about it, Sherlock."

"But Poppy, two women alone at sea. Storms flare up, Poppy. If the weather turns foul . . . the nature of the gales—"

"It will be fine. Until recently, almost everyone who travelled to India booked passage on a cargo ship. There were no ships just for passengers."

"But—"

"Thousands of ships use the Suez canal each year. It will be a great adventure. I'm going, Sherlock," I added.

"Poppy, such a voyage for two young women is risky."

"Did you not tell me once that to risk nothing is to risk losing everything?"

"I did, didn't I? You forget nothing." He glanced away, then asked, "You've really thought this through?"

Tears stinging that I refused to show, I said, "Yes, quite thoroughly. In spite of my efforts, my practice never did well.

Uncle and Aunt Susan are moving to Scotland. Father is gone; my best friend is dead."

"The clinic? Your mother. Michael and Kate and your nephew? And—" He paused, waited.

I was surprised at the emotional component to this series of questions. *What are you really thinking?* I thought. I shivered as if an icy draft had swept over me, but though the ballroom was chilly, I knew it was the fact that I was likely having my last conversation with Sherlock Holmes.

"Dr. Robertson will run the clinic and she is extremely capable. Michael will be fine now that he has Kate. Mum will live with them, at least for a time, and they will look after her."

"Well, it is an ambitious venture, I must say. But I know that you are very ambitious and determined. Otherwise, you would not have been able to become a doctor nor such an excellent assistant."

"I am ambitious, yes. And adventurous, I suppose. You brought that out in me." I paused. "Sherlock, ambition is fine but obsession . . . that can destroy everything in its path, especially when combined with the absolute license of great success. I will worry about you, I must admit."

"Worry? About me? Don't be ridiculous," he scoffed.

"Sherlock, you never stop working. And I've come to believe that relationships are not a relief for your work, or the point of your work but simply to augment your work . . . to inspire you or, oh, I don't know, keep the sexual side of existence from being a nagging distraction. At least that's how I felt after . . . after we—"

I could not finish the sentence or the painful thought. But then finally I said, "I know I was young, naive. Powerless against your studied exterior but—"

"No, no, Poppy!" he protested. "I am a difficult, exacting man. You asserted yourself into the center of my life in a way that no one else could. You didn't try to change me or keep up with me."

"You know that's not true. There are things I would have changed about you if I could."

"Perhaps, but you watched, you waited for your moments. You were astute. You knew when I needed library silence in the morning or when I needed complete aloneness when I was trying to determine the best way to approach a case. You knew I think I am the center of the universe, with everyone else orbiting in service of me . . . or that this is how I would have it. You knew that the slightest disruption to my strict regulation of emotions would threaten to crumble everything for me."

"Or at least your mood for the day," I replied softly.

"Do you know how very proud I am of you? How fortunate I feel to have been the companion of a woman who refuses to be pushed aside by men who smoke cigars and palaver about so-called important matters? A woman who is so strong . . . strong enough to stand up to a condescending fool like me?

"You determined . . . well, everything important about me, Poppy Stamford. It was never about control or surrender. I know who I am. I can lavish attention on something only to cite its flaws. I can be autocratic. But you never shrunk from me. I think you surreptitiously molded me despite my pathological eccentricities and my mania for logic."

"And your genius," I added. "Which is at the very heart of your incubus. I fear your genius, Sherlock. I fear that hunger which drives you, drives you like a madman, offers you nothing in the way of emotional nourishment. I fear it will—"

"Undo me?" he interrupted. He seemed to tremble. "I do not fear that. But I *have* feared self-immolation at your hands, Poppy. I feared being undone. I still do."

I did not know what to say or do. I simply sat there, quieted by the admission.

"All and all, it has been a most productive month for me," he said, abruptly changing the subject. "Littlecode and Barclay have been arrested. Their scheme to defraud people into investing in the cathedral is finished. That will look good on Lestrade's record. Loke is now a free man. The Yard is trying to track down John Carr, and his delinquent daughter has been shipped off to a convent."

"But Adam Worth—"

"He will be found, Poppy. I guarantee he will be found and brought to justice. He and his henchmen."

Then suddenly, he stood in front of me and I looked up. He extended his hands and I stood up. "Well, if you really are leaving, then I must make good on my debt."

"What?"

He put his right hand into his pocket and withdrew several coins. He placed them in my hand.

"What's this?"

"The seven pence I borrowed from you to buy a newspaper."

"What?"

"I bought a newspaper shortly after the paddleboat accident on the Thames. You loaned me the money."

Now I remembered. We'd had tea and were walking to Bart's. We had paused at a newspaper stand. The entire front page of *The London Times* was covered with a depiction of the paddleboat and the steamer and the crowds on the wharf. At that point, authorities continued to drag the river and many bodies had been recovered, but hundreds were still missing. Sherlock had asked me for seven pence to buy the papers.

"Sherlock, I—" But he interrupted me by drawing me into his arms. I put the coins in my pocket and we started to sway as if we were dancing.

"What will it be like, living on a tea plantation?" he asked. "You said you have read about it."

"There will be archery and croquet and tennis and golf and horseback riding and target shooting. Picnics and lavish dinners."

"And I suppose you will collect butterflies and dried flowers and play cricket."

"Oh yes," I laughed.

"Why, it sounds like you shall have no time for the practice of medicine."

"Absolutely not. I will be too busy painting with watercolors. I'll paint the peacocks who strut through the fields. Actually, from what I have been told and what I've read, India is very intriguing and beautiful. " I went on, suddenly at ease again with the easy rhythm of us, the comfortable conversation. "There are forests of tigers and elephants. Rhinos and swamp deer and water buffalo and grey monkeys. Perhaps I shall take a monkey for a pet. And there are beautiful trees and magnificent jungles and rolling hills. Victor says I will wake to the sounds of all the creatures . . . the cry of the peacock, the roar of the tiger, the bark of the spotted deer."

"Perhaps you should request some textbooks from Dr. McFadyean. It sounds like you may end up tending to as many animals as people."

"I'll at least have to sketch these exotic animals. But only when I am not busily hosting parties," I laughed. "Wearing beautiful afternoon party dresses and big hats, of course."

"Like Effie used to make."

Hearing him say her name stung. "Yes, like Effie's hats. And all the guests," I added quickly, "shall gather on Victor's verandah at twilight and drink gimlets. But only after a grand dinner of soup and turkey and fish and puddings and cakes."

Sherlock laughed.

"You know, Sherlock, I don't think I have eaten cake since Effie and Michael's wedding."

"I missed Michael and Effie's wedding. I regret that," he admitted.

"It's all right, Sherlock. It was a long time ago."

"I don't think I have ever attended a wedding except for Sherrinford's. What is it they say again?"

"What?"

His voice was very serious suddenly. "The vows, Poppy. The marital vows."

I was thunderstruck by the whiplash of the conversation. I could hardly speak. I stammered out, "The vows?"

"Yes," he said, giving my hand a slight squeeze.

"A lot of words, Sherlock. About love, comfort, honor."

"And the part about being bound for life—like the swans, Poppy? Like the swans?"

"The bride says, I take thee—and says the groom's name—to be my wedded husband, to have and to hold from this day forward, for better for worse, for richer, for poorer, in sickness and in health, to love, cherish, and to obey, till death us do part, according to God's holy ordinance; and thereto I give thee my troth."

He squeezed my hand more tightly and whispered, "And then the groom says the same thing. Til death us do part. Yes?"

I pulled my head back to look at him. "Yes, that's right."

"If you find the right person," he said. "I think it should be easy . . . logical to pledge until death, to never stray to another." His words were steady, deliberate. "For most people, at least."

"Yes, it would. With the right person, it would be easy to say til death us do part."

He kissed me lightly on the mouth and ran his hand across my cheek. I pulled him closer and I kissed him back, hard and desperate. For an instant, I wanted to parrot his own words back to him. "To risk nothing is to risk losing everything." But I made the instantaneous choice to keep silent.

My lips still wet from our kiss, I felt his lips move against my ear as he whispered, "You'll be late for surgery, Dr. Stamford, and that won't do."

He tore himself from my embrace and bolted from the room. I stood motionless in the empty room. Then tears ran down my cheeks as I went to the door and watched him quickly descend the stairs.

"Til death us do part," I whispered.

41

I had just two days to help my mother decide what she should take to London. She didn't know how long she would stay—maybe a few weeks, maybe much longer. Aunt Susan took charge, though, and by the time we needed to get ready to go back to London, I felt Mum was as prepared as she could be.

By the last day of December 1880, I had returned to London, packed only the essentials for my trip, and now it was time to say goodbye to Kate, her daughter Mary, little Billy, and Uncle and Aunt Susan.

The night before my departure to take the train to Folkestone where I would board the ship, Aunt Susan helped me finish packing. We kept my baggage light. She refused to talk about India. "I'm pretending that you are just going on holiday. I can't bear the thought of you living so far away. I had hoped you would visit us often in Scotland—and perhaps even move with us."

As I rolled up stockings and tossed them into a trunk, I said, "You can visit me in India. You love to travel."

"Not that far!" She lifted her hand up as if she were swatting a fly but I knew she was wiping a tear from her face.

Saying goodbye to Uncle Ormond was the hardest. He had been like a second father and in many ways, we had been closer than my father and I had ever been. We talked about India—the challenge of it, the loneliness I might face. But Uncle did not try to talk me out of it. He told me to use my brain and my skills to their fullest extent. "You have a good head on your shoulders, Poppy. While I may worry about you in this new, strange land, at least I can stop worrying about the dangerous escapades with Sherlock Holmes. And," he added, "Never forget that you can always come back to England. Or to Scotland. You will always have a home with us, you know."

To this day, it is difficult to speak of that parting. I did not know it at the time but I would never see Uncle Ormond and Aunt Susan again.

The morning of my departure, I asked Rattle to gather all of the street urchins so I might give them some coins and bid them adieu. It was hardest with Archie Wiggins. I had watched him grow up, seen him get in and out of scrapes.

"Archie," I said to him as I entered the room at the British Museum where I had asked him to meet me. It was there that he had assisted Sherlock and me with a very complicated case, and Archie and I had gone back many times.

He sauntered up to me and we stood in front of the statue that had introduced Archibald Wiggins to the wonders of the museum.

The goddess Tara was depicted in a large gilded bronze statue. Golden and luminous, it stood over 140 centimeters high. Her enviable hour-glass body was naked from the waist up. A lower garment, tied to her hips, hit her ankles at the hem. Her right hand reached out as if she were giving something away. Atop her head was a high crown with some kind of medallion.

From the moment he saw it, Archie had been mesmerized by the deity's large exposed breasts, her narrow waist and ample hips. He knew her legend by heart. Without looking at me, he recounted the legend back to me.

"At the beginning of time, the sea was churnin' and a poison was created that Lord Shiva drank. He saved the world from destruction. Like Jesus. Tara took Shiva on her lap and fed him with her own milk, a milk that could kill the poison."

"That's right, Archie."

"Will you never just call me Wiggins?

"You are always Archie to me," I said, smiling.

"Who will bring me here, Miss? Now that you're goin' away."

"Don't make me cry, Wiggins. Don't make me cry."

Late that morning, I went to Bart's to meet Michael in the chemistry lab. He and I wanted a few moments alone before we all headed to the train station.

As I entered the lab, at a distant table, I saw Sherlock's tousled dark hair falling forward over the microscope. Sherlock did not lift his eyes; he was totally absorbed in his work and did not hear the sound of my steps.

"Hello, Sherlock."

He looked up and stared at me in that particularly introspective fashion that I remembered so very well. Sometimes it was not possible to guess his thoughts, so far did he recede into his own secure fortress.

"Poppy," he said, his lips turning up in a smile. He moved away from the microscope, leapt to his feet and quickly stepped over to me.

"I came to meet Michael."

"He'll be back soon. He told me you were coming here to meet him. He . . . I think he wanted us to say a proper goodbye."

I felt his long fingers run through my hair as he pulled me close. For a moment, he rested his chin on the top of my head. I could smell the waft of his cologne.

I nodded. "Yes, it would be like Michael to arrange such a meeting, Sherlock."

"And you. Are you happy to be going? You deserve happiness, Dr. Priscilla Olympia Pamela Price Yavonna Stamford Trevor."

I blushed. "Trevor? Oh, no, just Dr. Stamford, Sherlock."

"You'll be married in India, then?"

"We may be but—"

"*May* be married? But I thought—"

"I am sure we will eventually," I lied, my voice faltering. I was not sure of that at all. Suddenly I was not very sure of anything.

"You are really leaving England then?"

I nodded.

"Poppy, I still do not understand. England is your home."

I sighed. "I told you. My practice is abysmal and Victor says that doctors are so needed in India that perhaps the fact that I am a woman will not stand in the way of being a doctor."

With a glint and a wry smile, he asked, "And have you arranged for someone to care for those social parasites of yours? The cat and that wretched dog?"

I laughed. "Michael is adopting Sappho and he has promised to find Little Elihu a home. Some people like bull terriers very much."

He smiled. "*I* am not one of them. Though I suppose a dog's acute olfactory sense could come in handy. So," he said heaving a big sigh, "we will have no more adventures then, Dr. Stamford?"

I touched his cheek. "Never say never, Mr. Holmes."

He thought a moment. "But I can in one regard. I shall likely never have—" He paused, rethinking his words. "I shall never have so good and loyal a friend as Victor was. I have missed him. Tell me, is he well satisfied with selling the estate? We did not talk about that much."

"Yes, Sherlock. He seems to have found great happiness in India and I believe he will be glad to be rid of the manor and the land. This will enable him to expand his holdings there. "

"And now you are back in his life."

I didn't say anything more about that. Instead, I said, "Promise that you will be more open to people, Sherlock. Do not turn your back on friendship if it is offered. Not all of us mere humans are unworthy. Some of us are very loyal."

"Yes, some."

"You have Michael. He is your friend."

"Michael is a wonderful man, but very engaged in his work and busy looking after Aleister Alexander, as he should be. And he has Kate in his life now."

"There is Inspector Lestrade . . . and Hopkins."

"Colleagues, acquaintances."

"There is your brother Mycroft."

He scoffed. "Indeed. Mycroft. Pray, spare me *that* as a friend." He paused, then said, "Poppy, you are one of the most remarkable individuals whom I have ever had the pleasure of knowing. I shall never again have anyone in my life like you."

I wanted so badly to tell him then that there would never be anyone like him for me, either. It was a simple fact, almost a scientific truth, a universal invariant.

"You will, Sherlock. You will find someone who is your intellectual equal, someone who challenges you. She will be *the* woman, Sherlock, the right woman for you."

He cupped my face with those lovely, pale, long fingers. His eyes took on a strange expression, one I had rarely seen and one that would haunt me for the rest of my life. He said, "No, I think not. If only—"

Then the door squeaked open and we quickly broke from our embrace. I have often wondered what he was about to say. I thought, *Almost. Almost is harder. Almost teases you with what could have been, with what you could have had, only to disappoint you.*

Michael popped his head in and called out, "Poppy!"

I turned. He was standing in the hall with another man, fair-haired with a mustache and a very stiff posture. He was a bit older than my brother. He had weary eyes and he held a cane in one hand.

"Your sister is deserting me. I shall be in need of a new assistant," Sherlock said.

I shook my head, then ran to Michael. He hugged me and twirled me around in the hallway.

"Poppy, I am sorry to interrupt you."

"Not at all, Michael," hoping that I was not blushing.

"I am going to miss you so very much," my brother said, his face contorted with pain.

"Don't make me cry, please. We should be going, Michael. I have a carriage waiting."

289

"I just have to do one thing before I leave. Oh," he added, "Apologies. John, this is my sister Dr. Priscilla Stamford."

I saw the man's eyebrows rise. The title 'doctor' for a woman was still so rare.

"Priscilla, this is Dr. John Watson. I knew him before he went into military service."

"Of course. My brother has spoken of you often, Dr. Watson. We share the same birthday, I believe, sir."

"That's right," Michael said, "You recall that John was attached to the Fifth Northumberland Fusiliers and he was wounded last year at the Battle of Maiwand."

"I was sorry to hear that, sir," I said. "Michael shared a letter from your orderly, Mr. Murray, about the battle."

"Oh, yes," Michael said. "I'd forgotten."

"A pleasure to meet you," Watson said in a pleasant voice.

"Likewise. I'm glad you are home safe, sir."

Michael placed the palm of his hand on Dr. Watson's shoulder. "Say, old chap, do you like dogs? My sister needs to find a home for her bull terrier."

"I like them well enough," John said.

Michael squeezed my hand and winked. "I'll be right back," he said. "Come along, John, I want to introduce you to the man I was telling you about earlier, the one who is looking for someone to share lodgings. He's found some rooms on Baker Street. He says they are quite nice and he knows the landlady." He pushed against the door, stopped and said, "Now remember, John, I told you, he's a rather hard nut to crack." Then Michael turned back to me. "Wait here, darling."

Michael pushed open the door to the lab and walked in. Dr. Watson followed.

I strained to catch one last glimpse of Sherlock Holmes before the door closed. I mouthed "Goodbye," and lifted my hand in a little wave. Sherlock mirrored my gesture. I thought again about our time at Holme-Next-the-Sea.

Almost is harder, because almost teases you with what could have been.

I ran before I could change my mind about leaving.

42

January sixth came quickly. It was time to board the ship.

Sarah and I had spent every evening in Folkestone, waiting for our departure day, poring over books and magazines about India. She was beyond excited. I was, I think, a little dazed. I wanted to believe that I was moving toward something, not running away. I wanted to believe that I was finally going to touch the wall that seemed to keep moving out of my reach . . . that I was going to place my palm against it and stand tall.

Mum and I called a truce. She was still angry. Angry about losing Papa, angry that I had told Uncle to proceed with the surgery, angry that I was leaving England, especially so soon after Papa's death. But Michael explained, many times, that Uncle had taken a chance to keep him alive a while longer but his days were numbered anyway. Her anger was nothing compared to mine when, just one month later, Michael sent me an article in a medical journal about the procedure. On January 29, 1881, Dr. Billroth performed the first successful resection for stomach cancer on a woman named Therese Heller. The surgery is known as the Billroth I to this day.

I hugged Michael and then Mum. She whispered, "You shouldn't be doing this, Poppy. Don't go."

I held her tight and said, "Mum, I'll be fine."

Michael took my bags and Sarah's to the ship and a sailor took them to our cabin while Michael spoke to the captain.

"Poppy," Mum choked out.

"No tears, Mum. I'll let you know as soon as I arrive."

She nodded.

As I walked with Sarah up to the gangway, it occurred to me that this was Sherlock's birthday. January 6, 1881. He was twenty-seven years old. I hoped he would celebrate with Mycroft but then I smiled to myself and said, "Of course he won't."

"What did you say, Poppy?" Sarah asked.

"Nothing, Sarah. Nothing."

Sarah went ahead and I stood at the edge of the platform. The gangway stretched out in front of me.

I didn't know when I would be home again. I didn't know what lay ahead. But then I remembered the young man from India I had met at the British Museum. The young law student who wanted to be a poet, Rabindranath Tagore. We had talked about many things. His dreams, my confusion. And I remembered something he'd told me once.

You can't cross the sea merely by staring at the water.

I crossed the gangway and stepped into the boat.

EPILOGUE

"Poppy" Stamford Trevor, my mother, always told me that when she moved to India, she never looked back. After her death, at the age of 91, I discovered otherwise.

In addition to journals, stacks and stacks of them, that detailed her life in India, she kept correspondence from Mr. Sherlock Holmes, as well as newspaper clippings and other memorabilia about him, in a chest beneath her bed. I read through them.

Reading Mum's journals was more like viewing a painting than reading a memoir or a story. How frightening and exhilarating her first sight of Calcutta was—seeing the colorful flags and masts of countless ships from all over the world, and the white palaces and bright green sun-shutters and the crowded strand of people who looked so different. Twenty years went by before she set foot on British soil again with my father, my brother Charles and me. I was still a young girl and I know how awestruck and terrified I was by the traffic on the Thames and the large, strange city that was waiting for me. But before that visit, Mum had so many experiences, some that may have caused her to regret her choice—cholera epidemics, witchcraft, uprisings.

One day I'll share all of it with the world . . . her adventures when she was an itinerant physician travelling throughout India with an assistant, a man named Will Murray . . . the man who had saved Dr. John Watson's life, and her 'cases' about which she often consulted with Mr. Sherlock Holmes. But those are stories for another time.

The most striking lines in any of the journals were these:

I kept that secret vow, that barely whispered vow that I made to Sherlock Holmes in Victor Trevor's ballroom — 'til death us do part'—for many, many years. I did not marry until I learned of the "death of Sherlock Holmes at Reichenbach Falls." It was in 1891, ten years after I left England.

Before that reckoning, I often thought of contacting him. More frequently than I ever admitted, and crazy as it might sound, I wondered, had he moved on? I always wondered if we could have been something, if we had missed our chance. I wondered, did he ever think of me and wonder that, too? Did he wonder if we could have been something extraordinary?

When I thought of him and our adventures, I would still get butterflies. I would remember how he looked at me that night at Mrs. Hudson's. How beautiful he made me feel. And I never forgot the way he kissed me and touched me that night in the cottage by the sea. I never forgot that I thought I heard him say he loved me that night.

And I never told him he was the one thing I wanted all those years.

But everyone thought that he had died in a struggle with Professor Moriarty at Reichenbach Falls.

Then he was 'resurrected' several years later. Contrary to what everyone believed, it was revealed that Holmes was alive. It was said that he won against Professor Moriarty at Reichenbach Falls by flinging him down the waterfall. It was said that he climbed up the cliff beside the path to make it appear as though he, too, had fallen to his death. This was a plan that Holmes had instantly conceived to defend against Moriarty's hoodlum colleagues. He explained to Dr. Watson that one of them knew that Holmes was still alive and tried to kill him by dropping rocks down on the ledge where he had taken refuge. Sherlock climbed back down the cliff, fell the last short distance to the path, and then ran for his life. The next week, he went to Florence and traveled for nearly three years. He told Dr. Watson the deception was required to outwit his enemies. He spent those years traveling to various parts of the world. He went to Tibet, to Persia and Khartoum. Before returning to England, he did some chemical research while visiting the French cousins, the relatives on his mother's side in Montpellier, France, who were sworn to secrecy. Along the way he purchased land in Sussex where he intended to retire and raise his precious bees. During all this time, the only people who knew that Sherlock Holmes was alive were Moriarty's henchmen, the distant cousins and his brother Mycroft. Even his brother Sherrinford thought Sherlock was dead.

A few years later he retired to the land he had purchased in Sussex.

But why all the travelling after Reichenbach Falls, I wondered. It was said he was tracking down all of Moriarty's cronies. But then I happened upon an article in the newspaper that said that Adam Worth, the Napoleon of Crime, had finally been captured and arrested in 1892, a year after the infamous "demise of Moriarty and Sherlock Holmes." I remembered 'Morrie Art' was one of the names that Maggie had whispered with her dying breaths. It was one of the many aliases by which Worth was called during his early criminal career.

What if? I wondered. What if "Moriarty" – Adam Worth? – had also survived the fall at Reichenbach Falls? What if during all that time that everyone thought Sherlock was dead, he was still hunting down the arch enemy himself, the Napoleon of Crime, as well as others in his crime syndicate?

Worth spent five years in jail. He was released from jail in 1897 and died in 1902. One might surmise that having fulfilled his vow to track down Maggie's killer and rid the world of the 'Napoleon of Crime,' Sherlock would finally feel he could leave the world of criminals behind. But it was only after Worth was dead, in 1903, that Sherlock finally retired to his country home in Sussex. I remembered his words to me in Aunt Susan's morning room when he came to see me shortly after Maggie's death. He said, "I shall not rest until he no longer walks among the living."

He made good on that vow.

And I believe I was one of the first to know. One day, several years after Sherlock Holmes had been declared dead, a large package arrived. It contained the portrait of Maggie that had been stolen from her safe. There was no note, no explanation. But I knew at once, he had found Worth and kept his promise.

I often wanted to reach out to Sherlock after I discovered he was still alive. But I knew that if he wanted to contact me, he knew where to find me. I knew that with all the changes in my life and all the mysteries in his, an unbreachable chasm had grown between us.

But we will meet again, Sherlock and I.

Until then, I rely on my sweet memories. I believe the words of Khalil Gibran . . .

"If in the twilight of memory we should meet once more, we shall speak again together and you shall sing to me a deeper song."

APPENDIX

The Real People of Before Watson, Book Four By First and/or Only Appearance

Prologue

Winston Churchill – Prime Minister of the United Kingdom from 1940 to 1945 and again from 1951 to 1955

Adolph Hitler - leader of the Nazi Party, Chancellor of Germany from 1933 to 1945 and Führer of Nazi Germany from 1934 to 1945. As dictator, Hitler initiated World War II

King George – King of the United Kingdom from 11 December 1936 – 6 February 1952

Chapter 1

King John – King of England from 1199 to1204

Chapter 2

Brig. General George Burrows – in charge at the Battle of Maiwand, July 27, 1879; had never commanded in battle before

General Roberts – marched with his men from Kabul with an army of 10,000 to relieve the garrison after the Battle of Maiwand so that British could withdraw to India in some safety

Chapter 6

Eizabeth Van Lew – spy for the Union Army during the American Civil War

Anna Bates – British spy during the Revolutionary War

Anna Smith Strong – spy for the Americans during the Revolutionary War

Chapter 7

Pablo Sarasote – concert violinist

Cardinal Manning – raised money for the Westminster Cathedral

Henry Clutton – architect who drew up original plans for Westminster Cathedral

Chapter 8

Oscar Wilde – author, poet, playwright

Bram Stoker – theater manager and author of *Dracula* and other novels

George Francis (Frank) Miles - a London-based British artist who specialised in pastel portraits of society ladies, also an architect; once a roommate of **Oscar Wilde**

Chapter 9

Sarah Bernhardt – actress

Giacomo Puccini – composer

Joseph Swan – physicist, scientist, inventor

William Armstrong – industrial magnate and millionaire

Henry Irving – actor

Chapter 10

Lily Langtry – actress

Chapter 13

William Gladstone – Four Time Prime Minister of United Kingdom (1868–74, 1880–85, 1886, 1892–94)

Chapter 16

Dr. A. T. Norton - Dean of the School of Medicine for Women in London in 1880

Mrs. Thorne – Dean of the School of Medicine for Women in London in 1874

Chapter 21

The Forty Thieves - a 19th-century New York street gang & a 19th-century London street gang – they terrorised both cities

The Forty Elephants - From 1873-1950s, an all-female London criminal gang, also known to use the name the Forty Thieves

Chapter 22

Mary Carr – aka Mary Crane, aka Polly Carr (born 1862). Became notorious 'Queen of the Forty Elephants, the exclusively female branch of the Forty Thieves. (**AUTHOR'S NOTE:** The author conjured the idea for the central plot of this novel—the burglary at The Pink Flamingo and Polly Carr's involvement—from a 'hole' in Carr's biography. In **1881**, the year that Poppy departs for India, Carr was an inmate at St. Mary the Virgin Penitentiary of Stone near Dartford, Kent. The complement at Stone was around sixty constantly changing inmates. Though Carr's life, crimes, arrests, etc. have been very well documented, why Carr is domiciled there is not known.)

Thomas Robert Linchin - Thirteen-year-old charged by his grandmother with 'repeated acts of thieving, endeavouring to set fire to her house, and threatening to take away her life.' The tattoo between thumb and forefinger distinguished him as one of the Forty Thieves

Edward Greyson- one of the first of the Forty Thieves gang to be brought before Surrey magistrates

John Craw – member of the Forty Thieves in the 1860's

John Carr – father of **Mary Carr**, first 'Queen of the Forty Thieves'; international bank burglar and associate of **Adam Worth**

Joseph Wilson – stole bonds with **John Carr**

Sir Edward John Poynter – Victorian artist

Adam Worth – widely considered the inspiration for Sir Arthur Conan Dole's fictional criminal mastermind James Moriarty in the Sherlock Holmes series, whom Conan Doyle calls "The Napoleon of Crime." Formed his own criminal network and organized major robberies and burglaries through several intermediaries. Those who worked in his schemes never knew his name.

Inspector John Shore - made **Worth's** capture his personal mission.

Jack Junka Phillips - a gargantuan Englishman employed by **Adam Worth** as a butler, bodyguard, and safecracker. Called Junka because of his habit of keeping his pockets leaden down with random junk.

Little Joe Elliott – American thief hosted by **John Carr** who lived at Carr's sister's home in Pimlico

Chapter 23

Dorothy Tennant - artist

George Frederick Watts - English Victorian painter and sculptor associated with the Symbolist movement

Chapter 24

Detective John Whicher –one of the original eight members of the newly formed Detective Branch which was established at Scotland Yard in 1842. In 1860 he was involved in the Constance Kent murder case; He was one of the inspirations for Charles Dickens's Inspector Bucket, Colin Dexter's Inspector Morse, Wilkie Collins's Sergeant Cuff and R. D. Wingfield's Jack Frost, among other fictional detectives.

Inspector Charles Frederick Field - a British police officer with Scotland Yard and, following his retirement, a private detective. Field is perhaps best known as the basis for Inspector Bucket in Charles Dickens's novel *Bleak House*.

Emily Laurence - went by the name Durant. Hotel and jewelry robberies

James Pearce – jewel thief who lived with **Laurence**

Chapter 25

Charles the Scratch Becker - the great forger whom police compared to "Michelangelo, Rembrandt and Whistler in artistic talent," was finally nabbed in 1900 for a counterfeiting spree involving some forty banks. In 1903 he emerged from San Quentin prison in a thoroughly cheerful mood, having spent his imprisonment perfecting a new type of forgery-proof paper and ink which he intended to sell to banks and paper firms

Inspector Robert Anderson - was the second Assistant Commissioner (Crime) of the London Metropolitan Police, from 1888 to 1901. He was also an intelligence officer, theologian and writer. Nicknamed criminal **Adam Worth** 'the Napoleon of Crime'

Joe Chapman – part of international crime syndicate

Henry Wade Wilkes – associate of **Adam Worth**

Lizzie Carr- John Carr's sister; hosted international thieves at her home

Chapter 26

Rose O'Neal Greenhow - female Rebel spy who used the Vigenère Cipher in 1861 when she warned **General Beauregard** that the Union Army was advancing toward Bull Run.

General P. G. T. Beauregard - Pierre Gustave Toutant-Beauregard was an American military officer who was the first prominent general of the Confederate States Army during the American Civil War.

Chapter 27

Judah P. Benjamin - Confederate secretary of state

Queen Victoria - Victoria was Queen of the United Kingdom of Great Britain and Ireland from 20 June 1837 until her death in 1901. On 1 May 1876, she adopted the additional title of Empress of India.

Henry John Temple, 3rd Viscount Palmerston – British statesman who served twice as Prime Minister in the mid-19th century

John Russell - British Foreign Secretary

Colonel James Archibald Stuart-Wortley-Mackenzie, 1st Baron Wharncliffe - a British soldier and politician and president of the Southern Independent Association of London, a group of very highly placed British men who favored independence for the Confederacy

Chapter 28

Granville Sharp, one of the first English campaigners for the abolition of the slave trade

William Wilberforce, the English politician, philanthropist, and abolitionist

Zachary Macauley - also leader of the movement to stop the slave trade.

Chapter 31

Richard Assheton Cross, 1st Viscount Cross – Home Secretary between 1874 and 1880 and 1885 and 1886.

Clara Barton - Clarissa "Clara" Harlowe Barton was a pioneering nurse who founded the American Red Cross. She was a hospital nurse in the American Civil War, a teacher, and patent clerk.

Chapter 34

Dr. Theodore Billroth - Christian Albert Theodor Billroth was a Prussian-born Austrian surgeon and amateur musician. As a surgeon, he is generally regarded as the founding father of modern abdominal surgery

Dr. John Lister - British surgeon and scientist, best known for spearheading the medical use of antiseptic medicine

Dr. William Cross – surgeon at Norfolk and Norwich Hospital

Chapter 35

General Henry Havelock - was nearing the city of Cawnore with relief troops during the 1857 uprising in India when an order was issued that all of the British women and children at the garrison were to be killed

Chapter 38

Dr. John Rothwell – British veterinarian in the Latham area of England

Dr. John McFadyan – Scottish veterinary surgeon

Chapter 42

Rabindranath Tagore – poet, author, activist

MX Publishing

www.sherlockholmesbooks.com

MX Publishing is the world's largest specialist Sherlock Holmes publisher, with over a hundred titles and fifty authors creating the latest in Sherlock Holmes fiction and non-fiction.

From traditional short stories and novels to travel guides and quiz books, MX Publishing cater for all Holmes fans.

The collection includes leading titles such as _Benedict Cumberbatch In Transition_ and _The Norwood Author_ which won the 2011 Howlett Award (Sherlock Holmes Book of the Year).

MX Publishing also has one of the largest communities of Holmes fans on Facebook with regular contributions from dozens of authors.

Also from MX Publishing

"Phil Growick's, 'The Secret Journal of Dr Watson', is an adventure which takes place in the latter part of Holmes and Watson's lives. They are entrusted by HM Government (although not officially) and the King no less to undertake a rescue mission to save the Romanovs, Russia's Royal family from a grisly end at the hand of the Bolsheviks. There is a wealth of detail in the story but not so much as would detract us from the enjoyment of the story. Espionage, counter-espionage, the ace of spies himself, double-agents, double-crossers...all these flit across the pages in a realistic and exciting way. All the characters are extremely well-drawn and Mr Growick, most importantly, does not falter with a very good ear for Holmesian dialogue indeed. Highly recommended. A five-star effort."

The Baker Street Society

www.sherlockholmesbooks.com

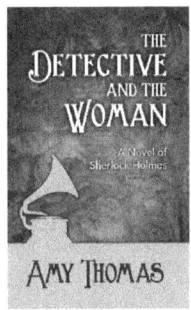